GHOST OF THE

5-15

La Riviere, Susan
Ghost of the Capitol Theatre

Capitol Theatre postcard, 1920. Courtesy: Glen and Valerie Thiesfeld.

OTHER BOOKS
by
Susan La Riviere

"Brother, if you ever think of scorning a female ghost,
the only advice I can give you is to run for cover!"

OZZIE GOLDSTEIN, Capitol Theatre's
entertainment manager

LA RIVIERE PRODUCTIONS
Yakima, Washington

ghost of the

Capitol Theatre

Susan La Riviere

YAKIMA, WASHINGTON

LA RIVIERE PRODUCTIONS
8 N. 36th Ave.
Yakima, WA 98902

Ghost of the Capitol Theatre

combines historical and fictional people, places and events.

For information, contact:
susanlariviere.com or SMareaux@aol.com
Copyright © 2011 by Susan La Riviere
ISBN 978-0-9793559-5-0

Manufactured in the United States of America
Second Edition

Book Design: Kathy Campbell, Gorham Printing
Back cover photo, courtesy of Rex Marble

To Frederick Mercy, Sr.
Your dream theatre is alive and well.

To the Capitol Theatre Committee
and the City of Yakima,
Thank you for restoring
Yakima's "treasure"

ACKNOWLEDGEMENTS

Ralph Woodall–Yakima historian

Capitol Theatre Historical fire photos
Gay Parker

Yakima Valley Museum
Yakimamemory.org
David Lynx: Capitol Theatre night photos

Postcard photo of Capitol Theatre,
courtesy of Glenn
and Valerie Thiesfeld

Rex Marble
Storyline

Therese D'Anjou La Lumiere
Storyline

Leonard La Lumiere
Photographer: Capitol Theatre interior

Laurie Moshier
French translation

The Roslyn Theatre
Jan, Lynne and Keith Donaldson,
Projection room photos

ghost of the

Capitol Theatre

Final stages of construction, 1920.
Courtesy: **Yakimamemory.org.**

Float to advertise the movie "Transatlantic", 1930. Courtesy: **Yakimamemory.org.**

CHAPTER ONE

The Monday Night Late Movie

The Capitol Theatre of Yakima, Washington was not a neighborhood theatre. Envisioning a grand vaudeville theatre located in the heart of downtown, Frederick Mercy, Sr. commissioned theatre architect, Marcus Priteca to begin construction on the Italian Renaissance palazzo in 1919 that would seat 1,500 people. The theatre interior was a combination of high Renaissance and classical elements, which displayed an air of opulence and grandeur. Tony Heinsbergen was hired to create the murals in the dome over the orchestra level of the audience. His assignment was to paint the muses of comedy, tragedy, music and art. The characters were painted in an artistic style similar to Michelangelo Buonarroti's, *The Creation of Adam.*

In the 1920s, vaudeville had its heyday at the Capitol Theatre with live musicians, singers, comedians, chorus lines and tap dancers. Exotic and domestic animal acts that an audience might see in a circus, freak acts like sword swallowers, acrobats and drag queens—anything and all that was crazy and wild could be found in a vaudeville show.

As the interest in vaudeville died, the theatre primarily showed movies with occasional live entertainment. In the mid-1960s, the theatre's manager, Albert Mallone, gave Rex Marvel permission to show popular reruns, mostly horror or sexy movies during the Monday evening shows. With the competition of television, the manager was desperate to bring in customers to the downtown Yakima movie palace.

Because Monday night was the slowest night of the week, Rex had scheduled Alfred Hitchcock's thrillers for the week: *The Birds,* starring Marnie Nickson, was a new movie in 1963 and would be shown at the 6:30 p.m. time slot. He had the same plan with *Psycho,* which was made in 1960 and stared Janet Leigh and Anthony Perkins. That movie would run at 9 p.m., the absolute slowest time of the week for the theatre. The scary Monday night movies, which were nearly X-Rated in the mid-sixties, were a strategy to bring in customers who happened to be night people.

In the projection booth, there were openings designated for the projectors as they pointed toward the screen. Through a large tinted window, Rex Marvel could see all of the seats in the balconies, and most of the main floor audience. The regulars who attended the Monday 9 p.m. movie always sat in the same areas and even in the same seats. There were quite a few loners, Rex noticed.

One couple met in the back seats then left during the movie. It was a no brainer to assume they didn't come to see the movie. The late Monday movie was their meeting destination. Who knew where they went after they hooked up? The couple didn't want to be seen in public. That much Rex guessed because they left the theatre through a side exit where a black vintage Jaguar was waiting. At least that's what Mike Hansen, an employee, reported after he had his regular smoke in the alley about 9:20 p.m. Each week, there would be a different high dollar automobile waiting for the couple. Vintage he guessed because Mike couldn't identify the vehicles as late model cars.

Mike Hansen told Rex about the strange couple who met in back. "Talk about clockwork! " Mike said as he and Rex smoked cigarettes in the alley.

"Now you got my curiosity," Rex said. "I want to see the Mystery Lady come into the theatre tonight. I've got film in the projector for the 9 p.m. movie so all I have to do is press ON! Once that's started, I'll come downstairs and stand by the snack bar. When she comes in and you take her ticket, scratch the right side of your face and I'll know it's the Mystery Lady."

When it was time for the movie to start, Rex rushed up the stairs, turned on the projector, made a few simple adjustments and started showing the newsreel. He didn't have to make any other adjustments when the movie previews followed the newsreel so he ran down the stairs and casually walked over to the snack bar.

A young woman, with shoulder length dark auburn hair bought her ticket at the ticket booth outside then walked into the lobby toward Mike who tore a portion of her ticket in half then touched the right side of his face. Her expert make-up and general appearance caused her to look like a movie star. An aura of aloofness, of being above everyone else who attended the late Monday movie, surrounded her. Rex couldn't help staring at the way her body moved inside her open, fur lined, full length black coat.

When she passed him to go to the ladies' room, their eyes met and Rex pretended to adjust his glasses but fumbled and knocked them across his face. As he tried to catch the glasses before they fell to the floor, Mystery Lady covered her mouth to keep from breaking out in laughter at Rex's embarrassed antics. Rex was surprised at his reaction to the Mystery Lady and reminded himself that it was time to rush back up the stairs and show the main feature.

About an hour elapsed as the suspense in Alfred Hitchcock's *Psycho* built up to the shower scene. Rex had to chuckle because he knew what was going to happen. The music became almost intolerable in intensity as an evil force entered the bathroom while Janet Leigh was taking a shower. The violins screeched in rhythm as Anthony Perkins slashed her.

Maybe the censors wouldn't allow the knife to actually puncture what looked like human flesh, and maybe they wouldn't allow the audience to see Janet Leigh naked and covered in blood. Rex thought the scene was lacking and would have directed it to be gorier with more blood. More nudity. Where was the blood as her hand slipped down the side of the tiled wall? For someone who'd been slashed to death, Rex figured there'd be blood everywhere. Each time he had seen the movie, he checked even closer to see if Janet Leigh was really nude but he was finally convinced she must have been wearing a skimpy flesh colored body suit as all actors had to do in the sixties if they wanted to appear nude.

Suddenly, a woman's scream filled the theater causing the hair on the back of Rex's neck to stand straight up. He had never heard such terror in anyone's scream like this one. Under his breath, he said, "Geez! Get a grip. It's only a movie." But the woman would not stop screaming. As he looked out his peep window, he observed people in the audience gathering around the woman while she pointed at something on the floor behind a row of seats and yelled, "She's there. She's there," as her hand covered her mouth. Two ushers were shining their flashlights at the location and trying to find what was terrifying her. A lot of commotion was happening in the dark theatre while the scene on the movie screen zoomed in on Janet Leigh's lifeless open-eyed face pressed on the bathroom's tiled floor.

Startling him, the phone rang and it was Albert Mallone, the manager, who was speaking on the other end. "Rex, stop the movie. Turn off the projectors and wait until further notice. I'm going to turn on the house lights."

"What's happening?"

"A customer in the audience spotted a body behind a row of back seats," was the explanation.

"A body? Are you telling me someone in the theatre is dead?"

"Yes. A young woman. The police are on the way so I've got to go to the front doors and let them in. Just hang tight until we figure this out. Go ahead and rewind the film. Movie time is over for the night."

Rex gently slipped the film out of the sprockets and wheels on the projector as he kept both reels in place. Reversing the reel on top, the film easily slid from the bottom reel until it was completely back in place and ready to roll for the next showing. He lifted the heavy reel off the projector and placed it between two metal cases. Looking like a huge compact, he took it over to the shelves and slid it vertically between other reel cases as if was replacing a book in a library stack.

By this time, the police had arrived and were keeping the moviegoers in the theatre for questioning.

"Okay, people. Try to stay calm," Albert Mallone was attempting to bring order to the general panic of the small audience as he stood on the stage. He didn't need a microphone when his booming voice gave instructions to the audience. The ushers were making sure nobody exited the theatre. "Everyone come up here and sit in the front rows. Let's go, folks. Lt. Paganelli needs to get your names and numbers so the sooner we get a few answers, the sooner you'll be able to leave."

Rex figured he'd stay up in the projection booth until the excitement blew over. No such luck as he heard footsteps coming up the stairs and a policeman appeared in the cramped space.

An intense looking police officer showed his badge and said "Lieutenant

Paganelli. Yakima P.D. We're questioning everyone in the theatre and need you to come downstairs."

"Why me? I was running the film," Rex responded and realized immediately that he sounded defensive.

As he examined the projection booth, Lt. Paganelli observed that the audience could be seen through the vertical windows.

"This process will go a lot faster if you cooperate. What's your name, sir?"

"Rex Marvel."

"Mr. Marvel, I'll follow you down the stairs. Go to the seats in front with the other people," Lt. Paganelli stepped back allowing Rex to cross in front of him and head toward the stairs.

The body had not been moved and was covered with a sheet while a cop was waiting for the coroner to arrive. Rex noted that the location of the body was in the usual spot where the couple met every Monday night before they exited the theatre. He was curious about what she looked like and what the man who met her looked like. As his mind whirled about what he would tell the officers, he decided he would tell them nothing. He saw nothing. He could not identify either of the persons in the couple so why get involved? It would be to his disadvantage if he did.

"Keep moving," Lt. Paganelli urged Rex. "Go right up to the front and take a seat."

"May I at least see what she looks like? Maybe I'd recognize her from other movies she's attended," Rex stopped at the site of the covered body.

Lt. Paganelli looked at the cop for permission who was guarding the corpse and got a head nod. The guard pulled back enough of the sheet to expose the young woman's face.

In a moment of shock, Rex gasped as he recognized Mystery Woman. He covered his mouth and couldn't take his eyes off the victim. Her alabaster skin and touch of make-up complimented her auburn shoulder length hair. The officer had mistakenly pulled the sheet back enough for Rex to see a red line around the woman's neck. Choked by a garrote he figured. That's why her mouth appeared to be gasping for air. Rex turned his head, gagged and staggered backwards as he bent over and put his hands on his knees to recover from seeing swimming black dots before his eyes, a sure sign that he was going to faint.

"That probably wasn't a good idea on my part. Sorry Mr. Marvel. Let's go up front and you can sit down."

"Okay people," Albert Mallone tried to get the attention of the audience as they watched the scene with Rex Marvel and the dead girl. "Lt. Paganelli is going to ask you for your I.D. information. Nothing personal. He just wants to know who is here in case you might remember something that'll help this case. So heads up, folks. Here's Lt. Paganelli."

Albert Mallone nodded at the lieutenant as they passed on the stage.

Lt. Paganelli began. "I know it's a shock to have someone murdered in the theatre where you come to relax and enjoy the movie. The young lady's circumstances are mysterious and we need to find out who she was and why this happened. We need your help to solve the crime so she can rest in peace."

Even though no one had cause to worry, there was silence in the group and an atmosphere of near panic to escape because a police officer was putting each person on the spot.

"Let's get started," Lt. Paganelli said.

In the next half hour, the moviegoers reluctantly gave their names, addresses and phone numbers. They were night people; those who wanted to escape their dreary realities and get lost in the darkness of a movie theatre to be in the world on the screen. For each person, that late night movie kept them on the brink between coping with their lonely, uneventful lives and desperation. All they had to do was survive one more week until the next Monday night movie. One could say their cover was blown in the lighted theater where their dysfunctions and vulnerabilities were revealed.

Once the audience was excused, the staff was next. Lt. Paganelli collected each person's name and other pertinent information. Then he asked for volunteers to tell what they knew about the dead woman.

Mike raised his hand briefly in a short wave.

"What's your name, sir?" Lt. Paganelli got his pencil ready to take notes.

"Mike Hansen."

"Mr. Hansen, what's your job here at the theatre?"

"I'm an usher. Sometimes take tickets. Fix things. I'm sort of a right hand guy for Al Mallone, the theatre manager."

"Did you know the girl?"

"Didn't know her exactly. I just watched what she did and who she did it with."

"What was her routine on Monday nights?"

"She was a regular at the 9 p.m. movie. Has been for a couple months. She was kinda weird if you ask me."

"Why?" Paganelli paused his pencil.

"She came right before the movie started and stayed in the ladies' room until the feature began then she'd go to the seats near the back."

"Maybe she was lonely," Lt. Paganelli wondered why a young woman followed the same routine every Monday night.

"Don't think so. A guy joined her as soon as she sat down."

"She met a date every Monday night at the movies. Why is that weird?"

"They left the movie about twenty minutes after the movie started. That's weird," Mike continued.

"How do you know that?"

"When I'd take a break in the alley for a smoke, I would see her and the guy come through the side exit and get into a car."

"What'd the guy look like?"

"I guess I need to back up on what I originally said. It wasn't the same guy each time. Each week, a different man showed up. Some were as young as her. Some could have been old enough to be her father. I couldn't possibly identify them because I made an effort not to look at them. Once I saw what was happening, I walked back into the lobby.

"What about the cars?"

"Old, expensive, maybe vintage ones. Not the same car every time. But always a classy lookin' rich guy's car. Lots of money type car."

"Anything else, Mr. Hansen?"

"Nope. Except to say if that beautiful chick was in my world, I would've treated her like a queen."

"Good. Very good, Mr. Hansen. Anybody else?" Lt. Paganelli looked from one person to another. The others commented that they briefly saw the woman pass through the lobby as she gave her ticket to the usher. Same thing with the men. Neither she nor the pick-up man bought popcorn or a drink. No one recalled them going out of the theatre through the front doors.

"Mr. Marvel, what can you tell me?" Lt. Paganelli looked at Rex.

"I can't see the audience in the back seats from the booth. Besides, I never have contact with anyone in the audience. My job is to keep the film going."

"What about the girl?"

"Tonight is the first time I've ever seen her."

Lt. Paganelli cornered Rex. "When you wanted to look at the girl, you said you might recognize her from her attendance at other movies. Which is it, Mr. Marvel? You don't have contact with anyone in the audience, like you said? Or you have the ability to recognize people when they attend the movies?"

"While I'm setting up the reels, I can see three quarters of the audience through the windows because the house lights are on. I can't see the seats directly under the balcony. Once the house lights are off, I can't see anyone. I never saw that woman when the house lights were on. Like Mike said, she must have gone to those back seats when the movie had already started."

Lt. Paganelli knew Rex Marvel weaseled his way out of that point. He wasn't a suspect but he also wasn't telling everything he had seen. No doubt about it.

The staff's names and numbers were as much information as Lt. Paganelli was going to get from the moviegoers and staff. He knew that no one in the theatre was the murderer. And he also knew that Mike Hansen's observations were a big break. Unfortunately, the police had little information on the victim's identity. In her purse, she carried keys to her apartment. There were no driver's license or car keys. No photos in her wallet. Just some small bills and a $100.00 bill, which seemed like an odd combination of cash.

However, there was a card from a local doctor for an appointment scheduled earlier that same Monday. The patient's name was on the card. It was Zizi Zeigler. Lt. Paganelli wondered what kind of parents would name their kid Zizi?

CHAPTER TWO

Mystery Woman

March 2, 1965   *Yakima Herald-Republic*

YAKIMA: On March 1, A young woman, approximately twenty-two-years-old, was found dead during the Monday late night 9 p.m. movie at the Capitol Theatre in Yakima, WA by a moviegoer as she walked down the aisle to her seat. Upon seeing someone laying on the floor behind a row of back seats, the moviegoer screamed and alerted the theatre ushers who confirmed that the woman between the rows was dead. The police were called immediately. In an effort to determine what time the murder happened, theatre manager, Albert Mallone, stated that all the aisles were cleared of popcorn and drink containers before the audience was allowed to take their seats before the late movie began. The balcony staircases had been roped off so no one was allowed beyond the main level. Mallone and Lt. Paganelli, Yakima Police Department, kept the audience in the theatre for questioning.

The name of the deceased will be withheld until her family has been contacted. She is described as approximately 5'6", auburn hair, Anglo and very thin. If you have any information about the missing young woman, please contact the Yakima Police Department, 555-1234.

A drawing of Zizi Zeigler's face was sent over the Associated Press wire service for publication in all major newspapers. The article that accompanied the young woman's drawing said that she was missing. If someone knew her, they were encouraged to contact the Yakima County Sheriff's Department or the Yakima Police Department, just as the obituary had stated.

Rather than being housed in the same building as the Yakima County Police Department downtown, the Yakima County Coroner's office was at the former location of the old Pizza Hut at 223 N. First Street.

Approximately 700 square feet, the vault-like room was lit with florescent lighting.

There were no windows and therefore no natural lighting.

A full size biological skeleton stood in the corner as the one silent visitor who consistently observed the coroner's business of dissecting a human body on the stainless steel autopsy table. Hoses, a drain sink, refrigerated drawers long enough to hold a body and a large refrigerator were part and parcel of the coroner's room. When the body in question was sliced, the coroner had the option to weigh the victim's body parts in a hanging scale similar to the fruit and vegetable scales that used to hang from grocery store ceilings of the past.

Along the wall was a counter with a microscope, reference books and a tall file cabinet. A light box for viewing x-rays hung over the counter topped by a utility clock, which was the highest feature in the room.

There was no observation window where a police officer or a family member could identify the body while standing in a separate enclosure. Since a homicide detective could be in the same room as the coroner to watch him perform autopsies, the incidents of pathogens, vapors, blood and body fluids from the victim to visitors was a valid concern not to mention that the coroner had someone in the room during the autopsy who distracted him from recording his findings as well as simply being in the way.

During the coroner's initial exam of the young female victim, Lt. Paganelli attended the autopsy as the coroner clicked on a tape recorder and placed it in the chest pocket of his white doctor's coat. He placed an x-ray up on the wall light box and gave some preliminary information to start the autopsy.

"This is an autopsy report for a female victim known as Zizi Zeigler who was found dead in the Capitol Theatre, March 15, 1965."

"What's the COD, doc?"

As the coroner pointed to the x-ray, he noted that, "The victim was strangled with a garrote."

"I've never heard of anyone in Yakima being killed that way," Lt.

Paganelli said. "How does it work?"

The coroner explained. "A garrote could be a ligature of a chain, rope, or scarf used to choke someone to death. A short wire, fishing line or piano wire with wooden handles on each end is the usual method. The murderer throws the wire over the victim's head, wraps the wire around her neck, pulls back and squeezes. Usually the victim is in a chair and struggles, to no avail, until a silent death occurs when the larynx is crushed and the victim dies from asphyxia."

"Isn't this a common method of execution used by the Mafia?"

"Using a garrote and blasting someone with a sawed off shotgun are both common with the Mafia. But you're right. This is the first time I've seen anyone in Yakima killed this way." The coroner turned from the x-ray and examined the body of Zizi Zeigler on the autopsy table. He rarely showed any emotion about the homicide victims he examined but this time was different and he was surprised by his surge of grief.

"Doc, you okay?" Lt. Paganelli searched the coroner's face to see what the matter was.

"Yeh, I'm okay." The coroner cleared his throat and continued speaking into the tape recorder. "Zizi Zeigler is approximately twenty-one-years-old, five-foot-six and weighs 110 pounds. She is white with shoulder-length auburn hair, hazel eyes, and straight teeth with no fillings. Appears to be in good health. I see bruises around both upper arms, which indicate that someone grasped her arms recently. Her breasts are larger than average but mature and she had a steady sex life." After cutting through abdominal tissue, the coroner made a discovery. "Upon examination, I'm finding that she was carrying a two-month-old fetus."

"Her face, eyes and mouth are healthy. I see nothing in this area of forensic interest. Her hands, fingers and fingernails indicate that she visited a manicurist regularly. Her toenails are also well manicured and her feet are perfectly groomed. Her hair is in good condition, which is an indicator of her grooming habits as well as her general health. She is built like an athlete but not a bulky athlete. She has a runner's body that's well muscled yet long and lean."

"That completes my examination of Zizi Zeigler's body and now I'll give a review of the clothes that she was wearing at the time of her death. Possibly, her garments will give us a clue as to where she shopped so we can contact the clothing stores for a clue about her identification."

The coroner continued to speak in his recorder as he walked over to a box of Zizi Zeigler's clothes, jewelry, shoes and purse.

"Her jewelry consists of: one diamond earring and what looks like a wedding band covered with diamonds that she was wearing on her right fourth finger. She was carrying a small velvet bag with ones and five dollar bills and a one hundred dollar bill. No checkbook or credit cards. She had a doctor's appointment card, a handkerchief, and a couple keys to her apartment building. A couple lipsticks. Mints."

Pausing for a second, the coroner said, "She was only wearing one earring. Where is the other earring?"

"I know the forensic team checked all the seat cushions and the carpet for any other evidence but they didn't find anything," Lt. Paganelli said. Changing the subject, he said, "She was wearing expensive clothes and jewelry but doesn't have a car, or at least there are no car keys in her purse. No photos or address book to indicate that she knows anyone. Note: her sweater has a Saks Fifth Avenue tag on it but there is no Saks Fifth Avenue in Yakima. Seattle, Washington and Portland, Oregon would be the closest outlets."

"What do you make of so little identification, Doc?" Lt. Paganelli shook his head while he rubbed his chin.

"She was not in a town where her family raised her. Even though she didn't have a job that we know about, she was wearing jewelry and clothes that were expensive. You can ask the apartment manager if she registered a car. If not, then she had no car, which is unheard of for a person this young and this wealthy. She was a beautiful young woman who had money but no employer. She was pregnant and dead. It doesn't take a rocket scientist to figure out that she was a mistress to someone who has lots—I'm talking a bundle—of money," Doc answered Lt. Paganelli's question.

The room was silent as both men looked at Jane Doe –aka Zizi Zeigler—for the last time.

"She's the same age as my daughter," the coroner held her hand for a moment.

"Mine too," Lt. Paganelli added.

As his voice cracked, the coroner said, "How could this young lady be a threat to anyone?"

Lt. Paganelli had never seen the coroner's heart so affected by a victim and he vowed to find out why this had happened. His first clue was the appointment card in the victim's purse listing a local doctor's name and office, located just a few blocks from downtown.

Dr. Richard Cannon, General Practitioner, pulled Ms. Zeigler's file.

"Looking at our records, Ms. Zeigler gave her address as an apartment downtown. Phone number too. Her general health was good except she was underweight. She didn't give any information about her family. No spouse. No work place or employer was listed. No driver's license. We do have a social security number on the application but usually don't check it unless an insurance company pays her bills," the doctor shared the information on the dead woman's application.

"What were the symptoms that prompted her to make an appointment with you?" Lt. Paganelli asked.

"She complained of morning nausea and thought she might be pregnant. It turned out that she was two months pregnant. I asked her if she had family nearby?" Dr. Cannon said.

"And?"

"She was thinking of moving back to the Seattle area to be with her family."

"Did she say where in Seattle or what town on the coast?" Lt. Paganelli was ready to write the name of the town.

"No."

"How did she pay for her visit?"

"Ms. Zeigler paid with a $100. bill and the receptionist had to scramble to find enough change to give back to the patient."

"Did she make an appointment to see you for another check-up?"

"No. She said she'd see her family's doctor in her hometown but didn't say what town that would be." The doctor shook his head and avoided Lt. Paganelli's eye contact while he tried to clear his throat. "I can't believe she's dead."

The next stop was the place where the victim lived. Lt. Paganelli drove to the downtown address given for her living quarters. He knew the address sounded familiar because it was The Chinook Hotel, 402 E. Yakima Avenue.

Known as the Skeleton Hotel from 1930 to 1946, construction on the

Chinook Hotel stopped dead in its tracks during the Great Depression when funds to complete the fourteen-story building simply were no longer available. The exterior was completed in 1944 and the hotel was open for business in 1949.

While other hotels in Yakima clung to their historic antique interiors, the Chinook Hotel was a trendsetter with modern, contemporary interior designs and amenities.

As Lt. Paganelli stepped through the doors, he noticed that the lobby was lit with recessed ceiling lights and electric wall sconces. The décor was contemporary and the walls were built with long narrow masonry called flagstone. The couches were sleek padded benches or half-moon, no frills seating arrangements. He walked across a red floral carpet to the check-in desk, which appeared to be an extra-terrestrial ship that had floated into the lobby. As if she was a teller in a bank, the receptionist was only visible from the chest up as she stood in the opening of the shielded countertop.

After he showed his badge and asked the receptionist if he could speak privately with the manager, the lieutenant was immediately escorted down a lighted hallway and into an office where a fashionably dressed man wearing a gold, chain bracelet stood up and extended his hand.

"Officer Paganelli, what can I do for you?"

"I see that you have overnight hotel guests. Do you also have people who rent a suite monthly?"

"Yes. We do have several guests who pay by the month," the manager answered.

"I'm looking for a renter who lives here by the name of Zizi Zeigler. Do you have any information on her?

The manager picked up his phone, pressed a button and said, "Vicki, will you look in the file cabinet and get Ms. Zizi Zeigler's file? Then bring it to me. Thanks."

He continued. "What's this all about, officer?"

"Ms. Zeigler was found dead on the floor behind the back seats of the Capitol Theatre last night during the 9 p.m. movie."

"Oh my word!" gasped the manager. She was so young and pretty. Do you have any idea why someone would go after her? Was it a robbery?" the manager gasped.

"All I can tell you is that we are trying to find out who she was. Did she list any family members on her application?"

Vicki walked in and handed the manager the file for Zizi Zeigler.

After browsing the sparse information on the application, the manager said, "She didn't list any friends or family members."

"Did she pay her rent with a check?"

"She paid us with a $100. bills in an envelope each month. Most of our guests stay one or two nights, maybe a couple days longer for conferences, so she didn't really have a chance to make friends. I didn't understand what she did with herself each day, to tell you the truth," the manager said. "She left a generous deposit so we weren't going to turn her away since she had no problem paying her first and last month's rent."

Lt. Paganelli stood up. "I need to see her apartment. Maybe we can get some information from her personal items like an address book or papers that she might have stored in her desk."

"She lived in apartment 218. Do you want to check the apartment now?"

"Yes. I'll call a forensic team who'll box up her belongings for storage. Although her room is not a crime scene, we need to take photos and pick up any evidence." Mainly, I'm trying to find someone who will identify her, particularly a family member who'll assume responsibility for her burial arrangements," Lt. Paganelli said.

The manager slid the phone toward the lieutenant and he called the Yakima Police Department. Within ten minutes, the CSI team walked through the front doors of the hotel carrying their equipment.

"I have the key to the victim's apartment," the lieutenant quietly told the team. "It's located on the second floor so we might as well go up the stairs."

To the left of the glass fronted gift shop, the team climbed the carpeted stairs that were exposed to the lobby. The wall alongside the staircase was covered in mirrored panels so that a visitor could see themselves in the glass until they stepped into a false lobby on the mezzanine level where more padded benches, that were supposed to be couches with no arms, lined the walls. Receded ceiling lights and end table lamps lit the way to conference rooms.

Tasteful framed prints of northwestern scenes occasionally lined the walls and matched the carpet, which was colored more like autumn than red like the lobby carpet. There was one more floor to go.

Lt. Paganelli noticed that his team of three people and himself made virtually no sound as they sunk into the wall-to-wall carpet on their way to the second floor. There was absolute silence as they walked down the wide hall to Zizi Zeigler's room. Maid service was nowhere in sight.

"216. 217. 218. Here we are." Lt. Paganelli turned the key in the lock, opened the door and all three men stood just inside the doorway with their mouths hanging open as they looked around.

Not one thing was out of place in the furnished apartment. It appeared that no one presently lived in the apartment or had recently resided there. The pillows on the rose patterned couch and burgundy stuffed chairs were in perfect order. The shiny cherry wood coffee table was bare and a lone lamp sat on the desk with no framed photos of family members.

As the team peeked into the bedroom, the double bed was covered with a light turquoise bedspread and matching décor pillows. The dresser was bare. When they opened the closet, only a variety of hangers were the content. There were no towels or toiletries in the bathroom.

The photographer got ready to shoot but turned to the lieutenant. "Are you sure we're in the right apartment? This place is empty."

"Murphy, go down and get the manager. It looks like he gave us the wrong key," Lt. Paganelli said and sent one of the investigators to the hotel office. "Let's look around. It's possible that someone cleaned this place out during the night so there wouldn't be any evidence connected to Ms. Zeigler. Kusske, see if you can find any prints."

Every dresser and desk drawer was empty. The storage and hall closets were empty. No cosmetics were in the bathroom—not even used soap. The refrigerator and pantry were empty. There were no sheets on the bed. The biggest clue was that someone who was worried about Ms. Zeigler being identified made sure there was no evidence to connect her to a person of interest.

"Officer, is there a problem?" the manager walked into the apartment.

"Are you sure Ms. Zeigler lived in this apartment?"

"Positive. Last week, she paid her rent for the month of March for apartment 218, this apartment."

"There is nothing to indicate that anyone has been living in this apartment. No unwashed dishes. No sheets on the bed. The bathroom is clean and dry as a bone. Does the hotel provide sheets and towels?"

"Yes. That's one of the services we offer our renters. The towels and sheets are changed several times a week," the manager couldn't believe his eyes when he saw that the apartment was empty.

"Is there a laundry service? Maybe some of Miss Zeigler's clothes are in the laundry," the lieutenant speculated.

"I'll step in the hall and ask my secretary to check the laundry room and get back to me," the manager wanted to get to the bottom of this puzzle as he lifted a walkie-talkie from a clip on his belt.

"Kusske, did you find any prints?"

"No prints, boss. Not even on the phone. Someone knew how to wipe prints on all the places that prints could be found. No hair in the bathroom or the bedroom dresser or bed. I'd say the fact that everything has been wiped clean is a big clue that someone was worried Ms. Zeigler's evidence would connect her murder to them," Kuskke said.

Murphy walked into the living room. "There're stairs going to the alley in back. Then there's a parking lot designated for the Chinook Hotel tenants. Anyone can go out this back staircase but a key is needed to get in. If a person carried all Ms. Zeigler's stuff out the door and down the back staircase, no one would have heard a thing. If he wedged the door open just a little, it'd be easy to get back into the hotel until all her belongings were removed."

The hotel manager stepped into the apartment. "Laundry service said they had a few garments that needed to be cleaned from room 218 but they're gone. The maid did not pick up towels or sheets from this apartment in the last forty-eight hours."

Lt. Paganelli nodded toward the manager in dismissal. "Here's the key. I'll close the apartment door on our way out. Thank you for your assistance."

As the manager left, he checked the number on the key and the number on the door just to make sure they matched.

Exasperated, Lt. Paganelli raised his voice enough to reach everyone on the team. "Have we got anything guys?"

Each person responded in the negative. The photographer indicated that he'd taken photos of every part of the apartment. The fingerprint expert found nothing.

Lt. Paganelli intended to have the coroner take Zizi Zeigler's fingerprints and send them through the F.B.I. system to see if she had any prior convictions. A forensic artist would sketch her face with her eyes open and that image would be sent on Associated Press, aka AP, to all the newspapers in the United States to see if anyone could identify her. In the meantime, the coroner would conduct an autopsy, record the results then her body would be refrigerated for a designated amount of time. If no family member claimed her body, she would have to be disposed, either by burial or cremation.

Since there were no clues in her apartment, Lt. Paganelli deduced that the lack of clues indicated a big clue. Someone wanted Ms. Zeigler wiped off the face of the earth and Lt. Paganelli was determined to prosecute the perpetrator.

Opening night, 1920. Courtesy: **Yakimamemory.org.**

CHAPTER THREE

Flashback to the 1950s

When Rex was growing up near the Boise Cascade Lumber Mill in Yakima he was different than most of the other kids in the neighborhood, who were Catholic and attended St. Joseph's Grade School on Fourth Street.

Rex's father was a Pentecostal Minister, which added to the daily pressure on Rex to be a perfect son who did God's will and most particularly his father's will. He felt kind of sorry for the Catholic kids in his neighborhood after he was told that if they managed to get to heaven, they would be on a lower level than the Pentecostal folks since they weren't under God's chosen religious umbrella of Protestantism. According to the church leaders, even Baptists would not be on as high a level in heaven as Pentecostals.

Rex had to watch his language around his father. Sometimes, he would say, "Gosh, what a lucky break!" about an event that seemed particularly serendipitous.

His father would respond, "That wasn't luck. That was God's providence."

Rex's father was an only child. Unfortunately, he had polio as a youngster and was picked on by the kids at school, which caused him to be sensitive to weak kids and particularly protective of his boys. Ben, the oldest son, followed his father's example by being his brother's protector. If Rex was scared or intimidated by a bully at school, Ben became the front man and handled the situation. He had little time for sports or much fun because he chose to spend his youth working as much as possible.

Lance, the middle son, was a star athlete in football and basketball and Rex was jealous of Lance's celebrity. It didn't help the brother's relationship when Lance reinforced the pecking order by monitoring Rex's slang language. Rex could not say "gee" because that sounded like a shortened version of "Jesus." He couldn't say "dang" because Lance said using that word would lead to Rex saying, "darn" then "damn" then "G-damn".

Rex was not big or athletic like his brothers. But he was smart and accurate when observing people's failures and successes. While others negatively commented about their family or friends, Rex never felt compelled to judge his classmates, teachers or family members. He never complained even when there was an event that didn't seem fair.

In the early 1950s, with the exception of the Pentecostal kids, most of Rex's friends looked forward to going to the Saturday matinees at the local neighborhood theaters, such as: the Roxy, the Liberty, the Avenue, the Yakima, the Empire—all owned by Fred Mercy, Sr. Kids as young as seven-years-old saved their chore money or money from delivering papers and paid twenty cents admission to enter the world of make believe at their favorite theater.

The Looney Toons cartoons with Tom and Jerry, Bugs Bunny, the Road Runner and Wily Coyote, Tweetie and Sylvester would start the movies. Then a comedy short would hit the screen with Abbott and Costello, or The Three Stooges, or Charley Chan.

The Saturday serials were continuing adventures of a particular hero like Buck Rogers or Flash Gordon facing certain doom from Ming the Merciless and the Rock People. The story and the characters were television on a big screen with lots of science fiction impossibilities. Each weekly episode portrayed the hero seconds from death then suddenly escaping the evildoers in an attempt to bring the bad guys to justice only to be betrayed and once again in dire straits at the program's end. The young audience was hooked and couldn't wait until the next week's installment.

Before the first main feature began, Ed Herlihy was the announcer of news about worldwide sports or war events that were shown on the Movie Tone Newsreel.

The adventures of the masked Spanish Zorro, England's Robin Hood, America's Davy Crocket and Africa's Tarzan were bigger than life heroes. Cowboy movies also included male heroes and their horses or companions, such as: Gene Autry and Champion, Roy Rogers and Trigger, The Lone Ranger and Tonto - "Hiyo Silver—Away". Movies that featured animal stars included: Lassie, My Friend Flicka, and National Velvet. Walt

Disney's animated productions were wholesome stories about animals, heroes and heroines whose lives duplicated the challenges faced by most real life humans with one exception.

Magic rescued those who were in perilous situations: Alice in Wonderland, Pinocchio, Dumbo, Bambi, Sleeping Beauty, Lady and the Tramp, Cinderella and Song of the South with uncle Remus. Godzilla, King Kong, the Creature from the Black Lagoon and The Blob were the horror movies that delighted screaming youngsters and gave them nightmares.

The Roxy Theater was located in a rough neighborhood on Yakima Avenue between First St. and Front. Next to the theater, the aroma of chili, onions, sauerkraut and foot long hot dogs at The New York Coney Island delicatessen tempted customers to purchase their little bit of heaven for twenty-five-cents.

If a kid couldn't afford a hot dog from the deli, soft drinks, popcorn, ice cream and candy bars were available at the snack bar in the theater lobby.

The reality that Rex and his Pentecostal playmates faced was that there were a lot of children who were eating popcorn and drinking Coca-Cola at the movies every Saturday and they weren't included. He asked himself what was the harm in seeing the Three Stooges or Bambi or Roy Rogers and Trigger? Then he'd ask his parents why he couldn't go to the movies with the other kids.

The answer was always the same. His parents told him that Pentecostals believed motion pictures were used to show the most corrupt passions and activities of men on a movie screen as entertainment about the ungodly world. If unrestricted use was permitted, movies would jeopardize and destroy the holy standards of separation from the world, which the United Pentecostal Church International had consistently upheld for many years.

His parents tried to console him by saying that God's people were permitted to take pictures of families and friends and to view educational, religious, or inspirational films.

The adults went one step further when it came to watching TV. If there were commercials that showed people smoking a cigarette or drinking beer, the children were ordered to step out of the room until the commercial was finished.

Even as a youngster, Rex observed the difference between what his elders said and what they did. Religious Jesus movies, sanctioned by Billy

Graham Productions, were shown in local theaters in order to accommodate large attendance from many Pentecostal churches. So the Pentecostal
viewers of the Jesus movies were sitting in a dark theater eating popcorn
and that was okay. But it wasn't okay for the Pentecostal youngsters to
see Cinderella in a dark theater and eat popcorn at the Saturday matinee.

Rex was beginning to understand the meaning of hypocrisy in the adult
world. When revivals were held in the spring and fall, people who were the
biggest sinners the rest of the year were also the loudest people to repent
as they stood before the revival audiences and yelled, "Give glory to God
... I'm a sinner, God. I'll change my evil ways if you'll just have mercy on
me." The hypocrisy galled Rex.

When he was in early grammar school, he and his pals invented their
own magical world by play-acting the adventures of Captain Marvel, a
comic book super-hero character. Rex, of course, was Captain Marvel. His
pal, Mike Hansen, was Captain Marvel, Jr. and sometimes played Captain
Marvel's alter ego, Billy Batson, a youth who worked as a radio news reporter and was chosen to be the champion of good by the wizard, Shazam.
Whenever Billy said the wizard's name, a magic lightning bolt transformed
him into the adult superhero, Captain Marvel.

His third pal, Sharon Meyer, played the wizard, Shazam, or the evil
Doctor Sivana. Although Rex had the most power, his two pals were legendary figures themselves. Their storylines came directly from the comic
books and were based on good versus evil.

Captain Marvel wore a bright red skintight body suit with a lightning
bolt insignia on the chest. The costume also included a white-collared
cape trimmed with gold that was thrown over his left shoulder and held
around his neck with a gold cord.

The only part of Captain Marvel's costume that Rex had was a white
blanket that he tied around his neck. Sometimes, he would wear a red
T-shirt and a red bandana wrapped around his forehead and tied in back.
During Halloween, he bought three black masks, which he, Mike and Sharon wore to portray their characters. The three of them took turns invent-
ing storylines to outsmart the evil villain, Doctor Sivana. The adventures
with Captain Marvel were played at home and also at school with other
children begging to play the various roles created by the threesome.

After the sixth grade, the three pals became more sophisticated in their make believe stories, not unlike becoming actors in movies. They were fascinated by the movies and vowed that when they entered high school, they would find a way to work at the snack counter or take tickets at one of the local neighborhood movie theaters. They were forbidden to work at the evening movies where adult movies were shown with stars such as: Elvis Presley, James Dean and Marlon Brando when they acted in movies that portrayed young men who were outcasts and acted in an immoral manner against society and God. Those story lines were totally unacceptable by the Pentecostal Church and Rex's parents.

Bank night, 1930. Courtesy: **Yakimamemory.org.**

CHAPTER FOUR

Ozzie Goldstein

Ozzie Goldstein had been called "the Wizard of Oz" most of his life.

Just like the contraption the wizard was operating behind the curtain in the movie, Ozzie was fascinated with all things that had wheels, sprockets, levers and operated with circular motion.

His passion was photographing home movies with his 8mm camera and splicing the film from several reels so that only the best of the story was shown. Back lighting, which caused people to appear as silhouettes, and bright side flares were problems that he avoided when he shot film outside. Using the spotlight on the camera as well as lights behind photographic umbrellas on each side of the person who was filmed inside allowed his videos to be as close to professional movies as an amateur could achieve.

In 1955 when Rex Marvel was fifteen-years-old, he, Mike Hansen and Sharon Meyer applied for work at the Capitol Theatre despite their parent's objection that theatres showed the most corrupt passions and anti-God activities of men on movie screens and called the films entertainment.

Al Mallone, the Capitol Theatre Manager, skimmed Rex's work information and at the same time took a good look at the three pals before him.

Rex was the rock-steady one of the bunch. Dressed in saddle shoes, a button-up plaid shirt tucked into his pegs—a type of cotton pant with a belt, Rex's hair was neatly parted and combed in place. His glasses gave him an appearance of being a young professor. Browns and greens were his colors, conservative and steady.

Mike was the entrepaneur, ready to try anything. He had a gift of gab, a born salesman, who could've sold ice cream to an Eskimo. His appearance was more casual with his Hawaiian shirt not tucked into his Levi's. With a sharp mind, Mike could remember people and details long forgotten by others. He could micromanage a number of tasks at a time with ease.

Sharon seemed like the boy's baby sister. They were protective of her but didn't need to be. She was more than capable of keeping cool under the stress of customers demanding candy, ice cream, popcorn and drinks. Sharon understood how money worked and could account for every penny.

Al started with Rex. "I see on your application that you had a paper route for the last three years, which means that you started very early in the morning to deliver papers before you went to school."

"I covered a two mile square area on my bike."

"You mentioned that you also fixed your own bike. Does that mean you took the bike apart, fixed the problem, then put it back together?"

"That's what it means. Once I understood how the bike chains and wheels worked together, it seemed easy," said Rex. "Then other people heard about me repairing my bike and asked me to fix their bikes."

Al Mallone did a double take on Rex's explanation of how easy it was for him to repair things. He checked the teen's applications, particularly their high-grade averages. "I think the three of you will work out just fine. We don't have large attendance at the movies but as you can see, the theatre is more like an opera house rather than a neighborhood movie theatre. So when we do have an entertainment event, we can easily seat 1,500 people. We'll need you to sell tickets, work as ushers, sell popcorn, candy and pop at the snack bar then be the cleanup crew after movies. How does that sound to you three?"

The teenagers looked at each other and tried to hide their excitement at working in such a glamorous theatre.

"Sounds fine," Rex was the spokesperson.

"We're going to have a movie tonight then a children's matinee tomorrow so let's go to the snack bar and I'll teach you how to make popcorn and work the cash register."

After repeating the information a couple times, the kids did some practice runs with the cash register and each of them took turns making popcorn. In the middle of the third popcorn run, Mallone got a phone call.

"Sharon, I need you to stay in the snack bar and clean the display counters and glass cases then organize the candy bars. Mike and Rex, let's go to the loading dock in the back of the theatre. We've got some heavy supplies coming in and the delivery truck is waiting for us." Mallone led the way.

The rest of the day, the trio became accustomed to their assigned duties and checked where various rooms were located in the theatre. In very short order, Al Mallone approached Rex and said, "I want you to meet Ozzie Goldstein. He's our resident genius when it comes to spot lighting live entertainment and operating the projectors. He needs an assistant who understands sprockets and wheels. Let's go up stairs to the projection booth and meet the wizard of Oz!!"

As they entered the top balcony and crossed over to the projection booth, Mallone alerted the projectionist, "Hey Oz, we're coming over."

"Come on in!" Rex heard a booming voice.

As they approached the entrance to the small booth, Rex caught a glimpse of the movie posters, such as: *Gone With The Wind* featuring Vivian Leigh and Clark Gable, James Dean in *Rebel Without A Cause and* Walt Disney's, *Treasure Island and Robin Hood.* The posters took the viewer into the wonderful world of make-believe and Rex knew he was entering a phase in his life that he had always dreamed about. If he couldn't be in the movies, showing them to an audience was the next best thing.

Rex saw that Ozzie Goldstein was wearing little round glasses on top of his head as he adjusted a small mechanism he held in his hands. He looked like he'd been shocked because his black wavy hair lifted in a puffed cloak around his face. His drooping Roman nose nearly reached the top of his lips, parted in a perpetual smile. His large eyes were dark with relaxed eyelids, friendly and welcoming. Although he didn't have an athlete's body, he was stout and sturdy, a person who rarely sat down and relaxed.

The manager said, "Rex, I'd like you to meet Mr. Ozzie Goldstein. Oz this is Rex Marvel. He had his own business repairing bikes and is familiar with mechanical parts," Mallone hoped the relationship would go well.

"Happy to meet you, Rex," Ozzie said as he reached out and shook Rex's hand. The handshake was firm and friendly.

"I've got a mess up here and need you to help me organize things. You're probably not going to do any lighting or projection work right away but for now, I'd like you to watch what I do and I'll explain things as we go along."

The three men looked at each other in agreement. Rex said, "Sounds good. I'm ready to work."

"Let's see. What shall I have you work on first?" Oz said as he held his glasses and put the tip of the ear stem in his mouth.

"Well, I've got some things to do." Al Mallone addressed Rex and said, "Looks like Ozzie will keep you busy from now on. Sharon and Mike will work with me downstairs."

"Thanks, Mr. Mallone. I'll see you later," Rex said to the theatre manager in parting.

Almost at the same time, Ozzie said, "Thanks for bringing Rex up. I'd like him to stay up here full time."

"He's all yours," Al Mallone said as he descended the stairs.

"Great. Well Rex, let's get the reel cases in order first." Shuffling papers around on a counter, Oz picked up a piece of paper with a list on it and handed it to Rex. "Here's a list of the movie titles that we'll be showing this week. There's new reels in those orange boxes that need to be taken out and put in order on the shelves. Just like books, the title is on the edge of each reel. We're gonna have to splice them later but for now I need you to match 'em to the list."

Oz wasn't a huge man; his height was a couple inches over six feet. As he showed Rex how to file the reel cases, he lifted them without effort. At 5' 8" with a slight build, the cases were heavier than Rex anticipated and he tried not to show that he was struggling with the reels' weight as he lifted them and slid the cases in the order they would be shown on each night of the week. Rex finished organizing the reels in twenty minutes and was ready for the next assignment.

"See all these scattered papers?" Ozzie referred to the stacks of papers on every counter and on the floor.

Rex looked around and lifted his feet since he was standing on papers that had been dropped on the floor.

"Yeah I know. I'm not a good housekeeper. What I need you to do is to gather all the loose papers and categorize them. When you get the piles organized, I'll take a look at them and see what needs to be thrown out and what needs to be filed," Oz said as he continued to work on a mechanical part.

After Oz and Rex worked together a couple hours, Oz said, "Let's see, it's 2 p.m. You drink coffee, Rex?" He continued without waiting for an answer. "I brought enough in my thermos for the two of us. We can't have coffee without some chocolate chip cookies, right? Good thing I made these last night so they're nice and fresh."

He found his favorite cup that said, "Boss Of The Sauce" on it and put it on a nearby counter then pulled up a folding chair. Rex noticed the inside of Ozzie's cup was stained to a deep brown color and he wondered if Oz ever washed his cup.

Reading Rex's mind, Oz said, "I have several cups up here that need to be washed. Don't worry; I won't give you a used cup. Here, you can have the thermos cup. It's shiny and clean. But we gotta get you your own cup if you're gonna be part of the team in the sky—the sky team. That's us. Pull up one of those chairs while I put on some tunes."

"I think we'll listen to the George Shearing Quintet today. Ever heard of Sir George Shearing? No? He's a British blind genius who plays the smoothest piano music this side of heaven." Oz took a record out of its protective paper cover and fitted it on a three-record-changer. The record gently dropped onto the spinning turntable then he placed the arm with the diamond needle cartridge on the record to start the music.

He listened for a few seconds and seemed satisfied as he recognized the melody. "This tune is called *Lullaby Of Birdland*. Very mellow, man, don't you think?"

Oz chuckled as he poured hot coffee into Rex's thermos cup then into his stained cup. He took a couple sugar cubes from a small bowl and dropped them into his cup.

"Sugar?"

Rex nodded and took two sugar cubes, like Oz, and dropped them into his cup.

Oz had taken a small container of milk out of his cooler and poured one second of milk into his cup.

"Milk?"

Rex nodded and copied Oz's drop of milk in his cup. They stirred their hot coffee, took a sip and were careful not to burn their lips. Oz picked up a cookie and consumed it in two bites before he picked up another one.

Rex shuddered a little as he sipped his hot coffee. It tasted bitter and he wondered if he would ever get used to the strange flavor.

"Your first cup of coffee, man? Don't your parents drink coffee?"

"My parents are Pentecostals. They don't drink coffee or go to movies,"

Rex smiled because he thought it was amusing that he was working in a theatre and drinking coffee.

"So this is totally a new world for you. That's cool, man. Who else is in your family?"

"Two older brothers: Ben the protector and Lance the athlete."

"I got ya. What's your title?" Oz thought the titles were a unique way of categorizing Rex's brothers.

"Rex means king. But that doesn't mean that I think of myself as a king. No. I'm just a kid who wants to know how things work in this world. I'm talking about how mechanical things work. I'm looking at those big projectors over there and I can hardly wait to see how the film goes through the sprockets. How you focus the projector. How you coordinate the sound."

"Yeah man, being a projectionist is sort of like being a magician. You're responsible for bringing images and sound to the big screen, which transports the audience into a world they will never see in reality. I'm gonna show a movie tonight at 6:30 p.m. Do you think you can stay that long?'

"I better go home and eat early then come back."

"Good deal," said Oz. "I'll be sure and have some more coffee and cookies waiting for you!" The two men laughed as Oz gave Rex a friendly punch in the shoulder.

CHAPTER FIVE

The Sky Team

A poster for *Twenty Leagues Under the Sea* was bigger than life size in the Capitol Theatre lobby and featured a narwhale as the menacing sea monster responsible for capsizing ships. Kirk Douglas, the Hollywood actor, was the explorer who was commissioned by the U.S. to find and destroy the creature. Innovative in underwater sea travel before its time, the science fiction movie featured a submarine called the Nautilus with Captain Nemo as the driving evil force.

Rex Marvel looked at the *Twenty Leagues* poster as well as the other movie posters in the lobby and knew that these science fiction movies were what his parents were talking about when they said all movies glorified evil forces in men and in God's creatures. But he didn't think the movies were evil. He thought they were fun and showed the extent of man's imagination, which in some cases turned out to be true.

His parents couldn't argue that his grades would suffer while he worked at the theatre. Like his older brother, he was making excellent grades without a lot of effort. Rex's mother tried a different approach. Her main trump card in controlling her children was to put guilt on them. It worked when they were children and they used that technique on each other. In summary, she told Rex that by working at a movie theater, he was retaliating against the Pentecostal Church's teachings.

Not one to argue, Rex always found a way to placate his parents.

"Your feelings are important to me," he told his parents. "My feelings are important to me, too. If the movie thing doesn't work out, I'll know it's time for me to find some other kind of work. I promise." Rather than telling them they were interfering, Rex always wanted to show his appreciation when he knew his parents were concerned about him. Still, his mother was unhappy that Rex rushed through dinner in order to run back to the theatre.

As he entered the theatre lobby, Al Mallone greeted Rex with a big smile. "There's my boy projectionist! How're you doing this evening?"

"Great. I can hardly wait to get started," Rex smiled as he headed for the projection booth stairs."

Ozzie's waiting for you. Go on up."

With each step, Rex hoped that he could remember the instructions and demonstrations that Ozzie Goldstein was about to show him."

"Mr. Goldstein? I didn't want to startle you."

"No problem, I heard you coming," Oz said as he carried a steaming cup of coffee in his hand. "Come on in."

Although Rex was eager to learn everything he could, he wasn't sure where to stand in the tiny room. It was almost as if he and Oz were doing a dance as their movements were coordinated with Rex trying to stay out of Oz's way.

"Now Rex, I'm getting the projector and film ready before we get the movie started. This is a good time to show you how the projector works. I'm going to give you some technical language before I show you how to wind the film. Ready?"

"I'm ready," Rex rubbed his hands together.

"I'm going to talk about three reels. The projector holds two reels. The reel on top holds film that will be viewed. We're going to call that reel one. As the movie is being shown, the used film winds around the reel at the bottom called the take-up reel. We'll call that reel two. That film will be rewound to a fresh reel so we can show the movie again if we wish. That reel on the counter is reel three. See the empty reel? Eventually, reel three will hold the original film. It's sort of a merry-go-round." Oz thought that was easy to understand.

"You might hear the term, 'spool'. That's another name for reel. In the U.S. we call it a reel. In England, they call it a spool. Reel has to do with film. To me, spool has to do with sewing or telephone wiring. So I'm going to refer to these film discs as reels."

"I understand," Rex said.

"I show several films each time we have a movie. For the Saturday matinee, I start with a cartoon, usually Looney Tunes. Then a comedy short, which means a shortened film that is not the main feature. It could be *The Three Stooges*, for instance. Next, is a serial like *Buck Rogers* that has a hook theme where the hero is in terrible peril and the movie audience has to come back to see what happens to their hero."

"For the evening shows, we don't feature a comedy short or Buck Rogers. Instead, we'll have previews of new movies and a newsreel about sports events and war activities. All those short features have to be spliced together with the main movie. Even the main movie has parts that have to be spliced and that's what I do during the day to get the film ready for a showing. I'll demonstrate how to splice film another time. Let's just concentrate on the projector for now, okay?" Oz knew the details of showing movies must be overwhelming Rex.

"We have two projectors. An alternative method would be to have those short films on one reel on the first projector. The main movie would be on a second projector so I would do a change over between the projectors."

"Wow, I see how the reels on two projectors would work better," Rex could figure out that much at least.

"Now let's look at the mechanics of how I put the film in the projector." The men were standing shoulder to shoulder as Oz held the main reel.

"We start by lifting reel one up high and matching the hole in the middle with a reel bar that keeps the reel in place inside the permanent half reel case. The film has several inches of clear film before the movie begins. So I'm going to take that lead film and slide it into this slit in the bottom reel. I don't want the film to touch the floor. The take-up reel is also protected in a permanent half case. Now, I'm going to spin the take-up reel around a couple times to make sure the lead film won't slip out. See that?"

"Yes, that makes sense," Rex thought it was simple so far.

"The main thing is that the film has to go in front of this lighted section of the projector. This little door opens so you can make sure the film is in the right places. But we have to keep the film secure before the projector light and after so it will thread into the take-up reel. That's why the film has to go through a number of rollers that will keep the tension nice and smooth."

"Let's count 'em as I thread the film." Oz made it seem like a game as he pulled roller covers out, threaded the film then clicked the covers back

Cartoons. Photo courtesy: Susan La Riviere.

Castle films. Photo courtesy: Susan La Riviere.

Film strips. Photo courtesy: Susan La Riviere.

Old projector. Photo courtesy: Susan La Riviere.

Reel boxes. Photo courtesy: Susan La Riviere.

Reel case. Photo courtesy: Susan La Riviere.

Reels. Photo courtesy: Susan La Riviere.

Reel lubricant. Photo courtesy: Susan La Riviere.

in place to secure the tension.

"I'm going to turn on the projector and look through this view finder at the first frame that'll go on the screen. I can adjust the focus this way. Come over and look at the first picture. I've turned the knob so it'll be out of focus. Then I'll adjust it so it will be in focus."

Rex looked through the viewfinder. "It's out of focus."

"How about now?" Oz adjusted the knob.

"Looks good. It's in focus," Rex said.

Oz said, "We have time for you to thread the film a couple times before we show the movie. I'd like you to put on these soft cotton gloves first so you don't leave prints on the film. I put the gloves on to rewind the film. Otherwise, I know how to touch only the edges of the film but the gloves are always a good idea."

"As we go along, I'll give you bits and pieces of additional information," Oz said. "I will tell you that we have a mono-sound system that includes a lower frequency range that the audience can hear through the woofer otherwise known as the electrostatic speaker system. The low bass sounds are important additions that dramatize the intensity of the sound throughout this large theatre."

"I'm impressed," Rex said. And that was saying a lot because he was not easily impressed.

"Once we show the main feature tonight and I carry the take-up reel over to the counter, I'll let you rewind it onto that empty reel that we identified as reel three. Then I'm going to transfer the empty reel on top of the projector to the bottom and it'll become the take-up reel. It's like a merry-go-round and it'll become second nature to you in a couple weeks. You understand how mechanics work so it should be easy for you," Oz said as he checked his watch.

"Everything at this theatre is done on time," Oz said. His casual demeanor and hip language was on hold. He was a professional projectionist in every sense of the word. "Our team has to be coordinated so that when those beautiful maroon curtains open and reveal the screen, the movie starts immediately."

The film in the projector was set and ready to go. He checked the focus a couple times. The main floor seating area had nearly filled to capacity to view *Twenty Leagues Under The Sea*, a science fiction thriller. As the lights dimmed to darkness, the heavy curtains opened, slid across the stage and disappeared into the wings.

When Oz pulled the ON lever, the screen lit up with the Movie Tone Newsreel as Ed Herlihy's voice described the new singing sensation, Elvis Presley. Oz turned toward Rex, flashed a smile and said, "IT'S SHOW-TIME!!!"

National Register of Historic Places, 1976.
Courtesy: **Yakimamemory.org.**

CHAPTER SIX

The Capitol Theatre

Ozzie Goldstein thought of Rex like a son and relished teaching him everything he knew. It never crossed Ozzie's mind that the theatre could not afford to pay two projectionists when attendance at movies and entertainment events dwindled during the 1950s and 1960s.

Television was one of the culprits that caused people to stay home. Lower ticket prices at neighborhood theaters were more attractive to an average or lower income person than the more expensive admission tickets at the Capitol Theatre, which was considered an uptown theatre. Still, the theater had a sizable share of youngsters who attended the matinee every Saturday.

Rex became an expert with the projectors and Ozzie was happy to be free of the restrictive schedule of showing every movie. Al Mallone remained the theatre's manager of the actual building maintenance and financial solvency. Ozzie Goldstein was in charge of all entertainment including the movies and he and Rex worked out a fluctuating schedule.

When Rex first began working at the Capitol Theatre, he promised his parents that if the job didn't work out, he would find other employment. They ignored his career as a projectionist and continued to give him the silent treatment when he attempted to discuss any part of his work.

By the time he was twenty-one, Rex was able to buy a small house on Naches Avenue, just a few blocks between his parent's home and the theatre. He was careful with his money and conscientious about the upkeep of his property. His house was painted robin's egg blue with white trim. Mostly perennials, decorative bushes and blooming trees, his landscaping was trimmed and his small lawn was lush and mowed. The interior of his house was clean and painted in pastel colors and featured movie posters and memorabilia. He had a gallery of photographs of the grand Capitol Theatre in his hallway.

One morning when Rex was visiting his parents, he decided to take a pro-active approach by inviting them to tour the Capitol Theatre. After they looked at each other, they surprised Rex by saying yes. They wanted to see the theater where their son had been working for the last ten years. Since their decision was a 180-degree turn-around, Rex had a feeling that his parents expected the tour to confirm their Pentecostal belief that all movies showed the diabolical worst in men and God's creatures.

On the appointed Saturday morning, Rex's parents took the bus downtown and walked part of the way. The day was sunny and he waited for them under the triple marquee. The middle lighted panel read TWO FEATURES TODAY. The panel on the right read: MATINEE: *Lassie Come Home.* The panel on the left read: *The Sound of Music starring Julie Andrews.* As he spotted his parents, Rex's heart fluttered with anxiety because of their past negative opinion of everything that had become so important to him.

After his mother hugged him briefly, she looked up at the movie selections and said, "Those look like wholesome movies." That was a good sign that things had a possibility of going well. He thanked his lucky stars that the movie selections weren't *Planet of The Apes* or *Creature From The Black Lagoon* for the evening movies.

It was a turnabout situation. Rex was the teacher and his parents were his students for the next hour. This was a moment that Rex would cherish for a long time.

"Mom and Dad before we go through the front doors, I want to tell you a little about Fred Mercy's dream of building a grand vaudeville theatre in 1919. I know you've heard the term vaudeville but maybe you didn't know that it was a live entertainment show that was kind of like a circus with performing animals and people who danced, sang and were crazy comedians or clowns. There was even a white guy with black make-up on his face to look like a black man while he sang, "Mammy, My Little Mammy!" This theatre was the largest live performance venue in the Pacific Northwest with sixty acts a week."

Rex paused at the front doors and continued his theatre history lesson.

"In the early 1900s, Mr. Mercy wanted the most beautiful theatre in the northwest because he loved vaudeville entertainment. That theatre was and is the Capitol Theatre, the grand lady of all theatres in Eastern Washington. And when we go through these beautifully carved doors, you're going to be in a theatre that many still call Yakima's Little Jewel Box."

Rex held the doors open for his parents to enter the lobby. The aroma of popcorn filled the reception area and they immediately saw the concession stand. "You're walking on a custom designed plush red patterned carpet that you'll see throughout the theatre. The art deco glass wall sconces are a sign that all of the art features in this theatre were made by artisans who dedicated their lives to creating beauty rather than concentrating only on function."

"Shall we go into the theatre?" Rex held the door open for his parents and they entered the lighted theatre.

His mother gasped at the vastness and beauty of the theatre's interior. "Oh my word," she said. "I've never seen anything like this and didn't know a theatre could be so beautiful."

Her comment reinforced Rex's feelings about the theatre and caused his heart to ache with thankfulness that his parents—or at least his mother—could finally see the ultimate beauty of a theatre that was one man's dream come true—Fred Mercy, Sr. He put his arm around his mother's shoulders and smiled down at her.

"There's so much to look at, son. And it's difficult for me to understand that all I see in this theatre was created by a team of people who had the same dream." She looked over at her husband to see if he was as impressed as she was. While he looked up at the murals in the dome, he had to hold on to a theatre seat to steady himself.

"I think you'll be able to see the whole theatre a little better if we walk up these side stairs to the stage," said Rex.

"You want us to stand on the stage?" his father wondered if visitors were allowed to stand on the stage because visitors to his church would not be allowed to stand in his pulpit.

"Sure, it's okay, Dad. There's a rail on the side of this narrow staircase if you need it."

Once the three of them were standing on the stage, Rex's mother brought her hand to her mouth and seemed overwhelmed, as she looked at the ceiling, the orchestra pit, the main level of seats and the two layers of balconies.

"Let's look at the dome first," Rex said. "I'm going to begin with Alexander Pantage, who was the biggest producer of vaudeville in the early 1900s. Together he and Fred Mercy, Sr. worked with designers and architects and supervised the construction of the Capitol Theatre."

"Theatres that Pantage designed can be found in Los Angeles, San Diego and Tacoma as well as western U.S. and Canada. When I say his theatres, what I'm referring to is the fancy curved Baroque style of art features that he liked and that means the features in the theatre are beautifully appointed and framed with columns on both sides of the stage. All his theatres have a rectangular lighted panel that is highlighted with decorative golden patterns. But his other theatres don't have the beautiful murals like the Capitol Theatre does," Rex pointed to the dome. "Aren't the paintings beautiful, Mom?"

"Yes, they are beautiful. Did the artist paint the ceiling on his back while he was on those tall platforms?"

"I'd have to say yes that he painted on his back just like many great artists. I can name one that you might recognize. That would be Michelangelo Buonarroti who painted the Sistine Chapel in Italy. Did you ever see a picture of his famous painting called The Creation of Adam?"

"Wasn't that the one where God and Adam's fingers are almost touching?" Rex's mother replied.

"Right again," Rex said. "Even though the murals in the Capitol Theatre look like Michelangelo's work, actually they were painted by Tony Heinsbergen to honor the muses of the theatre: comedy, tragedy, music, and art.

"Pardon me but I have no idea what a muse is," Rex's mother looked up at him for an explanation.

"That's a good question, Mother. I'll tell you that I had never heard the word muse or mythology until I started working here either. So I'll go back in time to Greek history and talk about two words. Mythology is the first word and has to do with gods and goddesses of all the natural occurrences in life. Like Zeus was the god of thunder and Hercules was the god of war."

"Goddesses and muses are words for the same thing. In mythology, there were nine goddesses, or muses, of the arts. Let's see if I can remember all nine," Rex started counting on his fingers. "First there was poetry, history, love, music, tragedy, hymns, dance, and comedy. That's eight. The last art was astrology, the study of the sky."

Rex continued. "The mural artist painted himself and his wife in the mural at the left end of the dome. See, Mom? He's in a brown jacket and she's in a green dress. Right over there."

"He had a sense of humor, didn't he?" Rex's mother commented.

"Yes, he did. I'm sure that you've seen the interior relief decorations that were highlighted with gold paint. That was another delicate job that Heinsbergen completed."

"Unfortunately, you can see that the round chandelier blocks some of the audience's view of portions of the murals so if a person really wanted to see the details, they'd have to walk around the orchestra floor or view the murals from the balconies. The paneling surrounding the murals is framed with lighted and molded friezes that appear to be gold gilded. Beyond that are layers of decorative carved molding."

Rex felt that most of his tour narration and choice of words were easy to understand yet, he also felt that it was necessary to mention the theatrical words that he had never heard of before he began working at the theatre.

Pantage's Face: "counting the house". Courtesy: Leonard La Lumiere.

"You know Mom and Dad, I had to learn many theatrical words that described various parts of the theatre and stage. For instance, where we are standing near the edge of the stage and where the curtains close, this opening is called a proscenium. And the middle decorative molding above us is called a cartouche that resembles the prow of a ship. At the base of the cartouche, you'll see a man's face looking at the audience. That's a carving of Alexander Pantage's face *counting the house.* In other words, he's figuring out how much money he made each night. It's funny don't you think?"

"I would never have noticed that little face without you pointing it out," his mother smiled. As she was looking up, she noted the opera boxes similar in placement to the balconies at Ford's Theater where President Lincoln was shot.

"Can a person sit in those small balconies on either side, son?"

"During the time of vaudeville, the opera boxes were excellent seats because the performers played downstage, which was right on the front of the stage. Now that we're showing mostly movies the boxes are more for decoration but the theatre can use them for a lighting position," Rex answered. "Stage technicians are the only ones allowed to reach the opera boxes by ladders.

"People sitting in the middle balcony have an excellent position to see everything that is happening on stage from a little higher position. You'll find the same thing with the upper balcony. This theatre seats about 1,500 people and was designed with the thought in mind that there are no bad seats. See how the seats are rounded?"

"Notice that the walls of the theatre are curved, which allows sound to be channeled up instead of bouncing. The acoustics in the Capitol Theatre are considered to be some of the best in the Pacific Northwest," Rex was proud to be associated with such a beautifully constructed theatre.

"The orchestra pit is right in front of us. The whole unit raises and lowers and can be accessed in the basement. Hopefully, in the future when we can book ballet in this theatre again, the orchestra pit will stay low and the audience will not be able to see the musicians. Since the pit is an elevator, it's used to transport equipment down to the dressing room level, which is below us."

Rex could see that his parents needed to move around after standing in one place for twenty minutes. "I want to point out where the sound booth and the projection booth are before we explore the stage. The sound booth is located in the back row on the main floor. But the projection booth is located where you see that panel of windows way high up under the ceiling? Above the last row of seats in the highest balcony?"

"Dad, do you see the windows?"

"Those windows are so high. Is that where you work, son?"

"Yes. The projection booth will be our last stop. Before we do that, I want to show you the giraffe door."

At the same time, both his parents said, "The giraffe door? You mean where a tall animal could walk on the stage?"

"Precisely."

As the trio walked toward the back of the stage, Rex guided them to the right and said, "May I present the giraffe door. This was a doorway where animals that were in cages or tall trailers could be led on stage to do a circus performance. The stage crew had to cut out a doorway tall enough to accommodate a giraffe act at one time. Probably the only exotic giraffe act ever. Don't even ask me what a giraffe could do. My guess is that a trainer simply led the giraffe on stage and hoped that it wouldn't panic and try to run."

"The cables, ropes, grand piano, rigging, pipes, arbors and a variety of curtains, were all used when there was live entertainment at the theatre. The Grand Drape that traveled across the front of the stage weighs 2,000 pounds."

Rex was surprised when his parents walked around the wings of the stage and took a closer look at the operations part of the theatre. They looked up at the hanging stage lights, the catwalks, the cables and ropes. Although they didn't ask any other questions, they could see that the Capitol Theatre had been the Grande Dame of Yakima, no question about it. They could also see that the equipment was sitting idle.

Rex interrupted their reverie. "Now Mom and Dad, Fred Mercy loved the idea of entertaining people. That's why he owned so many of the neighborhood theaters around town like the Majestic, the Liberty, the Roxy, the Yakima, the Ave and the Empire. Unfortunately, in the 1950s, television slowed the desire for audiences to pay to see vaudeville in person when they could see the same kind of acts on the Ed Sullivan Show and other variety shows."

"Are you saying that all this stage equipment hasn't been used since then?" Rex's mother asked.

"It's almost like the equipment has been put back in place until the next performance. Maybe in the future, stage entertainment will come back to the Capitol Theatre. For now, we are only showing movies. And to tell you the truth, we keep the audience on the main floor and hope the attendance and the sale of concessions will pay the rent," Rex said with regret.

"I see that our hour is at hand so let's skip the dressing rooms and go up to the projection booth," Rex started to lead the way and his parents followed. "Having a second thought, he said, "We can climb the stairs or go up the elevator."

"Oh I want to view all the levels," said his mother." His father always went along with his mother so they both agreed to climb the stairs on the side of each balcony. First, they had to walk up one flight of stairs to the mezzanine.

"This is where people use to take a break between performances when there was vaudeville acts. It really is a second lobby and rather than a concession stand, the house would serve drinks from a permanent bar. Movie goers are not allowed up here except to use the bathrooms," Rex informed his parents. "Let's go up the stairs to the top balcony."

Once the threesome was at the top of the theatre, Rex's mother said, "Oh, this is very scary up this high. I can't imagine people sitting in that first row because it would be so easy for them to stumble and go over the top."

Rex was concerned about his mother's comfort. "The projection booth is over here and up a little. Will you be okay to take a few more steps?"

"No need to fuss over me. I can take care of myself," his mother became defensive. "I'll follow you."

Within a few steps, Rex was in the booth and walked out to help his parents up the few steps. He had adjusted the posters so that *Cleopatra, Born Free, Funny Girl* and *The Pink Panther* were the featured films. "Come in. Come in. I know the booth is small but there's room to move around. Take a look at the view. Don't you feel like a bird about to take flight?"

His mother couldn't continue her gaze over the theater. She stepped back and knocked over a reel. "Gosh, a-mighty! I'm a bull in a china shop," she said as she tried to pick up the reel and bumped into a counter.

"Mom, here's a chair. If you'll take a seat, I'll explain the merry-go-round of showing a film," Rex said. "Dad?"

Leaning against a counter, Rex's father waved to indicate that he was fine and to get on with the projector lecture. As brief as he could manage, Rex gave a simplified version of Ozzie's first lecture to him about operating the projectors. His parents nodded until their eyes fluttered and they tried not to doze in the middle of his explanation.

"Well, I think that wraps it up," Rex said to alert his parents that he wouldn't give them any more information that they could not understand. "Watch your step as we leave the booth. We're going back to the stairs that will take us into the lobby and out the front."

As the family carefully made their way down the flights of stairs, they chatted about things other than the theatre. There was going to be a revival coming up and they wanted to know if Rex planned to attend. Although his parents didn't want to come to the theatre, they had come because they loved him. Although he didn't want to go to the revival, he told his parents that he would go because he loved them.

That's how it was in his family. They loved each other and attended events and places that otherwise they would never have considered. In the end, they were always glad about their choices.

The Capitol Theatre Lobby: wall sconces are handcrafted.
All interior photos courtesy: Leonard La Lumiere.

Heinsbergen murals around relight on dome.

Dome, balcony and opera box.

Relight and art mural: Heinsbergen painted himself in the mural.

Art murals

Music mural

Comedy and tragedy mural

Three balconies and projection room

Top balcony

The cartouche: the prow of a ship.

Bronze theatre mask

Stage and opera box

CHAPTER SEVEN

The Cremation

It was mid-March and the falling snow covered all the patrol cars in the downtown parking lot outside the brick building housing the Yakima County Police Department.

One of the detectives had arrived before 7:30 a.m. and made coffee in the tiny combination kitchen and photocopy room. The aroma of brewed coffee filled the offices and Lt. Paganelli tried not to spill the coffee in his filled-to-the-brim cup while he walked to his desk. He checked his list of priorities for the day and Zizi Zeigler was at the top of the list.

The phone rang as he took a sip of hot coffee and burned his tongue as usual.

It was the coroner. "I got your note that today is the day we're transferring Miss Zeigler's body to Shaw and Sons Funeral Home."

Lt. Paganelli checked his information. "They'll be ready for her any time after 8 a.m. Since this is the first Jane Doe case I've handled, I'm guessing that she has to be embalmed before her burial. Right?"

"Unfortunately, her body is unclaimed and cannot be buried unless family members can identify her and will pay for her internment," answered the coroner.

Trying to show that the police department was doing everything possible to identify her, the lieutenant said, "We've got the artist's drawing of her face and her description on Associated Press but still haven't gotten a bite. If the family finally comes to us after searching for her, where will they find her?"

"I know you haven't had a case like this before so you wouldn't know that the family will find her ashes in a lined box in the coroner's storage unit along with countless other boxes of unclaimed ashes. She's considered a cold case for the time being," the coroner said.

"So you're telling me that today is the day she will be cremated, not buried?"

"Correct. The ambulance is here now so I need you to come over and escort her body to Shaw and Sons as soon as you're ready."

"What a tragedy," Lt. Paganelli had to swallow a couple times as he thought about her situation and how he'd feel if she were his daughter. He left his hot coffee and put on his overcoat.

He had no way of knowing her birthdate but the coroner figured she was at least twenty-one-years-old. Lt. Paganelli knew that guess was on the money since his own daughter was the same age. If this girl had a father who loved her, his heart must have broken when she left home and didn't tell her parents where she was going or finally, where she lived. From all that he could see, the girl, Zizi, cut herself off from her family just as surely as if she had been kidnapped. As a father, the lieutenant made these assumptions with no proof to back up his opinions.

There was no indication that she had a daily job yet she paid her rent and doctor with $100. bills. The money was coming from somewhere or someone. So the deduction was that she was providing a service that warranted being paid big bucks. The guy that picked her up at the theatre wasn't her main squeeze. Like Mike Hansen from the Capitol Theatre had said, the pickup man paid her no mind. Lt. Paganelli figured the chauffer or the assistant worked for the main man who she was ultimately meeting.

She had enough money to keep her in expensive clothes and jewelry but not enough money to buy her own car. No car meant that the man who was keeping her in $100. bills did not want her to have access to a vehicle that would allow her to leave town. Lt. Paganelli wondered why this pretty girl would allow her life to be controlled by someone else?

The only thing he could figure is that women who are mistresses to married men usually make a gross mistake of expecting to be the only love interest in the lives of their man. A mistress believes that once the boyfriend divorces his wife, they will be married. Lt. Paganelli wanted to tell mistresses that they should expect their lives to be a waiting game until they are discarded, like so much excess baggage.

"What kind of man would destroy such a beautiful, naïve young woman,"

Lt. Paganelli said to the air. "And what about the baby? Now we're talking about a double homicide," he reminded himself.

Still trying to figure out the scenario, the lieutenant considered the facts. An expensive car came to pick her up. It wasn't the same car each time so the owner wanted to make sure the cars could not be connected to him. In other words, he had something to hide. This young girl, who was truly influenced by money, was a mistress. Her man was a prominent figure in Yakima and didn't want anyone to know that he had a mistress.

Why? Most likely, he was married. Maybe he was a public figure who needed public support to keep his job. Maybe he was a minister of a church. All these possibilities needed to be narrowed down until the man responsible for Zizi Zeigler's murder was brought to justice. And it didn't make one bit of difference who the perpetrator was.

Lt. Paganelli exited his office, approached the back staircase and lightly touched the wooden handrail as he quickly descended one floor. He pushed open the swinging door, finished another staircase and went to his car. After he opened the door, he pulled out a snowbrush on a long handle and removed the snow from his car windows.

He pulled out on Third Street and headed to Lincoln Avenue where he turned left until he hit First Street then he turned right and within a few minutes spotted the waiting ambulance. One of the drivers indicated that he should go inside the coroner's autopsy room.

The coroner was somber as he waited by a black body bag lying on a rolling stretcher. "Ready?"

"Go ahead and unzip the top so I can see her face. Then I'll sign the release papers," the lieutenant said.

The coroner unzipped the bag enough to reveal the girl's once lovely face whose skin now resembled the color of clay. Her vibrant auburn hair and natural autumn colored eyebrows were testimony to the promise she had held in her young life.

"She's ready to go and I'm ready to sign the papers," the lieutenant looked for the clipboard holding the release document. He scribbled his name and handed it back to the coroner as the two drivers rolled the stretcher out the door and slid it into the ambulance. As they shut the double doors, the lieutenant said, "Wait for me to get in my car and I'll follow you."

Looking at the coroner, he said, "The ashes?"

The coroner said, "I'll pick them up and put them in the storage unit. I'll send you a copy of the release papers from Shaw and Sons."

"Release papers. That's the sum of this young girl's life?" the lieutenant already knew the answer.

"Hopefully, we'll find some answers in the next few months. If she's looking down from Heaven, she knows that at least she had two dads who would have protected her if we had only known about her situation. All we can do now, is to find the predator who did this to her," the coroner said as he turned and brushed the snow off his head and shoulders before he entered the building.

CHAPTER EIGHT

The Dream

Seldom did Rex Marvel have dreams. That's why he was struck when he remembered the clear image in his dream of finding a jewel near the chair where Zizi Zeigler was murdered.

"Nonsense," he thought. "Let the police investigate the murder. I have my responsibilities up here and the last thing I need is to become involved with the death of that beautiful young beauty I saw in the lobby. Geez, who'd ever thought that she'd be such a knockout!"

"Okay! Okay!" he continued talking to himself in response to his inner voice that was nagging him to hunt for the jewel. "I'll just look around and when I don't find anything, I won't think about it one more second."

As he came down the stairs into the lobby, he saw Sharon cleaning the popcorn machine and the display cases. "Hi, how's it going this morning," Rex said trying to act casual.

"I'm working. And you?"

"I'm waiting for several boxes of reels to be delivered. Will you let me know when the truck gets here?" Rex said.

"You should see Al about that. How am I supposed to know when the delivery truck has arrived?" Sharon said.

"I'll check the loading dock and see if there's a delivery schedule posted on the bulletin board. I'm gonna turn on the house lights for a little while," he said as he approached the theatre doors.

The theatre was pitch black with the exception of the ghost light glowing on the stage. Sort of like a night light for a theatre, the ghost light was similar to a tall lamp without a shade that gave a person a faint light to approach the stage from the audience or if they were approaching the stage from the rear, they would have enough light to see the edge of the stage.

Rex stood at the light panel after all the theatre lights were on. He knew exactly where the murder chair was located yet he hesitated about approaching that row of seats.

"What if I do find something? Then what?" he said to himself. "If I don't look, then I won't be involved. If I do find a jewel, I'll have to take some kind of action and give it to the police. The earring will prove nothing except that it came off her ear during the struggle. Geez, I don't want to think about the panic she felt before she lost consciousness. The poor girl!" he shook his head. He finally got his nerve and told himself, "Just go look then it'll be over and you can go to the loading dock."

Rex slipped a flashlight out of his back pocket, clicked it on and walked to the murder chair. "I'll check all the seats first," he thought as he held the flashlight with his left hand and slid his right hand between the bottom cushions and backs of a half dozen seats around the murder chair.

As he stood up, he said, "Nothing there." He got on his hands and knees and searched the carpet of the murder row and a couple rows in front and in back. "Nothing there. I guess I'm done," he said as he stood up. Out of the corner of his eye, a tiny flash made him jerk his head to the left. He immediately saw that the flash was wedged in a crease in the carpet at the base of a seat leg across the main aisle.

"What the ...?" he mumbled as he bent down and picked up the round diamond earring.

Just as he straightened up and looked at the sparkling gem in his palm, the delivery bell buzzed, signaling that a delivery truck was waiting at the loading dock. He shoved the diamond earring in his Levi's pocket and headed toward the back of the theatre.

He could only carry four orange-colored boxes containing reels of cartoons, comedy shorts and the newsreels. During the second trip from the loading dock to the projection booth, he carried the main feature reels above the highest balcony to his projection booth. All the reels needed to be spliced and ready for the weekend by the end of the day so he settled into working for a couple hours.

At his first break, Rex took the diamond earring out of his pocket and placed it in a small clean cereal bowl for the time being. Since he'd never seen a diamond before, he was amazed at the sparkling brilliance of the gem as he rolled it around in the dish near his face. He noted that Zizi had worn earrings that clipped on her ears rather than wearing pierced earrings and he was amazed that the other earring stayed on her ear.

Just like Ozzie who like to listen to either records or the PBS station on the radio, Rex had the radio on. Suddenly, he thought he heard a commotion in the theatre. Someone crying? He turned his radio down and heard nothing but the ticking of his wall clock. He turned the dial back up and reached for a second pair of scissors that were hanging on his work wall above the splicing counter. He heard someone opening and closing a door and walking on a floor above him. How could that be? Could someone be walking on the roof to make repairs? Again, he turned the radio down and heard nothing.

"I need a break and a cookie," Rex talked to himself per usual. He had adapted many of Ozzie rituals and brought a thermos of coffee to work plus homemade cookies every day. While he was getting the thermos and cup ready, a small movement caught his peripheral vision. The bowl with the diamond ring was vibrating and moving across the counter.

Rex knocked over his chair as he back-pedaled and moved as far away from the dancing bowl as possible. He stared at the vibrating bowl in disbelief. "Is this an earthquake?" In panic, he stepped through the door opening and across the top rows of the balcony. His feet barely touched the stairway as he descended into the lobby.

"We've got an earthquake going on!" he practically yelled at Sharon.

"What are you talking about?" she regarded him as if he were mental.

"The earthquake! Didn't you feel it down here? Things are vibrating and moving around in the booth. You guys must have felt some movement down here too. Didn't you feel anything?"

Al Mallone came through the front doors and caught the end of the conversation. "What's going on, kids? Is something the matter? Rex, did you get your delivery this morning?"

"Did you feel that earthquake a few minutes ago?" he asked Al.

"No. I didn't feel a thing. Did you feel something up in the booth?"

"Yeh. I definitely felt and saw something moving around up there. Are there workmen on the roof?"

"No workmen. Say, we've got to have those films ready for tonight so I'll check with you in an hour to see if you finished the splicing. Everything okay, Rex? I'll listen to the news and see if anyone else might have felt the tremors," Mallone talked to Rex like a reassuring parent.

Rex mumbled to himself as he headed toward the stairs. "I need to get out more often. I'm seeing things."

Rearview of the Capitol Theatre, 1960s. Photo courtesy: **Yakimamemory.org.**

CHAPTER NINE

The Earring

Rex regretted finding the murdered woman's earring because its existence pulled him into the case and he did not want the police to interrogate him. Before he picked up the phone to call Lt. Paganelli and tell him he had found an earring, he reminded himself that his parents had taught him to do the right thing and that's what he was doing.

He wrapped the earring in a handkerchief and checked to make sure there were no holes in the left pocket of his Levi's before he left the projection booth. "Why did I have to be the one to find it?" he asked himself. "The cleaning crew probably would have found it and put it in lost and found along with other jewelry, glasses and odd and ends. I should have just ignored the darn dream," he chided himself as he walked two blocks to the police station.

Rex paused in the doorway when he saw that Lt. Paganelli was waiting for him behind the front desk. He had a feeling of dread as if he were stepping into a den of snakes. If he turned around and left the building, the police would come after him so he figured he might as well give them the earring and get rid of it.

Seeing that Rex was hesitating about entering the police lobby, Lt. Paganelli said, "Come in, Rex."

Haltingly, Rex approached the window at the police counter and the lieutenant asked him, "So you found an earring that you think might have belonged to Zizi Zeigler?"

"I really don't know who the earring belongs to. I think it's safe to say that none of our Monday late night customers wear diamonds," Rex said.

As Rex and the lieutenant were talking, the door burst opened and several upset people shot into the lobby. The most vocal lady of the party was determined to report criminal activities of a family member and the rest of the party was determined to stop her and change her mind. Rex stepped out of the way of the turbulent shouting mob and waited by the door until the group had completely filled the lobby.

Lt. Paganelli called for assistance when he saw that the group's physical turmoil was increasing. "Kuskke, get out here and bring Murphy with you to control these people. Take the lady in black to room three and find out what the problem is. Get rid of the rest of this mob unless they shut their mouths."

The two police officers entered the lobby and separated the woman in black from the group. "Ma'am, you can tell me all about it in private," said Sgt. Kuskke. "Just go through those double doors and turn right at the second room where you see the desk. I'm right behind you."

"All right folks," officer Murphy raised his voice. "You can be quiet and sit here or go outside." He towered over the group and kept them from sitting on the benches until they made some attempt to settle down. Instead, they continued to argue and he could see that there might be a fight. "Okay, let's take it outside. Go outside all of you." He pushed them through the door toward the sidewalk with his bulky presence. Rather then getting run over, they complied and moved out of his way.

Rex was about to exit the lobby also and had his hand on the doorknob when the lieutenant called him. "Rex, come back. I have some forms that need to be filled out. It'll just take a second. C'mon, we'll go to my office and I'll help you get this over with."

Reluctantly, Rex turned and followed the lieutenant through two swinging doors and down a dismal hallway into a neat bare bones office with an Italian flare. A variety of Italian humorous items decorated the bookshelf along with a brand new black T-shirt that was framed and probably given to the lieutenant as a joke. Big bold white letters said: GOOM-BA, an affectionate term between Italian American men, meaning friend. There were a few framed black and white photos of the lieutenant with Italian-American movie celebrities and also one of him behind a spaghetti covered birthday cake ablaze with flaming candles.

"Have a chair there, Rex. We'll get this straightened out in no time and look at anything that might help us figure out who Zizi Zeigler was."

"Is she gone?" Rex asked.

"Is she gone? You mean is she buried or cremated?"

"Yes, that's what I mean. What happened to her?"

"I guess I can tell you that when a murdered person's body is not claimed by any family members, we eventually have to dispose of it. We have no proof that Zizi Zeigler was the dead woman's real name. So she was put into a Jane Doe category and her case *is* or I should say *was* a cold case. Now, if you have some new evidence that can help us, we'll pull her case as a priority. Even if you do have an earring, we also have a matching earring."

"Well, I don't know why I bothered to come over here then if what I have isn't going to help," Rex shifted to the edge of his chair.

"Hold on! I didn't exactly say the earring wouldn't help. Here's what I would say would help. Where you found the earring might give us a clue about something we didn't know before. Maybe we could take a photo of exactly where you found the earring," the lieutenant said.

"Yeh, maybe," Rex was looking for the door.

"In the meantime, I'd like you to fill out this form that gives the date, time of discovery and where the earring was located. You'll see the questions are easy so I'm going to give you a moment to write in the answers. Here's a pen. In the meantime, I'm going to check on the woman who came into the lobby right after you. I'll be right back," the lieutenant stood up and exited his office.

Rex saw that the questions actually were straightforward and he answered them as simply as possible and signed his name and the date. When he was finished, he thought about autopsy scenes that he'd seen in the movies and he forced himself to form a mental picture about what he had to do back at the theatre.

Lt. Paganelli walked back into the office; looked at the form Rex had filled out and opened his drawer for an envelope. "Looks good. All the questions are answered real good. Now, I just need to put the earring in this envelope and we'll add it to Ms. Zeigler's box of possessions. So let's see the earring."

Rex reached into his left Levi's pocket and pulled out the handkerchief. He could feel a small lump so he knew the earring was still there. "I can finally get rid of this darn thing," he said to himself.

When he opened the fabric, instead of the earring, there was a brass screw. He stood up and frantically pulled out all the linings to his pockets thinking it might be stuck in a fold or, even worse, that it might have dropped through a hole. There was no earring.

"Is this your idea of a joke?" Lt. Paganelli became irate. You made such a g-damn deal about the earring and then you come here and take up my time with a screw?" He stood up and went to the hall door. "When you find the earring, let me know. We'll come get it. Now, I've got other things to do."

Rex's face was flaming with embarrassment as he shoved the handkerchief and screw back in his pocket, walked out the door and rushed toward Yakima Avenue then turned left. He chided himself and thought, "I must have grabbed the screw and thought it was the earring. That's never going to happen again. Let them do their own research." He walked into the theatre lobby with his head down.

"Are you sunburned, Rex? Your face is so red!" Sharon said.

He passed her without speaking and climbed the stairs to the projection booth. Before he started working, he reached in his pocket to throw the handkerchief and screw into the small tin trashcan. He dropped the flimsy package and something metal clicked on the tin. "Oh well, I might as well save the screw. I can always use it," Rex said to himself. He reached down, pulled out the tissue and opened it to reveal the earring. As if a hot poker had struck him, he dropped the hanky and the earring bounced and settled on top of the splice counter.

He had already jerked back from the counter and looked around as if there was an entity watching his movements. "Am I losing my mind? What the sh -t is going on!!!"

CHAPTER TEN

Contact

"I can't find Rex," Ozzie said to Sharon as she arranged candy bars in the display case and filled the freezer with popsicles and ice cream cups.

Looking at his watch, Ozzie said, "Do you have any idea where he might be? We're going to open the doors and start the movie in one hour. I want to make sure that all the films are ready."

"Maybe the alley? Smoking?" Sharon said.

Oz walked to the end of the lobby and out the side door. As he looked down the alley, he saw a cloud of smoke billowing from an exit alcove covered by a striped awning. Many mornings, Oz would find bums who had slept overnight in the deep alcoves and he mumbled to himself that the theatre had to fill those alcoves in. "Maybe it's just another loiterer in the alcove," he thought to himself. "But maybe it's Rex." He figured that he might as well check.

As he walked toward the smoke, he saw that it was Rex dragging on a cigarette and deep in thought.

"Rex? You okay, man?" Oz approached Rex and saw that he wasn't his usual smiling self. Rather, he was pensive and somber. "Rex? Are you gonna talk to me, man? What's going on?"

Rex looked at his friend and mentor and paused as if he wanted to tell him something but knew his message would not be believed. He most definitely did not want his credibility to be doubted because he might lose his job.

As if he had mental telepathy, Oz said, "Unless you've set the projectors on fire, you can tell me anything and I'll listen. You know that, Rex."

Rex dropped his cigarette, stepped on it and headed toward the lobby entrance of the theatre. "Do you have a few minutes to come up to the booth with me?" he asked Oz.

As they made their way up the stairs, Oz kept a conversation going about some new films that he'd ordered as well as general trivial information. When they arrived at the projection booth, Oz asked, "Have you got everything ready for the movies tonight?" It was a question that he asked every night. And every night that had Rex worked, he answered in the affirmative.

Once the usual question was answered, Rex got to the point. "This has to do with the girl that was murdered here in the theatre."

"I thought the police were taking care of that," Oz responded.

"It's considered a cold case because they don't really know who the girl was. They think the name she used at the hotel was a fake name."

"Geez, who would ever name their kid Zizi?" Oz said. "So how are they gonna find out her real name?"

"They've run into a wall so they're calling her a Jane Doe and her ashes are stored in a box at the coroner's office," Rex said.

"What's that got to do with you?" Oz asked.

"I found her earring wedged against one of the seats in the theatre and took it to the police station."

"That was the right thing to do," Oz crossed his arms. "But something else is going on. I can feel it."

"I wrapped the earring in a handkerchief and put it in my pocket here in the booth. When I pulled it out of my pocket to give it to Lt. Paganelli at the police station, the earring was gone. Instead, there was a brass screw."

"No way, man!!" Oz uncrossed his arms and put his hands on his hips.

"That's not all. When I got back to the booth, I threw the handkerchief and screw in that little trashcan. I heard something click and thought I'd better double check. When I opened the handkerchief, the earring was there."

"Get outta here!!" Oz stepped back as if he was hearing something diabolical and put his hand to his mouth. There was silence for a moment until Oz wanted proof. "Have you got the earring here?"

Rex made a move over to the shelves. He reached for a Folger's Coffee tin, opened the top and dumped the contents on the splice shelf. A Kleenex and the earring spilled out onto the counter. Oz picked up the earring, examined it and put it back on top of the Kleenex.

"That's a diamond earring, man, for sure. It's definitely not a Wool-worth's ring. Looks like 24-Carat gold too," Oz commented as the diamond expert that he thought he was.

"I can't get rid of it and when I try, the thing comes right back like it wants to live here," Rex rubbed his hand over his face.

"Man, you got a situation going on here. You got a ring with a mind of its own. Not that I don't believe you," Oz put his hand out to assure Rex that he sort of believed the story but it didn't make sense.

"Let me try something. Would you trust me with the earring for an evening? Then I'll bring it right back to you?" Oz was trying to figure out a plan.

"Trust you? Are you kidding? I would like you to throw the earring in the trash or better yet, leave it in the alcove where I was smoking and let a bum pick it up. Then let's see if he can get rid of it!" Rex was at his wit's end. "In other words, don't bring it back. I'm serious. I don't want to ever see the g-damn thing again!"

"How 'bout if I pawn it?"

"The police will trace it to you and that'll connect you to the murder. They'll think that you're trying to get rid of evidence."

"So if a bum finds it and tries to pawn it, he'll run into the same thing." It was a statement from Oz rather than a question.

"Why ruin another person's life that's already having a hard time?"

"No problem, man. Let me have it and I guarantee that you won't see it again if that's what you want."

As Rex picked up the Kleenex and the earring, he handed it to Oz. "I never want to see this earring again. Get rid of it!"

Oz held it in his hand and both men saw him put the Kleenex and the earring in his pant's pocket. I'll check with you after the last movie about tomorrow's delivery schedule. I just have to find out the time the truck will be here."

With relief, Rex showed his movies and got a call from Oz. "The truck will be here at 8:30 a.m. and I'll carry the reel boxes up to the booth. I'll see you tomorrow after 4 p.m. Get a good night's rest."

Rex hadn't slept well since he found the ring. He figured that night he'd finally sleep through the night. All went well at the theatre for the next day. While he was splicing one of the new films together, he heard Oz's familiar voice as he walked toward the projection booth. "Rex, I'm coming to see you."

Rex stood up and thought Oz might be delivering some equipment he ordered.

Oz stepped into the booth with his hands in his pockets, reluctant to have eye contact with Rex. "You're not gonna like what I have to tell you, man."

Rex felt a flash of heat shoot through his body and he did not want to hear what Oz had to tell him because he knew it was about the earring.

"I tried to get rid of the earring, man, and it was guaranteed to work."

"What did you do?" Rex was afraid to ask.

"When the delivery truck arrived, I knew those other boxes were going to the Princess Theatre in Prosser. So my idea was to stick the earring in one of the boxes that the truck hadn't delivered yet. I pulled the couple Kleenex's outta my pocket and got ready to stuff it into a little opening I found in one of the boxes. I checked it to make sure the earring was still there."

"And? Was it?"

"No. I'm sorry to tell you that there was only a brass screw in the Kleenex."

Both men were dumbfounded and braced themselves against the counters as they realized that a force was trying to make contact with them. Oz was the first one to speak.

"Have you looked in the Folger's Coffee tin today?"

"I didn't think I needed to look."

"We might as well take a look. I'm sure there's nothing there. The earring has just disappeared. So your wish has been answered," Oz smiled not believing what he had just said.

Rex walked over to the shelf and picked up the Folger's Coffee tin, opened it and dumped the contents on the splice counter. The Kleenex and earring spilled out.

CHAPTER ELEVEN

The First Shadow

"What're you gonna do, man?" Ozzie asked somewhat alarmed. " What do you think this means?"

Perplexed, Rex returned the question. "This isn't a magic trick because there's no magician. This is Zizi Zeigler's earring and she does not want it to leave the booth. I'm talking about … "

"What? What are you talking about?" Oz knew that Rex would find it difficult to consider that they were experiencing paranormal activity. But there it was. The earring seemed like it had a mind of its own. Or rather, some THING had control of it and the only person that could be was Zizi. She was dead wasn't she? How then could she control anything?

Rex finished his thought. "You know what I'm talking about. The question I'm asking you is do you think that we're dealing with Zizi's ghost?"

"What else could this be? You see the earring here in the booth. But when you take it in a handkerchief somewhere else, it turns into a screw. Then when you bring it back to the booth, it becomes the earring again. Tell me about it!!!" Oz raised his voice.

"I gotta ask myself why? She was never up here. I didn't know her and the only time I saw her was the night she was murdered," Rex said.

"You were about her age, maybe a few years older. She's looking for a sympathetic person to help her," Oz said.

"It sounds like you're saying somebody was blackmailing her. Or maybe she was doing the blackmailing."

"If she had a real boyfriend, you would've seen them being lovey-dovey in the theatre. But she had this weird situation going on with the man who met her at the same time every Monday night. He didn't act like her lover.

He was taking her to 'the real man,' a guy who didn't want to be seen with her in public. Ask yourself. What kind of man wouldn't want to be seen in public with that beautiful lady?"

"Could be someone who's married, or a minister, a politician, a mob boss or the mayor."

"You said mob boss. Why'd you say that?" Oz asked.

"I was reading about the Alaska Corral Club in the paper yesterday. There's girls who are go-go dancers, which is legit. But there was a raid on dancers who were performing topless and completely nude. I also heard there's gambling in the back and other mob activities," Rex seemed informed.

"Like what other activities?"

"Money laundering."

"Ever heard of the northwest triangle? Seattle, Yakima, Spokane. The Seattle mob wants to keep things moving one step ahead of the feds," Rex said.

"What's this got to do with the lady that was murdered?" Oz asked.

"Have you ever known anyone whose name was Zizi?"

"Can't say that I have. What are you getting at, mister detective?" Oz smiled.

"Dancing girls? Zizi? You think those dancing girls call themselves ordinary names like Dorothy, Pauline or Esther? Nah. Their names are strictly fiction such as Bitty, Fifi, Trixie or Peaches, names that you'd call a poodle," Rex said. "Maybe that's where Zizi used to work."

The second Rex finished that sentence, the men looked up as they heard a woman's voice whimpering and softly crying above them. They stood against the counters and looked at each other as if to say this can't be happening! Breathless, they waited, afraid to make the slightest move. Next, they heard a woman's steps and the sound of a door opening and closing. Then nothing. At least they thought nothing else would happen but the counters and small table in the middle of the room began to softly tremble. Pencils, spoons, pieces of film started sliding and turning as if they were on top of a washing machine going into the spin cycle.

When the action ceased, the pencils and spoons were in the shapes of arrows.

Both men were stunned as they looked at the makeshift arrows and tried to figure out what just happened.

Oz was the first to rub his face and look at Rex as if he was some kind of freak. Then he made a guess at the meaning of the arrows. "You got a ghost, man. And she's into you! You must have hit the nail on the head when you mentioned the Alaska Corral. Look at what direction the arrows are pointing.

"Okay. Okay. They're pointing west. What am I supposed to do about all this?" Rex sounded desperate.

"Don't you get it, man? She wants you to go there?"

"Then what?" Rex could not believe this was happening to him.

"I don't know the answer. Maybe we should go together as customers," Oz said.

"It would be our civic duty to go to the Corral and see the dancing girls so we could figure out what happened to Zizi?"

"Right on!" Oz was smiling in complete agreement and nodding his head.

"What about Lt. Paganelli? Shouldn't we tell him?"

"The owners of the Corral know the lieutenant. Why hasn't the owner of the Corral come forward with information that she worked there? The answer is simple. They don't want her murder to be connected with them in any way. If they did know who her boyfriend was or anything about that situation and they didn't tell the police, they could be held as accessories to the murder or charged with hiding evidence. Both are punishable by a stiff jail term."

"So what's the next step?" Rex asked.

"The movies here at the theatre have to be shown. I can do that. The people at the Corral know that I'm from the Capitol Theatre because of the publicity I've done around town. But they don't know you." Oz was leading up to an assignment.

"Are you saying that this Pentecostal kid should go to a strip-joint run by the Seattle mafia to get information on a murdered girl?" Rex could not believe that Oz was making that suggestion.

"Well, now that you've volunteered to be a sleuth, I'll stay and run the movies," Oz settled it.

"It ain't gonna happen," Rex said firmly. I don't have the answers to the disappearing earring and the spooky things we heard and saw. I hope everyone in the universe hears that statement. This whole deal is strictly a police matter."

"It's your funeral, man," Oz said as he shook his head and headed toward the door. "I'd hate to be in your shoes if the ghost gets angry at you for not helping her reveal who murdered her."

Raising his voice out of frustration and fear of the unknown, Rex said, "Let's get this straight. It's not my funeral or my so-called situation. I'm not into ghosts and I am not going to get involved. So adios, Mr. Wizard! You're not gonna get me killed by the mafia today. I don't want to join Miss Zizi while she walks around an imaginary floor that doesn't exist. And if I do get shot helping her, you'll be the first one I haunt!" Both men laughed from the ridiculousness of the situation.

Oz didn't even try to suppress a snicker as he turned his back, waved goodbye backwards and stepped into the theatre. He knew this matter was not over. In fact, it was just beginning.

Not one to dwell on things he didn't understand, Rex got to work. He had to splice the new shorts together before the 6:30 p.m. movie, *Some Like It Hot*. This was the Monday night special—his choice—so he thought he'd lighten things up with a Marilyn Monroe movie.

"Geez," he thought to himself, "look how her life turned out. One of the most beautiful women in the world, a movie star, and her life was a mess. Rumors of affairs with the Kennedy brothers, a marriage to a baseball star and a play writer, she just couldn't find a place for herself in the world. Such a tragic figure," Rex shook his head at the desperate life of Marilyn Monroe.

"Maybe Zizi was like that too. She was so beautiful with her alabaster skin and auburn hair. What good did it do her in the end? She left her family and allowed her life to be controlled by someone else. She probably started making demands or maybe she wanted to go home and the man wouldn't let her 'cause she knew too much about him. I thought I heard she was expecting a baby. That must've been the reason she was killed. She would be required to put the father's name on the birth certificate and I'm guessing the man didn't want that information to be revealed. I hope Lt. Paganelli finds her killer." Rex's thoughts were going round and round in his head about Zizi.

The evening passed without further incidents and it was time to rerun

Some Like It Hot in the 9 p.m. movie slot. All the regulars who attended the late Monday night movies were in their usual theatre seats. Out of fifty people, there were five couples and the rest were singles, some who came together and some who sat alone.

Even though the movie was going well, Rex liked to check either what was on the screen or the focus on the projector. About an hour after the main feature had started, Rex was watching the screen. For a brief second, a shadow of a human figure walked to the middle of the screen and stopped as if looking back at the projector. If someone were walking behind the screen, their silhouette would be small. No, this was as if someone was walking directly in front of the projector and their shadow was projected onto the screen.

Rex panicked and rushed out of the booth to see what was blocking the light on the projector but there was nothing there. Just as he was returning to the projection booth, he spotted Oz stepping onto the balcony and rushing toward the booth.

"What the hell is going on?" Rex had never seen Oz so upset. "Is this your idea of a joke?"

Rex looked at Oz with his mouth hanging open as if his face was paralyzed.

"Oh my God, you have no idea what just happened either, do you?" Oz put his hands on his hips. "There is no possible way a person could walk in front of the projector," Oz said as he stood in the highest room that overlooked the theatre. He looked at his watch. "The shadow thing happened at precisely 10:22 p.m., the exact time the police figured that Zizi was killed on a Monday night."

Oz looked at Rex, who was looking down with his hand covering his mouth. "She's trying to get your attention and now she's all over the theatre. If you don't do something to help her, she's gonna start lifting people outta their seats. Rex, do you hear me? You can't hide from Zizi Zeigler anymore, man!"

CHAPTER TWELVE

Northwest Mafia Hits Yakima

During the 1960s, while the United States was distracted with an internal war of civil rights, the Bay of Pigs, assassinations of political figures, the Vietnam War, landing on the moon, the Woodstock Festival, Dr. Timothy Leary's mantra of 'turn on, tune out and drop out,' Frank Colacurcio, Sr., his son and associates were often portrayed by law-enforcement officials and the news media as two of Seattle's most notorious racketeering figures.

Frank senior was born in America to Italian immigrants who were farmers on land called "garlic gulch" and was developed into Boeing Field Airport. They hauled produce to Pike Place Market, one of the oldest public farmer's markets in the U.S.. The main and lower arcades were famous for fishmongers, crafts people, exotic antiquities and oddities, fresh flowers and international cafes. The market, which overlooked Elliott Bay, was located in a low income housing area. Within walking distance, tourists were regularly approached for money. Strip joints, sex shops, tattoo, piercing and massage parlors shared the historic area with antique shops and European cafes.

In the 1950s, Colacurcio changed occupations from hauling produce to becoming an entrepreneur when he got into the jukebox, cigarette, and vending machine businesses. Rivals claimed that his thugs threatened storeowners to install the machines and pay him the profits. Historically, those types of businesses attracted organized crime because of their easily skimmed cash.

Once considered Seattle's connection to the Mafia, he duplicated their intimidation tactics to become a racketeer who slipped by federal and local law enforcement officials. Feeling that he was untouchable by the law,

Colacurcio invested in bars, restaurants and clubs. To avoid obtaining liquor licenses for his establishments, his relatives and associates posed as the business owners. He attempted to expand his existing businesses into Portland, which drew the attention of Robert Kennedy and the U.S. Senate committee investigating organized crime. A Portland crime figure, told the committee that Colacurcio wanted to set up houses of prostitution there.

Committee Counsel Robert Kennedy questioned him about his alleged racketeering activities in Seattle and his failure to pay taxes on the profits from his businesses. Since the majority of his businesses had names of other people as the owners, the committee couldn't find enough solid evidence to bring charges against him that would stick.

Rock and roll entertainment changed along the west coast in the mid-1960s when go-go dancing and discotheques were hot in San Francisco. Colacurcio heated Seattle's night scene with his own version of go-go dancing and discotheques when he introduced go-go dancing in the Fire-lite Room at the Moore Hotel with scantily costumed girls dancing in cages. Some of the dancing girls were underage and he served a six-month suspended sentence for contributing to the delinquency of minors. He was found guilty by the local Municipal Court for kicking a bartender, who worked at the Firelite, when he found out the man was an informer about the racketeer's illegal activities.

After disco dancing became a popular drawing card for clubs in west coast cities, Colacurcio took go-go dancing one step beyond the others by introducing topless dancing. Eventually, the dancers stepped out of the cage and danced on customers' tables. Since the police didn't seem to have a problem with his mostly naked dancers, Colacurcio forced his dancers into prostitution. In 1967, at one of his clubs, the police arrested a twenty-three-year old cocktail waitress with the charge that she was also working as a prostitute.

Colacuricio was the moving force behind strip clubs and prostitution in all his business endeavors and paid the police thousands of dollars monthly for "police protection." Taking advantage of his agreeable relationship with the law, he added illegal bingo cards and gambling at his bars and restaurants.

He ran his operations from Talents West, a hiring agency and business office in a small building on Lake City Way. The walls displayed photographs of scantily dressed women and they became his main source of income whether they were go-go dancers, topless dancers, call girls, hookers or streetwalkers. Like cattle, the women were channeled into an area of service that best fit Colacurcio's need for income. Girls from foreign countries were attracted to the promise of citizenship in exchange for dancing in nightclubs. Their dreams turned to nightmares when they were forced to become prostitutes or face deportation.

Eventually, his tentacles of crime reached beyond Seattle to Yakima clubs that traditionally invited customers to dance and party to live entertainment. Ray and Larry Orteig, former professional baseball players, owned the Alaska Corral in the early sixties and featured country and western music from The Chancellors composed of local musicians: Dan Bardes, Bob Homan, Darwin Evans and Jim Cartwright. Their bands also entertained downtown at the Chieftain Hotel.

Once Colacurcio became the owner of The Alaska Corral, he introduced go-go dancers and discotheque music replaced a portion of the country and western music. The Corral became a trademark of Colacurcio's Seattle establishments: a centrally located scene of human excesses with strippers, alcohol, drugs, fights, gambling surrounded by adult porn shops, tattoo, piercing and massage parlors and general mayhem.

State patrol investigators reported that Colacurcio had met in Yakima with Salvatore "Bill" Bonanno, the son of the legendary New York Mafia boss Joseph "Joe Bananas" Bonanno, to discuss a business relationship. Colacurcio famously responded to a reporter that he and his family had gone to Yakima to pick hot peppers, "but I didn't pick no bananas."

If Colacurcio wanted to expand his businesses in Yakima, he had a choice of bars, clubs and restaurants that were concentrated in a two square block area between Front Street and First Street as well as north and south of Yakima Avenue. For service men from the Firing Center on R & R and other local men, there were plenty of girls' sexual services for sale whether they danced, waitressed, worked upstairs or solicited customers on the street.

Next to The Corral was Van's Billiards Hall and two doors over was a porn shop called The Room. On the other side of the Union Gospel Mission was Victory Tavern, a gathering spot for African-Americans known as Blacks in the sixties. The Montana and the Pacific Hotels were in the red light district due to the red lights in the stairways and fire exits and most particularly because of the prostitutes who walked the streets on Front and First Streets on both sides of Yakima Avenue.

The Jade Room at The Dragon Inn was another popular spot for country and western live music and dancing. The Golden Wheel and the Lotus Room were separate hot spots conjoined so that a customer could walk through the Golden Wheel into the Lotus Room.

Stockman's Café and bar was like a little Chicago. Pimps and their girls hung out there with prospective customers. The Blue Banjo was notorious for drugs and stabbings. The Roza Hotel was at the end of the block and around the corner on Front Street were the Senator Hotel and the old opera house.

The Sports Center was on the block between the historic district and the downtown establishments. Customers could play cards or billiards as well as gamble on sports games and horse races. The team names and racing scores were posted on an upper wall above display cases that sold cigarettes and cigars. Rumors reported that the upstairs was used for male customers and "working girls."

When Colacurcio was interested in buying a bar or restaurant, his method of operation was to make an offer to the proprietor. If the owner refused to sell the business establishment, a series of incidents could follow: the business could experience an expensive mishap that required police or insurance inquiry; the business could be torched or a business owner could be shot.

It was open season in the sixties and darkness wasn't needed to hide the trades of the time. Just two square blocks on and off the Ave. and a man could purchase anything or anybody he desired. In the historic part of Yakima, every night was alive with human consumption.

CHAPTER THIRTEEN

Impasse

"So what have you decided to do, man," Oz asked Rex when they headed out to the alley for their morning smoke.

"About what?" Rex knew full well what Oz was talking about but he played dumb to postpone the inevitable conversation about the "ghost."

"Don't play dumb with me, man. You know what I'm talking about. Fine. You want me to spell it out? I told you the girl's ghost is into you and she's trying to tell you who murdered her. The only way you can find some answers is to know who she was to start with. What was her real name? Who knew her? Where did she work? Or maybe she only worked on Monday nights for one man," Oz turned to Rex to see if he had any emotional response to the situation.

"You want to know what my response is?" Rex anticipated. "My response is to stay out of it. Do nothing. Let the police deal with the matter. Once the ghost sees that I'm not willing to become involved, she's gonna be into you instead of me. You have the passion to solve this mystery and with your proactive personality, you're the best choice. She can try to kill me with her wizardry but I know I'd be killed if I inquired about her in the red light district."

Oz was quick to respond. "If she did want me, I would help her. You're right about that. But that's not the case. For some unknown reason, she wants you."

"Can we please end the discussion about the ghost?" Rex dropped his cigarette and smashed it with the sole of his shoe.

"No problem, man," Oz started to get heated because of Rex's feigned indifference. "But hear me now and remember these words. You're scorning her desperate need to seek revenge on the person who murdered her and her spirit will not rest until that is accomplished. If you don't help her, you're gonna see her raise the roof on this theatre and knock the people against the walls. Are you ready to be responsible for that kind of action because of your indifference?"

"What? Are you the expert on ghost behavior these days?" Rex's sarcastic remark made light of Ozzie's warnings. " I thought I was hired to show movies. Now you're telling me that I have to be responsible for the antics of a ghost? Let me ask you one question."

"Fire away!"

"What makes you think that the paranormal activity is coming from the girl and not the devil?" Rex brought up a new thought on the situation.

"Probably my own experience with the earring made it seem like the girl was trying to send us a message," Oz was rationalizing that the girl was causing all the action. "Didn't we hear her crying and walking as she opened and closed the door above us? You think the devil would be capable of fooling us by making girl sounds?"

"The devil is God's antithesis and was one of God's cherished angels until he challenged God's power," Rex sounded like his father delivering a sermon.

"What the hell does antithesis mean?"

"It means the opposition. The devil opposes God and has powers that are beyond our imagination. He can appear to be a person who is benevolent, sweet, needy and desperate in order to gain our sympathy. He never appears as the devil because that would scare us. He appears in a way that we need to see—like a weeping woman who needs us to solve her murder. See what I mean?" Rex's explanation about why he didn't want to become involved suddenly became clear to Oz.

"Far out, man. This deal is becoming too heavy for me. I gotta take a break from it all and go back to work. See you later."

Rex definitely had to take a break from the ghostly nonsense and see if the expected shipment of new reels was due as expected at 10 a.m. Just as soon as Rex entered the lobby, Oz popped out of his office near the front of the theatre.

"The delivery truck is here. Go ahead and sign the delivery papers and have the guy unload the new reel boxes. After you guys put the old reel boxes in his truck, I'll help you carry the new boxes upstairs. I'm still on the phone with a guy in Los Angeles. Be right there as soon as I hang up."

Rex walked through the theatre, up the side stairs and behind the stage where sets were stored that would go on stage in a live production, except there were no sets these days. He walked across a huge receiving area that was as large or larger than the stage and was flanked by theatre paraphernalia on the sides—sort of like a warehouse. The delivery guy had just rolled open the back door of the truck when a couple dozen boxes started to lift and roll in a circle as if there was a tornado inside the truck.

Rex and the delivery guy stepped back because it appeared that the rocking truck and its contents were about to explode. A sound like a buzzing roar accelerated the turmoil of the boxes and shot them out of the truck and onto the loading dock.

As if there was a timer on each of them, the packing tape on the tops of the boxes simultaneously ripped off and shot open from the internal pressure created by some rocketing force. All the reels rolled out at one time and the scene was similar to Mickey Mouse's *The Sorcerer's Apprentice* in the movie *Fantasia*, where he commanded the brooms to dance in unison.

However, the reels were not moving in unison. Rather they moved as if they had motors and an invisible force at the wheel was commanding them to roll, lift, spin in the air, and reverse their forward action to shoot backwards or simply stay in place and spin as if they were showing a movie on a projector. It seemed a magnetic force had taken possession of the movement of the reels and their action was scattered and erratic.

An imaginary phenomenon switched the action and the reels lined up in a small army. Slowly at first then picking up speed, the spinning reels headed toward the terrified truck driver and Rex, who were holding on to each other—spellbound with terror and disbelief at what was happening and what was about to happen. They were standing against the wall and inside the back of the stage.

Oz stepped into the set warehouse and could not believe his eyes. The truck driver and Rex were about to be sliced to pieces if the reels collided with them. What he was witnessing was insanity but it had to be stopped. Without hesitating, Oz ran to the side where the sliding doors had been pulled back that separated the stage and the set warehouse. With all his might, he pushed a two-story door on rollers and kept pushing it across the back of the stage. The two men caught his intention of putting a barrier in front of the rolling reels and pulled the door while he pushed.

The metal reels clanged against wood and steel braces, bouncing off the stage door and spinning on their sides until their force was quieted and they flattened like cookies on a sheet about to go in the oven.

The men were gasping for air from pushing the heavy door shut. The deliveryman collapsed into a sitting position on the floor and rocked as he tried to comfort himself. "Dear God, what just happened? What happened? Can somebody tell me what just happened?" he repeated to himself over and over.

Rex rested his hands on his knees in order to get his breath under control. He was trembling and tears welled in his eyes at what he had just witnessed.

Oz didn't know whether to comfort Rex and the delivery man or to shake Rex and tell him that the explosive reels were the tip of the iceberg at what the ghost was capable of doing as long as Rex refused to help Zizi.

After Rex stood up, Oz put a hand on his friend's shoulder to comfort him. "Are you all right, man? Those reels could have chewed you and the delivery guy up. Zizi was after you for sure 'cause she's angry with you. You're the only person she wants to help her!"

Rex wiped the tears out of his eyes. "What could be more clear about the power of the devil? You think that little girl who was murdered could make those reels try to kill us? Think again!! That was the devil taking advantage of her situation and showing us his power."

"What would be the devil's purpose in doing all that? What does he want? Your theory about the devil doing all this doesn't make sense, man. No sir! You better change your thinking and help her or the next time she comes after you, I might not be around to save you."

CHAPTER FOURTEEN

The Visitor

"All I can say, man, is that we've been experiencing some tremors in and around the theatre," Oz explained to the deliveryman. Did you know this area has some hidden tunnels? Yeah, it does. I'm gonna ask Yakima utilities what the hell was happening underground to make those reels seem like they were alive. Had to be some kinda magnetic situation with underground cables and wiring."

The deliveryman nodded at Ozzie's explanation but there was no way he believed anything Oz was telling him. He knew what he saw and experienced; reels that had the intention to rip him and Rex apart. His face remained blanched and there was a certain expression that Oz had seen on people's faces after they had witnessed an atrocity. It was shock, denial of seeing the scene with the dancing reels, the possibility that a ghostly force was making all the boxes and reels go crazy. The only comfort that the deliveryman had was that two other people were witnesses and had watched the reels take on a life of their own.

Oz tried to make light of the dancing reels as if those kind of crazy things happened all the time at the theatre. Rex and the deliveryman were silent and attended to the job of getting the reels back into their correct boxes. They loaded the old reels into the truck as well as reel boxes for delivery to the other Mercy theaters in Yakima and the Princess Theatre in Prosser.

Life at the Capitol Theatre seemed to be back to normal as the men threw themselves into their respective schedules. Even though they were doing their jobs, their minds never rested as they hashed over the power the ghost had over inanimate objects—the boxes and reels. They both knew that she could tear the theatre apart at any time unless someone paid attention to her need to avenge the man who had her murdered.

Rex said the dancing reels were the work of the devil when he knew that was not the truth. He didn't want to acknowledge the presence of the ghost because that would mean he was convinced she was real. If he had mentioned these incidents to his parents and that he believed a female ghost caused them, his parents would have thought that he was possessed by the devil, that he was insane. And frankly, he was beginning to wonder if he was insane. Paranoid-schizophrenic people had conversations with imaginary people and that's exactly what this situation was becoming.

Ignore it. It will go away. She will go away. That had been Rex's motto when it came to pain or mental anguish. So that was exactly what he intended to do. Do nothing. Get back to work and stay busy. All of this insanity would leave the premises.

It was time to prepare for the two evening movies and since Rex was given the freedom to choose the Monday night movies, he decided to show *The Sandpiper*, a movie that was filmed near Carmel, California in 1965 and starred Elizabeth Taylor and Richard Burton. The story was about a married school administrator (Burton) who fell in love with a single mother (Taylor). Their love story was forbidden and ends with both their hearts being broken.

The theme song, *A Shadow Of Your Smile*, seemed particularly haunting to Rex and he tried to stop himself from thinking about how beautiful Zizi had been when he saw her in the lobby and how their eyes had met and how he tried to act casual in her presence but instead he nearly broke his glasses as he fumbled to adjust them.

Our wistful little star
Was far too high
A teardrop kissed your lips
And so did I
Now when I remember spring,
All the joy that love can bring
I will be remembering,
The shadow of your smile.

His reverie was broken when the phone rang. It was Mike Hansen on the other end calling from the lobby.

"What's up?" Rex asked.

"A woman is sitting in the same exact seat that Zizi used to sit in."

"That's bound to happen, I guess," Rex didn't think it was a big deal.

"The woman could pass for Zizi's sister. That's how much she looks like Zizi," Mike said. "Why don't you come down and take a look at her when the movie is over and the customers are coming out of the theatre."

"Is Oz here?"

"Yes, he's standing right here and he saw her too. We want you to see her so he said to tell you that he'd be up and take care of the end of the movie reel if you wanted to stand in the lobby and check out this look-alike woman," Mike said.

"Okay, we're about a half hour from the end of the movie. Tell Oz to come up in fifteen minutes so I can come down to the lobby," Rex said.

"Will do," Mike said.

The exchange took place near the end of the movie and since Rex had already played the movie at 6:30 p.m., he recognized the final scene and finale' music.

As the first customers exited the theatre through the lobby, Rex, Mike and Sharon were standing nearly shoulder-to-shoulder just to make sure that they didn't miss the woman who looked like Zizi's sister. It appeared that everyone had left the theatre and the woman in question was not part of the crowd.

"She didn't come out," Mike said. "I'll go inside and see if she's still there," he made a move to enter the theatre. He saw that she was still sitting in Zizi's seat and was gathering her small suitcase, purse and sweater.

"Ma'am, are you okay?" Mike asked her and couldn't believe his eyes. She didn't have the fashion sense that Zizi had because she was wearing plain clothes. But the shape of her face, her eyes, the chestnut colored hair and her petite build nearly duplicated Zizi.

The minute she began to speak, she had a heavy accent that Mike didn't recognize right away.

"My sister loved this theatre," she said. "I was hoping that she would be here tonight but I didn't see her. Maybe tomorrow night ..."

"Are you looking for your sister?" Mike already knew the answer.

"Yes. Maybe you know her. Therese D'Anjou. She's a couple years younger than me and people say that we could pass for twins." The woman stood up, stepped into the aisle and walked beside Mike toward the lobby.

"Maybe someone else who works here might remember her. What is your name, Ma'am?" Mike asked while he tried to act casual.

"Oh, I'm Louise D'Anjou from Montreal, Canada. Do you think you could help me find my sister?"

"Do you have time to talk to the staff here at the theatre? I know it's kinda late," Mike wasn't about to tell her that her sister had been murdered.

"Yes. I can stay for a while," she said.

As Mike and Louise entered the lobby, he said, "This is Louise D'Anjou. She's looking for her sister, Therese, who comes to the movies here."

By this time, Oz had run down the stairs and stood next to Rex and Sharon. Rex was spellbound and told himself to stop staring at this woman who was close to Zizi's age but almost seemed like a mother figure.

Mike walked with Louise over to Oz and said, "Mrs. D'Anjou, this is Ozzie Goldstein who is one of the managers of the theatre. Would you like to talk to him about your sister?"

Oz smiled at her and shook her hand. "Ma'am, let's see if we can get some information from you about your sister. I think it would be quieter if we talked in my office. Would that be all right with you?"

She nodded in the affirmative.

"Go right in through that door where the light is shining and have a seat. Could I get you some hot tea?"

"That would be very nice," Louise was all smiles and seemed receptive to anyone who could help her.

"I'll be right back. I have to check on something first. Yes, that's my office. Go right in," Oz said. As soon as she had disappeared in Oz's office, he said, "Sharon, get her some tea and stay in there with her once you bring it to her. Don't let her out of your sight. I'll be there in a few minutes."

Oz went into Al Mallone's office and called the emergency number at the Yakima Police station and got an operator. "Yes, this Oz Goldstein, manager of the Capitol Theatre. We have an emergency here and I need Lt. Paganelli to come here immediately. Tell him we have the sister of Zizi Zeigler in my office. Also tell him not to turn on his siren. He just needs to get here before the woman decides to leave."

Therese. Photo courtesy: Therese La Lumiere.

Louise, Martine, Therese. Photo courtesy: Therese La Lumiere.

After Oz came out of Mallone's office, he told Rex and Mike, "Once the lieutenant gets here, hold him in the lobby until I make sure that this woman really is Zizi's sister."

Madam D'Anjou had taken a pack of cigarettes out of her purse and shook one out. When Sharon entered the room, a cigarette was hanging out of the side of the sister's tight mouth. In a hurry to get a flame from her lighter, her hand was shaking so much that she could only get a spark each time she rolled the striker. Sharon put a cup of tea on a lamp table by the chair where Louise D'Anjou was sitting and said, "Ma'am, there's no smoking in the theatre" just as Oz entered his office. He sat in the chair on the other side of the table and smiled without saying anything until Sharon left.

Louise D'Anjou wanted to smoke. Reluctantly, she took the cigarette out of her mouth, slipped it back in the pack, and then put the pack in her purse. After a small cough, she took a big breath in order to deepen her smoker's cough and couldn't seem to stop hacking.

Oz recognized her stress and said, "Ma'am, take a sip of your tea. That'll help you stop coughing." She obeyed Oz and in the act of drinking her tea, the coughing stopped. She took a handkerchief out of her purse and wiped her mouth then nodded that she had recovered and could talk.

"I see that you have a suitcase. Are you planning to stay in Yakima a while?" he asked.

"Yes, I was going to ask a cab driver where to stay but it's getting late. Maybe I should go. I don't have a hotel room," Louise said as she looked at her watch.

"There's a hotel around the corner called The Commercial Hotel. I could call them right now and get a room for you. Would you like that?" Oz offered.

She nodded and smiled. "That would be very nice," she said. "If it's not a problem for you."

Oz picked up the phone and got ready to dial. "No problem at all. I know the staff over there and they'll take good care of you." He made the arrangements for Louise and she said "three days" so he passed on that information to the desk clerk.

Once the hotel arrangements were made, Oz got down to business. "Ma'am, do you have a picture of your sister. Therese D'Anjou? Was that her name?"

Louise nodded and started digging in her purse. She brought out her wallet and opened it to show a photo of her smiling sister, Zizi Zeigler. She also showed a photo of the two sisters together, her and Zizi.

"Do you recognize her, sir?" she asked.

Oz felt that he had to be careful about what he told the sister. This was a police matter after all and now Zizi's story was about to be revealed.

"I do recognize her as a lady who came to the late movies each Monday night. I don't understand why you believed that your sister was here in Yakima and why you came to the Capitol Theatre tonight. You're a long way from home in Canada," Oz needed some answers.

There was a knock on the door. Then the door cracked open and Mike peeked through and caught Oz's attention.

"Excuse me a second, ma'am," Oz said as he closed the door behind him. He stepped out in the lobby and saw Lt. Paganelli waiting for him.

Lt. Paganelli spoke softly. "This better be good, Goldstein. I've had a long day and I hear you've got a lead on the Zizi Zeigler case. What's up?"

"What's up is that I've got Zizi Zeigler's sister in my office. That's what's up!" Oz was looking for a positive reaction from Lt. Paganelli.

Believing this was a hoax like Rex's diamond earring that turned into a screw, Lt. Paganelli responded by saying, "Is that right? Well, I've got a winery in the Okefenokee Swamp that I'd like to sell you!" He shook his head and turned in the direction of the front doors.

CHAPTER FIFTEEN

The Letter

Oz quickly stepped to block Lt. Paganelli's exit from the theatre.

"Look," Oz was getting heated that Lt. Paganelli didn't regard the sister as being a break in Zizi's cold case. "I wouldn't have called you if I didn't think this sister was going to tell us who Zizi Zeigler really was. This lady is searching for her sister and doesn't know that Zizi is dead. I wasn't sure how to handle it so I wanted you to meet her before we lose the chance to find out who Zizi was. If this person is Zizi's sister, she's got to be told that her sister is dead. And she is entitled to claim Zizi's ashes. That's the job of the police," Oz said and backed off.

"Thank you for telling me what my job is," Lt. Paganelli said. "Have you got a meeting room where we could talk to the woman?"

"Al has a meeting room just off his office. Do you want to go in there and I'll bring her into the room?" Oz said.

"Yes. That would be best."

"Oz said, "Sharon, I want you to stay with Louise during this meeting. She's gonna cry and I think she'll feel better with you beside her. Go get her and bring her into Al's room. I'll get Rex and Mike to go in there too."

Everybody knew where to meet. They just needed Zizi's sister to give them enough information to show that she truly was a family member.

Sharon entered Ozzie's office and saw that Louise D'Anjou was enjoying the hot tea. But she was also looking at her watch and checking the late time.

"Miss D'Anjou? We've got some folks in a different room who are going to talk to you about your sister. All of us can't fit in here. You can take your tea or I can make another cup for you. I see that you have a lot to carry."

"Do you want me to go to the other room now?" Louise D'Anjou asked.

"Yes. Follow me. I'll stay with you and if there's anything you need to have explained, I'll be able to tell you in French," Sharon said.

Louise got a grip on her suitcase and purse and followed Sharon into the meeting room where Lt. Paganelli, Ozzie, Rex and Mike were already sitting around the table.

"What is this?" Louise started to panic when she saw so many people waiting for her.

Sharon said, "I'm going to stay with you, remember? We just want to help you get some answers about your sister. Let me introduce everyone. You've seen all of us except Lt. Paganelli, who is with the Yakima Police Department."

The lieutenant stood and offered his hand to Louise. "Madam D'Anjou?" he said.

She couldn't remember his name so she nodded and tried to smile but the idea that there was something coming up that would be painful had already shot through her mind.

"This is Rex, who runs the projector, and Mike, the assistant manager and me, Sharon, I make the popcorn." Everybody chuckled.

Lt. Paganelli addressed Louise D'Anjou. "Ma'am, do you have a photo of your sister?"

She dug in her purse for her wallet, found the photos and opened the wallet so he could see a picture of three girls. "That's me on the left. Martine is in the middle and that Therese on the right."

"You and Therese could pass for twins. Now, is there anything else you can show us that proves what your sister's name is, her age, where she worked and when she entered the United States? I'm trying to find out if she was a citizen of Canada or the United States."

This time the sister pulled open the zipper on the outside of her suitcase and lifted out a pack of papers, which she put on the table. Sharon was watching her every move to make sure that she showed all of the papers rather than only showing some of them.

"I have the letters she wrote to me. When her letters stopped, I came to the town where her letters were postmarked," Louise began.

"Why did you think your sister might be at the Capitol Theatre?" the lieutenant asked.

"You can see it in her letters. She described The Capitol Theatre. How beautiful she thought the theatre was. And the movies, she mentioned how she would have loved to be in the movies," Louise said. "I have the last letter I received from her but it's in French. Would you like to know what she is saying?"

"It would help us know something about her," Lt. Paganelli said. "Can you read the words aloud to us in English?"

'I'll do my best," Louise said.

"I think that would help," the lieutenant sat back and touched his fingers to his closed eyes in order to concentrate on Therese's message.

This is how the letter was written.

Chère Louise

Ce soir je vais voir un film qui donne le frisson au beau Capitol Theatre. C'est dans ce film, qui s'appelle Psycho, où il arrive que la voiture d'une jolie jeune femme tombe en panne. Il n'y a qu'un hôtel dans les environs pour passer la nuit. L'hôtel Bateman. Le propriétaire de cet hôtel est vraiment fou et, d'après ce qu'on m'a dit, il est arrivé quelque chose de mauvais à la jeune femme.

Ces derniers temps il m'est arrivé quelque chose de mauvais et je ne sais pas quoi faire.

Je suis allée chez le médecin il y a quelques jours et il m'a dit que je suis enceinte de deux mois. Je sais ce qu'on appelait des femmes célibataires qui se sont retrouvées enceintes. Donc je te prie de ne pas raconter mes nouvelles à Papa. Il serait déçu par moi. Et il songerait à l'homme qui m'a mise enceinte. Il demanderait: "Pourquoi ne sont-ils pas mariés?" C'est notre secret à nous, Louise. L'homme dont je te parle est un juge ici dans cette ville et il est déjà marié. Je croyais qu'il quitterait sa femme et se marierait avec moi. Mais il a dit non. Il veut que je me fasse avorter. Je lui ai dit que l'enfant est à moi. Je ne le tuerais jamais.

L'homme me dit que je suis sa maîtresse et qu'il gardera mon passeport et mes papiers d'identité en lieu sûr. Je ne peux pas travailler n'importe où parce qu'il ne me les rendra pas. Et je ne peux pas voyager parce qu'il refuse de me rendre mon passeport. Je lui ai dit que je ferais quelque chose d'illégal afin d'être déportée. Il m'a répondu que, si je le faisais, on me mettrait en prison au lieu de me déporter. Je ne sais que croire.

La seule chose à faire pour moi est de m'arranger un nouveau passeport; donc il me faudra un extrait de naissance afin de le faire. S'il te plaît, envoie–le–moi à l'hôtel Chinook, situé dans l'Avenue de Yakima dans le Washington.

> *Je veux revenir dans mon pays.*
> *Je t'embrasse,*
> *Therese*

Louise read it in English.

Dear Louise,

I'm going to see a scary movie at the beautiful Capitol Theatre tonight. Psycho is the name of the movie where a pretty woman's car breaks down and there's only one place to stay, The Bateman Hotel. The owner of the hotel is insane and I heard some bad things happen to the lady.

I've had some bad things happen to me lately and I don't know what to do.

A few days ago, I went to the doctor and he said I was two months pregnant. I know what we use to call women who got pregnant and weren't married. So I'm asking you not to tell Papa my news. He would be disappointed in me. And he would wonder about the man who got me pregnant. He would ask, why aren't they married? This is our secret, Louise. The man is a judge here in this town and he is married. I thought he would leave his wife and marry me. But he said no. He wants me to have an abortion. I said the baby is mine. I would never kill it.

I have illegal citizenship papers. The man says I am his mistress and he will keep the papers and my passport in a safe place. I can't work anywhere because he won't give me my papers. And I can't travel because he refuses to give me my passport. I told him that I would do something illegal so I would get deported. He said if I did that, rather than deporting me, they would put me in jail. I don't know what to believe.

The only thing I can think to do is get a new passport so I need a copy of my birth certificate to do that. Please send it to the Chinook Hotel on Yakima Avenue in Yakima, Washington.

I want to come home.

> *Love, Therese*

The lieutenant tried not to show his excitement about so many questions being answered in this letter. He finally had a solid lead about the murdered woman.

"Thank you for sharing your sister's letter with me," the lieutenant said. "Sharon knows some French and can make notes on a separate tablet. Do you mind if she and the others read the letter?"

"No, I don't mind," Louise said.

"Now, I have an important question to ask you. Who is Zizi Zeigler?"

"That was the name my sister used when she was dancing. Mostly, she just used her first name, Zizi," Louise said.

"Your sister was a dancer here in Yakima? What kind of dancer?" the lieutenant asked.

"Pardon me. I didn't say she was a dancer in Yakima. She was a strip tease dancer at the Chez Paris in Montreal when she was a teenager." Louise looked at the body language of the policeman and the theatre people. They all looked down except Oz. "I must tell you that Therese only stripped during the day for businessmen who enjoyed a free buffet. You must understand the difference between the attitude of Frenchmen who live in Montreal and appreciate the beauty of the dance and dancer and the attitude of American men who consider strip tease dancers to be prostitutes."

Louise continued. "I'm going to speak for my sister and tell you that she loved her work. The beautiful costumes and sets were similar to the dance productions you would see in Las Vegas. The money that she earned for her career in Montreal gave her personal freedom and allowed her to travel to Europe, across Canada and around the United States. She use to tell me that one of her dreams was to ride on a motorcycle with a boyfriend into Mexico and Central America."

The lieutenant commented, "I didn't know striptease dancing was considered a performing art in Montreal. How about Seattle? Did she work there?"

"She did dance in Seattle but I don't know why she would leave Seattle to come here. What I do know is that I came to Yakima to bring her birth certificate and see if there was some way to bring her home to Montreal. I didn't want to send it through the mail and take a chance that it might get lost. She wanted to come home and she needed a passport to do that," Louise said.

"You have her birth certificate?" the lieutenant asked.

Louise shuffled the papers and pulled out an envelope with THERESE'S BIRTH CERTIFICATE written on the outside. She handed it to the lieutenant.

The writing was in French but at least he could recognize the name of the hospital, the year of her birth and who her mother and father were. She was twenty-two years old when she died. Her father's name was Roland. Her mother's name was Laura.

"What about your parents? Why aren't they here to help their daughter?" the lieutenant figured he had nothing to lose by asking questions about the family dynamics.

Oz, Rex, Mike and Sharon were looking at Lt. Paganelli to see what his next move would be. At some point, he was going to have to tell Louise what happened to her sister. The four of them were glad that they didn't have to pass on the bad news.

Louise broke the momentary silence. "I have given you valuable information now I need some information from you. Can you please tell me if you know my sister? I want to see her," Louise looked at each person imploring them to tell her where her sister was.

Lt. Paganelli cleared his throat and looked directly at Louise. Rex held his breath because he knew the lieutenant was going to tell Louise the bad news. The lieutenant covered his mouth with his fingers then gave her the news. "Madam D'Angou, I regret telling you that I have some bad news about your sister." Sharon put her hand on Louise's shoulder and knew the worst was to come.

"A couple months ago, your sister was found on the floor between the back seats of this theatre. She came to the 9 p.m. movie every Monday night and met a man who took her to a waiting car in the alley. We figured that the man wasn't her boyfriend but most likely took her to see her boyfriend. When we found her, she had been strangled and was dead."

Louise believed the lieutenant and cried out, "Oh no!! She's dead! And the baby too!" She sobbed and ranted to herself saying that her sister didn't have a chance to have a happy life. Their rotten parents didn't take care of their children so Therese survived the only way she could by showing her beautiful body.

The lieutenant stood up. "Madam, Sharon is going to stay with you. We'll leave this meeting room and take a break in the lobby for a few minutes. When you recover a bit, Sharon will come get us and I'll let you know what the next step is. Sharon?"

CHAPTER SIXTEEN

Therese's Story

After fifteen minutes, Sharon came into the lobby and said, "Louise is ready to tell you about her sister, Therese.

The lieutenant, Oz, Rex and Mike followed Sharon back into the meeting room. She had made another cup of tea for Louise and the sister's face was puffy and red but she attempted to smile as the group entered the room.

"Please accept our condolences," Madam D'Anjou Lt. Paganelli referred to her in a formal manner.

"We went to your sister's apartment at the Chinook Hotel the next morning after her death to see if we could find anything that would identify her, such as a driver's license, passport or address book. During the night, someone got into her apartment and took all her personal belongings. Her clothes, her makeup, her address book and her food were gone. They even took the sheets off her bed. The manager told us Zizi Zeigler occupied apartment 218. But the place could have been occupied by anyone because there was absolutely nothing personal in those empty rooms."

He continued. "It became clear to us that another person did not want us to find anything that might connect your sister to them. That person had knowledge about how to remove fingerprints. There was not even one hair that we could find that would reveal that your sister had lived there. As a consequence, if a judge asked us for evidence that Zizi Zeigler had lived there, we would have to say that we could not find any evidence that anyone lived in that apartment."

"I have a letter with her return address of the hotel and her room number. Will that help?" Louise D'Anjou handed the lieutenant an envelope with the complete return address. It clearly listed 218 as Zizi Zeigler's apartment.

"Yes, this envelope will help. And the hotel manager also said she lived in that room. So that also will help. However, unless we found her personal evidence, we couldn't be forensically certain that your sister lived in apartment 218."

"Did your sister have a Washington State driver's license?"

"She had one in Quebec because she drove a Saab. But we never talked about whether she had a U.S.A. driver's license," Louise said.

The lieutenant was thinking out loud. "We checked with the Washington Department of Motor Vehicles and Licensing and didn't find a driver's license under the name Zizi Zeigler. Now that we know her real name, we'll check under the D'Anjou name."

"What kind of work did she do in Quebec?" the lieutenant asked.

"Therese and I were both strippers. Actually, we'd been apart for years because of our attempts to deal with our parent's inability to act like normal parents. Finally, when we did reunite, we danced together on stage in Toronto. Our strip club allowed the girls to be paid to sit with customers after they were dressed. But neither Therese or I did that," Louise said.

"The next question is was she employed here in Yakima? What brought her to this town? Can you help us with that information?" Lt. Paganelli asked Louise.

"The best I can do is to tell you where she worked in Seattle. Even though I asked her about working in Yakima, she avoided answering that question," Louise said.

"Where did she work in Seattle?" the lieutenant was writing all the information in his small notebook.

"She worked as a stripper at the Raz-Ma-Taz Club on Aurora. The club was known as a strip club so the police didn't bother the owner, Frank Colacurcio, Jr.," Louise said.

"Do you think your sister was into drugs or alcohol?"

"Therese was a runner and long distance swimmer. She had the body of the Goddess Atalanta because she was athletic. She ran from the top of the Grand Canyon to the bottom then ran back up to the top and passed people who were fainting from heat exhaustion. I know she tried marijuana when she was a teenager but hated it. She was not a prostitute. I don't know what her relationship was with this man in Yakima but she was in no way a call girl. She was making plenty of money as a stripper and use to send money to our father." Louise emphasized that a woman could be a stripper and not a prostitute.

"Someone brought her here to Yakima either through blackmail or giving her a better deal than she had in Seattle. I think once we find out what that reason was, we'll have a better direction to find her killer." When the lieutenant looked up from his notebook, he saw that Louise's eyes were closed and she was nodding from exhaustion.

"Madam D'Anjou? Ma'am?"

Sharon rubbed Louise's back to wake her. "Wha ... ? Oh sorry, I'm so sleepy."

"I think we've covered enough for the night. You are staying at the Commercial Hotel?"

Oz said, "Yes, I made reservations for her."

"I'm going to take you to the hotel and walk you to your room. I'll come by for you in the morning at 8:00 a.m. to take you to breakfast. Then I'll need you to come to the station and identify the sketch that an artist drew of your sister and her clothes. Don't be alarmed if there's a man sitting in the hall outside your room. He'll be one of the detectives who'll be guarding you," Lt. Paganelli said.

"You think I need to be guarded?"

"Yes ma'am. Your information may lead us to the killer and believe me when I say that whoever that man is, you are a serious threat to him. So we need to get your information then make sure you are safely returned to Canada. "For now, this meeting is over."

Everyone stood up. Rex approached Louise and said, "Ma'am, when you have some time, would you like to come up to the projection booth in the theatre? I have something that I think belonged to your sister and I would like to give it to you."

"Will I be allowed to do that, Lieutenant?"

"Since the hotel is closer to the theatre than the police station, why don't we visit the projection booth first thing after breakfast then walk over to the station?" Lt. Paganelli said. "I'll be with you in a minute, Madam D'Anjou. I need to make a phone call."

While Sharon and Louise went to the ladies' room, Lt. Paganelli returned to Ozzie's office and called the police station. "Get detective Kusske over to the Commercial Hotel immediately. Tell him he's gonna be on alert overnight. Make sure he's packing and has a back-up clip. We need to keep this witness alive."

When the ladies came back, Lt. Paganelli approached Sharon off to the side. "Sharon, I know you're not working for the police department. But as of now, you are. That is if you'll consent to spend the night in the same room with Louise. Oz told me the room has twin beds and a little kitchenette. I need you to keep a line-of-sight on Louise during the night until I pick her up in the morning. Will you do that for me? You'll be compensated, no problem."

"Wow. This sounds serious. If her safety is in jeopardy, I'll stay with her," Sharon said.

"Congratulations, detective Sharon Meyers. You are officially working for the Yakima Police Department."

CHAPTER SEVENTEEN

The Reunion

Madam D'Anjou lived through the night. Not that there seemed to be any real danger from the man who had her sister killed but Lt. Paganelli didn't want to take any chances. When he arrived at the hotel room, he said, "Just a moment Madam D'Anjou. I have to talk to Sharon in the hall for a second and let her know what's on the schedule."

In his softest voice, he asked, "Did she give you any other information?"

"Not really. She'd had enough stress for the night. Listen lieutenant, you'll have to get someone else to stay with her. She is a chain smoker and a drinker. This air that I'm breathing in this hall is the first clean air I've had in about nine hours. My hair and my clothes stink from her cigarette smoke. I'm going home to take a shower and get some real sleep before I have to go to work at the theatre. In other words, I'm not going to breakfast with the two of you."

"Send my check to the theatre," Sharon said as she headed for the stairs.

Next door to the Commercial Hotel, the Turf Café attracted customers by their attraction in the display window of a turkey on a rotisserie. The roasting turkey was not only appetizing to look at but the aroma was like smelling Thanksgiving dinner every day of the week. Madam D'Anjou and the lieutenant stepped into the café' for breakfast and talked mostly about the D'Anjou family members, particularly Therese.

As promised, after breakfast the lieutenant brought Louise D'Anjou back to the theatre so she could visit with Rex. Mike called Rex on the phone from the lobby to make sure he was in his booth and he was. So the lieutenant walked with Louise up the stairs to the highest balcony then across the back of the theatre seats. The door was open and once Rex saw them, he walked to the last stairs leading into the booth.

"Good morning. Lieutenant, there's very little room in the booth. I wonder if I can have some privacy with Louise?"

"How long with this take?" The lieutenant had things to do.

"Hard to say. Not more than a half hour. If we visit longer, you'll know she's here with me."

"Yeah. Go ahead. I'll be downstairs drinking coffee. When you're done, will you walk Louise down the stairs into the lobby?"

"Sure thing. I'll take excellent care of her. C'mon Louise. Come into my booth." Rex helped Louise up the few stairs and she stepped into the projection booth. She seemed wide-eyed as she looked at his colorful posters, the big projectors and the shelves of reels and the splicing counter.

After Louise briefly looked out the windows and saw the vastness of the rest of the theatre, she staggered from a rush of vertigo and reached for a chair to sit in.

Rex told her about the amusing incident in the lobby when he and Zizi's eyes met. "I just felt like we had an instant connection and the whole evening I was trying to figure out a way to strike up a conversation with your sister. I didn't realize that it was too late. We're you and your sister very close?"

"I guess you could say that we wanted to be close but at times we were separated because of our desperate family situation," Louise tried to rub the nicotine stains off her fingers.

"Your mother and father didn't take care of you?"

"I have my own memories about the abuse at home since our mother was paranoid-schizophrenic and our father was an alcoholic when he wasn't working."

Rex couldn't imagine how the sisters' parents could raise their children.

"When Therese was seven-years-old, she had been living with our auntie. Mother wanted her to live at home so not long after she started living there, she had an opportunity to bring some of her little girl friends home to play. When she and the girls walked through the door, our mother was talking to the 'voice' and had a butcher knife in her hands. She had sliced the curtains, which were in shreds. The kitchen was a mess with pieces of dishes, fruit and vegetables, papers on the table and floor and our mother was still slicing everything in sight. So the little girls ran away. At school, they wouldn't play with Therese anymore and teased her about her crazy mother. She was humiliated."

"Sounds like a horror movie," Rex said.

Louise continued. "Another time when Therese was eight-years-old, she was at school when our mother came into the classroom and gave her a jar of macaroni and cheese and a jar of milk. She announced that she wanted to make sure her daughter had enough to eat. Therese was mortified when the teacher had to ask our mother to leave the classroom."

"Couldn't your father help you?" Rex asked.

"Our father was a welder. When he came home, he was the one who had to clean up after our mother's rampages. It was too much for him and he found solace in the bottle. So at night and on the weekends, he was so drunk that we children had to become the parents and feed ourselves when we could find food."

"As if the tragedy wasn't enough," Louise continued. "My brother, Mario, was a very introverted child and quite often was bullied at school. He wouldn't stand up for himself and eventually was placed in remedial classes for the retarded. He was what you might call a delicate boy and to make matters worse, he went to live with priests because our parents weren't capable of taking care of themselves much less their children. At his school, he was sodomized and was a young man when he committed suicide." Therese went to live with the nuns and was sexually abused.

Louise felt that Rex was a sympathetic soul so she opened up to him. Once she began the story of the D'Anjou family, she could not stop.

"Therese was also an alcoholic?" Rex wondered.

"No. She turned to athletics and dancing in front of audiences," Louise answered.

"My word, what a sad story about your family. I'm so sorry. And now, you have even more sadness with the passing of your beloved sister, Therese." Rex had barely given his condolences to Louise when they both became alert because of a voice they heard whimpering and crying above them. They looked up expecting that the lady who was crying would come into the booth. That's how close she seemed to be.

"*Oh mon Dieu! C'est ma sœur qui pleure! Où est-elle? Je veux aller la voir.* Oh my God! That's my sister crying! Where is she? I want to go to her!"

They both continued to listen to the feminine footsteps as a door opened and closed. Then the sounds stopped.

Louise's eyes were wide with tearful disbelief at what she had just heard and she looked to Rex for an explanation. "There's no floor above us, only the rooftop. Your sister has made quite a few appearances. Not that I could see her. But she's made things move around and on one occasion, she nearly scared us to death when she put some power on movie reels to come after the delivery guy and me. When I refused to help her because I thought she was the devil, she became angry with me."

"Elle ne peut pas se reposer parce que quelqu'un l'a assassinée. She cannot rest because someone has murdered her."

Louise was alarmed that her sister was trapped in a lost world. She asked, "Is she appearing to anyone else?

"Mostly, she appears to me. Like I said, she did scare the deliveryman and me when she made those reels of film come after us. Oz saved us by pushing the stage door shut. Then the reels bounced on the door and stopped spinning." Rex thought it would be safe to share the story with Therese's sister.

"She's trying to make contact with you. Are you going to find the man who murdered her? That's what she wants you to do. I implore you. Please help her!!!" Louise broke down in tears and Rex tried to comfort her.

"Would you feel better if I searched for Therese's killer?" he was finally willing to be Therese's warrior.

"Oh, would you?" Louise lifted her red and puffy face in an expression of premature gratitude.

"To tell you the truth, we don't know if she worked in Yakima. But she must have gone some place other than the hotel and her boyfriend's place. Her nails were manicured regularly. Maybe I should start at local beauty shops. Women always tell their beauticians about their lives and their troubles. Right?" Rex wanted assurance that he was on the right track.

Louise's face lit up. "That would be a good start. How about if I went with you? People who knew Therese would recognize me and think that I was her. You would know that they had contact with her just from the look on their faces."

"I hope Lt. Paganelli would let us do that."

"Why does he have to know?" Louise made a good point.

"Well, if you are willing, I think that would be a good idea." Rex finally had a partner who could help him get started on finding Therese's killer.

The phone rang and it was Mike. "The lieutenant wants Louise to come down to the lobby. He's got to take her to the station."

Rex said, "Tell him she's on her way. I just have one more thing that I have to do."

Louise looked expectantly at Rex thinking that he wanted to get started immediately.

"The lieutenant wants you to come to the lobby but I want to give you something before we walk down the stairs." Rex took a few steps to the shelves above the splice counter. He opened the lid on the Folger's Coffee tin where he was keeping Therese's earring. He picked up the tin and turned it upside down so the earring could slide out on the table. But the brass screw tumbled out.

"What the...? I had your sister's earring in this tin and I wanted to give it to you but it has disappeared." He looked at Louise with an apology and disappointment in his voice.

She looked down at her closed hand and gasped. When she opened her fist, the gold and diamond earring sparkled in her palm.

CHAPTER EIGHTEEN

Cold Case Box

Louise D'Anjou did not have a clear idea of what to expect at the police station. She thought maybe she would identify the sketch of her sister as being both Zizi Zeigler and Therese D'Anjou or maybe she'd pick up a few of her sister's clothes. It was a sad event for Louise to return to Montreal with her sister's possessions and not her sister.

The lieutenant wanted privacy in a conference room rather than an interrogation room where people could watch Louise through the one sided glass. She would need some time to weep over the loss of her sister, especially when she touched Therese's clothes and smelled her perfume on the fabric.

"Let's go in here, Madam D'Anjou. I think you'll be comfortable." Once they had settled in their chairs, the lieutenant picked up the phone and called his secretary. "Sally, bring in the cold case box for Therese D'Anjou . Thanks."

"How long will you be able to stay in Yakima?" the lieutenant asked Louise.

Her answer was unexpectedly to the point. "I'm not leaving until you have the murderer in custody. I look enough like Therese that I can go around to places where I think she might have been a client or customer and see if anyone thinks I'm her."

"You plan to do this by yourself?"

"I would like to have Rex accompany me because he said that no one would recognize him. We'll be able to see what people's reactions are and that will help us find out where my sister was a customer," Louise said.

"The only way I'd permit that plan is for you to have undercover backup from us or you're likely to get shot. Do you have any idea of the dangerous people you're facing? You're a threat to the murderer." The lieutenant was alarmed at the possibility of losing Louise as a key witness. "Let's put that plan on the back burner for now."

The lieutenant had to get the forensics out of the way immediately before they got into the cold case box. The most conclusive evidence that Louise and Therese D'Anjou were sisters was through blood tests and fingerprints.

"Bring your purse and your bag with you. Leave the sweater here. We've got to go to the admissions section of the jail to have your fingerprints taken. We'll also take a couple photographs there and we'll take a few drops of your blood out of your finger so that we have a complete forensic profile of you. We've already done this with your sister. Yes, that's right. We have her fingerprints and a blood sample on file and of course photographs of her face and body. If we have to appear in court, we want to have all the evidence possible to show that the two of you were sisters." The lieutenant stood up and opened the door for Louise.

She followed him down and up a number of stairs, which led to admissions where a female expert was waiting to take her prints. "Hello. I'm officer Kendall and I need you to just relax and let me place each finger exactly where it needs to go on this chart. I'll press each finger on an ink-pad first. It'll be messy but not painful."

With efficiency, the finger printing process was completed. She also took a front and side shot of Louise for the record. A medic came in next and pricked her finger to gather a blood sample. Louise felt like a criminal and tried to keep from weeping.

Lt. Paganelli said, "You're very brave to let us do all these procedures. Thank you. We're going to return to the conference room and look through a box that has your sister's belongings so follow me."

Once the two of them returned to the conference room, Lt. Paganelli said, "I'm going to ask you to give me Therese's birth certificate, her letters and photos. They will go in a locked safe but we've got to have them in order to identify your sister. Right now, she's considered what we call a Jane Doe. That means, she's a person who has no identity. By giving us these documents, we will be able to open her case and prove that Zizi Zeigler and Therese D'Anjou are the same person. We'll also have a small clue that there is a judge involved. We just have to find him. As soon as the case is solved and we have brought the murderer to justice, all your sister's possessions will be returned to you," the lieutenant explained.

"You want to take my sister's letters, her photos and passport from me and put them into custody?" Louise could not understand that thinking.

"If you're uncomfortable with that idea, think about how you'd feel if those same items were stolen from you and you never saw them again because the murderer had destroyed them." After Louise handed over the needed documents to the lieutenant, he called his secretary on the phone. Within five minutes, she knocked and brought in a box labeled Zizi Zeigler—deceased March 1, 1965.

The box was placed on the conference room table and Louise brought her hands to her mouth and began to weep. "I can smell Channel 5, the perfume Therese use to wear."

"I'm so sorry for your loss, Madam D'Anjou," the lieutenant said as he lifted out a large manila envelope. Your sister's sketch is in this file as well as a photograph of her that was taken in the autopsy room. I need you to identify both the sketch and photograph as being your sister, Therese D'Anjou and Zizi Zeigler. We'll start with the artist's sketch."

He laid the artist's sketch on the table and watched Louise's reaction. As it always was when a family member identified a loved one who had been murdered, the sister's reaction was immediately mournful. "Is that a drawing of your sister?" the lieutenant asked.

"Yes, that's Therese, my sweet sister," Louise answered.

The photograph of the deceased was going to be difficult for Louise to look at but there was no other way for her to make the identification of a person who had already been cremated. The lieutenant laid a black and white photograph on the table that showed Therese D'Anjou at eternal rest. The ligature cut on her neck had been covered up for this photo. But there were other photos that showed a close-up of her neck that the lieutenant would not show Louise.

"Oh my God," she really is dead! She didn't deserve to die this way. And the baby died too. My God, she finally had the beginning of her own family and now they've both been murdered!" Louise sobbed and repeated various laments in French. "Therese wasn't going to bother anyone. She just wanted to come home and raise her baby. Papa would have been a grandfather and he would have been so proud."

While Louise was mourning her sister, the lieutenant picked up the telephone and punched a connection to his secretary. "Sally, can you make some hot tea and bring it in for Madam D'Anjou? Thanks."

Lt. Paganelli was filling out a form as Louise identified her sister's sketch and photos. There was more to go so he proceeded to show Louise her sister's clothes and jewelry.

"Let's take a look at her clothes and jewelry and see if you recognize anything." Therese's cashmere sweater, wool pants, fur lined wool coat, scarf, underwear, boots and gloves were laid on the table.

"I've never seen these clothes before," Louise said. "But they are a size ten, which is the correct size. She wore a size eight shoe and that also is the correct size for Therese."

"Here's a box of the jewelry she was wearing. Take a look at the pieces. Maybe you'll recognize some of them." The lieutenant had rolled the jewelry inside a black cloth and stuffed it into a shoebox just to make sure none of the jewelry was misplaced. As he unrolled the cloth, he displayed a gold bracelet, a gold ring with five diamond chips and a gold hoop earring with one diamond.

"I don't recognize this jewelry as anything that I've seen Therese wear but I do know that she loved beautiful jewelry. By the way, I have the matching earring," Louise said as she reached in her purse and took out a handkerchief, which she laid on the black cloth and opened to reveal a brass screw. Her mouth dropped open as she gasped in disbelief.

"What is this? I had the earring in my hand just an hour ago in the projection booth," she said before she dug in her purse to see if the earring might have fallen out of the handkerchief.

"What do you mean?" the lieutenant asked. This scene was like *deja vu* when Rex thought he was bringing the earring to give to the police department. Instead, when he opened his handkerchief, it was a brass screw.

"When I was visiting Rex in the projection booth this morning, we heard Therese crying on a floor above us. I recognized her voice. Then we could hear her walking and opening and closing a door. That's when Rex went over to a coffee tin to take out the diamond earring that he found in the theatre near where she was killed. But the earring wasn't in the tin. Somehow, it appeared when I opened my hand. After I looked at it a while,

I put it in my hanky, rolled it up and stuck it in my purse. This is the first time that I have looked at what I thought would be the earring since then. How could something that was an earring turn into a screw? Can you answer that question for me?"

Louise D'Anjou needed an explanation. Because if no one could answer the question, she would understand that her sister was a ghost who had powers that no human could ever possess.

Since this scene had happened already between Rex and the lieutenant, the thought that he was dealing with a ghost finally rang true. "This isn't happening to anyone else," the lieutenant thought. "The disappearing earring is only happening to Rex. The ghost does not want the earring to leave the projection booth, not even with the ghost's sister." That was a message from the ghost to Rex, as well as the lieutenant. The ghost wanted Rex to solve her murder. The lieutenant reasoned that there could be no other explanation.

"Madam D'Anjou, I know this thing with the earring that turns into a screw is a puzzle. My job is solving one puzzle after another and this situation is no exception. The missing earring and your sister's murder will be solved. I don't feel you are safe in this town because you look just like her and your plan to see who recognizes you as being Therese will work. Once it does, your life will really be in danger."

"If it's the only way that we can find my sister's murderer, I will consent to being the sacrificial lamb as we wait for the lion to attack."

The door opened and Sally walked in with a teacup of hot water, a bag of Earl Grey tea, a tiny pitcher of milk, a few cubes of sugar and a spoon on a tray that said, YAKIMA—THE FRUIT BOWL OF THE U.S.A.

"Sally, will you go get a camera in the supply room and we'll get a few pictures of Louise?" the lieutenant needed to get her photographs and it was also a way of easing up the situation.

"Now, Madam D'Anjou, I need you to sign this document that you have seen all the evidence we have on your sister. The most important thing that you'll be signing is that the sketch and the autopsy photo is both Therese D'Anjou and Zizi Zeigler, the same person who is your sister. Sign in these two spots, please. While Louise D'Anjou was signing the next-of-kin document, Sally returned and asked Louise to stand against a blank wall so her photo could be taken for the record."

"I'm going to ask you if you will hold up the sketch of your sister next to your face on one side and the photograph on the other side. We want to have a record of the similarity of the two sisters on file."

The photos were taken and there was one more matter to settle.

"We sent your sister's sketch on Associated Press to the major papers across the United States and didn't receive an answer. We also fingerprinted her and sent her prints to the FBI with no results. Your sister has never committed a crime because her prints were not on file. After a couple months, a body that's being held at the morgue without being identified or claimed, is cremated."

"You cremated my sister's body?"

The lieutenant felt this was an accusation of sorts. "Yes. Since no one claimed her body, by law we were within our rights to dispose of the body. I'm sorry. I know that's hard to hear."

"Where are my sister's ashes? I want to claim them," Louise said as she started to rise.

"We'll send the sealed box of ashes by air express to your address in Montreal after you have flown home and we know you will be there to receive them."

"I understand. I think that is the best way to bring her home," Louise said and sat back in her chair. She reached in her purse for her pack of cigarettes and started to pull one out.

The lieutenant said, "You can't smoke here. But I'll join you for a smoke if you'd like to go outside."

After Louise put the pack of cigarettes back in her purse, her face hardened as she looked at the lieutenant. "My sister wants Rex to find her killer. I think I can help him do that. I want the bastard executed for killing my sister and her baby."

The lieutenant replied. "Washington State's method of execution is hanging or lethal injection. Once we find the killer, your wish has every possibility of coming true."

CHAPTER NINETEEN

The Bodyguard

Lt. Paganelli knew that the presence of Louise D'Anjou in Yakima was a life-threatening problem for her and the police department.

After the police received Therese's letters, birth certificate and photographs as well as information about her family's address in Montreal and the names of several of her relatives, her murder was no longer a cold case. However, even at a police station, people gossiped. The lieutenant feared that because the sister had pertinent information, the murderer might try to eliminate her.

"Madam D'Anjou, if the person who murdered your sister discovers the fact that you look so much like Therese, he will feel threatened. Since I believe your life is in danger, I'm going to make arrangements for you to return to Montreal where you'll be more protected. I need you to return home and let me concentrate on finding your sister's murderer."

"Until you leave Yakima, officer Kusske will be your bodyguard,' the lieutenant added. "You were brave enough to come to Yakima and give the police department information about your sister and I don't want anything to happen to you. The lieutenant picked up the phone and called his secretary. "Sally, get officer Kuskke in here. I think he's doing some paperwork at his desk. Thank you."

Within a couple minutes, there was a soft knock on the door and officer Vince Kusske looked in. "Did you want to see me, lieutenant?"

"Come in." Officiating the introductions, the lieutenant said, "Officer Kusske I'd like you to meet Louise D'Anjou. She is the sister of Therese D'Anjou, the lady from the Capitol Theatre." Officer Kusske had been on the CSI team investigating the murder of Louise's sister and knew the police department had run into a wall since there had been no identification on Therese. Now that this sister had brought new information, the case had become hot and Kuskke figured she was in great jeopardy.

"I'm sorry about your sister," the officer said as he shook hands with Louise. Unlike the other detectives who were sharp and crude in their language and treatment of people, Lt. Paganelli chose Vince Kusske because of his gentle and caring nature with people, a character trait that didn't last very long in the police business of dealing with degenerates, drug dealers, abusers of women and children and who thought nothing of taking a human life because they were insulted. In his forties, tall, dark with puppy dog eyes, it was impossible not to trust Vince Kusske with a person's life. Instinctively, he could read a dangerous situation or a criminal's intentions before the action started and keep his assigned person out of harm's way.

Louise D'Anjou smiled at the officer and offered her hand. They shook hands briefly then she gathered her sweater and purse. As officer Kusske held the door open for her, she walked through and turned toward Lt. Paganelli for final instructions.

"I'm going to have my secretary make plane reservations for you immediately and we'll see if we can get you on a flight before tonight. I'll get a squad car to take you to the airport and we'll stay with you until you board the plane," the lieutenant needed Louise to leave as soon as possible.

Since the police station was only a few blocks from the Commercial Hotel, Louise and detective Kusske decided to walk. He knew a squad car would pick them up at the hotel and drive Louise and him to the airport later that afternoon.

"I want to pick up a couple things at the Bon Marche before I leave," she smiled.

"No problem," Kusske said. We'll go over one block then walk down Third Street toward Yakima Avenue. The entrance doors are right there."

"Aren't you the detective who was outside my door at the hotel last night?" Louise asked.

"Yes, and I'll be with you until you fly out today," he answered. The two of them chatted about the differences and similarities between life in Washington State and life in Quebec during their walk.

Within a few minutes, they were at the front doors of the Bon Marche and the two of them entered the store through the glass double doors. The intermingling fragrances from the cosmetic and perfume departments filled the air. The smell of leather from women's purses and shoes added to the variety of pleasant aromas. Beyond the cosmetic department, the officer could see the men's wear department, both clothing and shoes.

Without asking permission, Louise bee-lined for the escalator to the second floor. So many women buyers milling around the cosmetic department had momentarily distracted the detective and he had to make his way through the customers quickly without causing a scene in order to keep up with Louise. He boarded the escalator and saw her walk to the left as she reached the clothing level of the store. Because her quick actions alerted him that she was not paying attention to her safety in a crowd, he noted to himself that he would make sure she didn't get beyond a couple yards from his side. Even that short distance was no assurance that he could reach her in time if she was attacked. He expected that somehow she would be assaulted but he didn't know how or where. He just felt that it was guaranteed to happen.

All sizes and all prices of ladies ready-to-wear clothing filled the majority of the space on the second floor. Without hesitation, Louise walked through the women's lingerie section and approached the beauty salon where the odor of ammonia from a woman getting a permanent stung her nose. Louise approached the appointment desk to see if she would be recognized as her sister, Therese, and was already talking to the receptionist as officer Kusske stood against the entrance opening to the salon. He wanted to be within earshot so that he could be a witness to her conversation.

Once the receptionist laid eyes on Louise, there was an immediate response of recognition of the person she thought was Zizi Zeigler.

"Holy crimminy! Where have you been? Someone saw your picture in the paper and the police wanted to know who you were!" cried the receptionist. She came around the counter and gave Louise a big hug. Her hair looked like a two-toned mop; the top half was bleached and high on her head in a straw colored hill. The bottom half was long stringy dark hair that extended down her back like a witch's hair-do. She smelled like incense and cigarette smoke at the same time.

Louise responded. "I took care of my dying sister in her last few months and had to make her funeral arrangements. But I'm back and could use a hair trim. Is my regular lady available?"

"You're in luck! Kitty has an opening. Let me see if she can do you?" the receptionist looked over to station two and saw that the hairdresser was killing time by cleaning her mirror. "Kitty! You got an opening for Zizi? Yeah, I know! Can you believe she's back with us? She had a big illness with a sister in Montreal." Getting back to Louise, she said, "Go ahead, hon, she's ready for you."

Kitty was waiting for Louise with open arms. "Well, it's sure good to see you. So sorry about your sister in Montreal. We thought you might have moved. C'mon hon, looks like you can use the works. What? You just want a trim today. Sure, no problem. Let's go get 'er washed."

Officer Kusske knew there was only one way out of the beauty salon and it was his job to wait. He found a chair and looked like any patient husband, as he became a sentinel in an out-of-the-way spot where he could watch Louise's every move. She had a rather loud voice, typical of many smokers and alcoholics, so it was with no effort that officer Kusske could hear her conversation.

Kitty started the conversation with an inquiry about Louise's accent. "Seems stronger since you visited Montreal."

"I have to adjust my brain to speak English again," Louise said.

"Your boyfriend must have really missed you. The judge? He still married?"

Louise nodded and watched Kitty in the mirror to see if she would give any further information about Zizi-Therese's relationship with a judge.

"Don't waste your time, hon. He's just in love with your beauty. Who wouldn't be?"

Louise wanted to keep the conversation going. "He says he loves me and he's given me diamonds."

"Yeah, I was wondering where your diamonds were?" Kitty commented. "But hon, you have to be careful. I don't know if your judge is straight or connected with the mob and I bet you don't know either."

"What mob?" Louise played dumb.

"They're into that whole scene down on First and Front Streets." Kitty whispered in Louise's ear. "Somebody is getting paid big bucks to ignore on all those naked dancers and prostitutes in that district. Could be the police. Could be certain judges too. I just hope it isn't your guy that's in the pocket of the Seattle mob."

"How could I find out if my guy is a bad guy?" Louise asked.

"Tell him you want the two of you to have some fun at The Corral. See some of your old friends there. If he refuses, be suspicious about why he doesn't want to be seen with you there. If you do go, see who talks to him."

Kitty put the finishing touches on the comb-out then sprayed the hairdo with a cloud of Spray-Net. "Well, how's that look? You're all spruced up and ready to rock and roll. Good luck with your guy. Let me know what happens." Kitty gave Louise a hug before she went to the receptionist and paid her bill.

Officer Kusske heard everything. He did not want it to seem like he was waiting for Louise so he walked over to a woman about his same age, who was looking at lingerie and stood near her in order to make it look like he was waiting for her. After she walked away from him, he kept some distance until he followed her into the ready-to-wear section and out of the staring eyes of the hairdressers. Louise understood his method of operation and allowed herself to be available near the escalator where officer Kusske joined her.

The two of them exited the store and officer Kusske kept the tone of his voice low as he talked to Louise. "Now we know that your sister was involved with a judge here in Yakima. If you think about how she could have been involved with him, there are only a few choices. Tell me what you think they are."

Louise was agitated about the information she received from her hairdresser regarding the judge being connected to the Seattle mob. "Since Therese had no identification, it's possible that the judge was keeping it from her. I'm talking about him keeping her illegal citizenship papers, her passport, her address and phone book, maybe her social security number. I don't know if he knew her real name. But he must have if she had a social security number. I know one thing. He doesn't have her birth certificate. There was only one and now the Yakima police department has it."

Kusske encouraged her to continue. "What else do you think your sister's relationship with the judge was?"

"She had to be his mistress. Why else would she be picked up at the same time every Monday night at the Capitol Theatre? But Therese was smart. She wouldn't stay with a man who forced her to be his mistress in order to get her identification papers back. She would threaten to tell the authorities about his illegal deals." Louise was thinking out loud.

"If she threatened to tell the police on him, wouldn't he stop her?" Kusske asked.

"Once she found out she was pregnant, her plan to turn him into the police was no longer important. She just wanted to come home to Montreal and raise her baby," Louise summed it up. "But he obviously didn't want to be named as the father on the baby's birth certificate. He didn't kill her himself. He had her killed by one of his men. But why was it done in that beautiful theatre—the Capitol Theatre, a public place?"

As they got ready to cross Yakima Avenue at Third, two men ran past them and were rushing toward the Capitol Theatre. The first man was yelling HELP! HELP ME!! The second man was running just as fast and was shooting at the first man; his shots were hitting the sidewalk and people were screaming and huddling together. The first man was dressed like a businessman with his suit coat flying and his head covered by a hat. The man chasing him was dressed in a hooded sweatshirt and appeared to be younger and more athletic.

Instinctively, officer Kusske drew his weapon, a .38 Special. He yelled at Louise, "Run inside the hotel and call Lt. Paganelli!!

Even though the men had a sizable head start on him, he joined the chase and saw them turn into the alley between the theatre and the back of the Wilson Building and the Commercial Hotel. By the time he reached the alley, the two men were nowhere in sight. He continued to run and came out to a parking lot behind the theatre on the right where a deliveryman was carrying boxes into the theatre. Officer Kusske trotted up to the man and asked, "Did you see two men run by here? One was shooting at the other man?"

While holding a small box, the deliveryman was startled by the police officer holding a gun. "I haven't seen anybody back here this morning and I've been working out of the truck for about a half hour. What's going on?"

Without hesitation, officer Kusske ran to Fourth Street and looked toward Yakima Avenue and down Fourth. A few ordinary people were walking into businesses but no one was running. The men involved in the chase had simply disappeared. As if lightening had struck him, officer Kusske realized he'd been distracted from protecting Louise D'Anjou by his efforts to apprehend the man shooting his gun at the first runner. He experienced an adrenaline rush when he understood that this was the assault he'd been expecting where Louise would be killed.

He hustled down the alley toward Third Street and turned toward Yakima Avenue. Once he reached the intersection, he veered toward the right and went into the Commercial Hotel. There was no lobby but there was a receptionist.

"Did Louise D'Anjou run in here just a few minutes ago and ask you to call the police?" he tried to catch his breath.

The receptionist was startled into immobility. "Sir, I've been at this desk since I came to work this morning. I saw Louise D'Anjou leave with Lt. Paganelli when I came on duty and I saw you leave too. But I haven't seen either of them since. No one's come into the hotel except the mailman."

"I need to use your phone," officer Kusske said. While he was dialing, he could feel beads of sweat covering his forehead. "This is officer Kusske. Get Lt. Paganelli on the phone immediately. Louise D'Anjou has disappeared!"

Back of the Capitol Theatre. Photo courtesy: David Lynx.

CHAPTER TWENTY

The Reward

Rex saw Oz come across the top of the balcony toward the projection booth with the intention of helping unload and file the new reels. The two men could read each other's thoughts when it came to work and were compatible in their uncle and nephew type relationship.

Oz hesitated while Rex was trying to clear some space so he could walk around the boxes and the large projectors. "Have you heard the latest news, man?"

"About what?" Rex answered, which meant no, he hadn't heard the latest news.

"Louise D'Anjou is missing."

"What!! How can that be?" Rex straightened up to make sure he heard Oz correctly. "She had police protection and Lt. Paganelli was intent on getting her on the next plane outta town.

"It was a sting, man, plain and simple. Two men ran past the bodyguard and Louise and they were shooting at each other. The bodyguard got his gun out and chased them. When he got back, Louise was gone. She didn't get shot or killed that the police know of because they haven't found her body. She just disappeared off the face of the earth," Oz said while he had his hands on his hips and rolled his head from side to side still not believing the news himself.

"Where'd you hear this information?" Rex asked.

"On the radio. Anyone with information is asked to call the police. It'll never happen, man. No one will ever have any information. The ones who got 'er will make sure that no one has any information. She's toast, I'm sorry to say," said Oz.

Not knowing what to say about the news, the men stood in place and seemed dumbfounded about what to do next.

Both men's eyebrows shot up and Rex pointed up with his index finger as they heard a woman softly crying. Then he put his finger in front of his lips as if to say, "Be quiet! Maybe the ghost won't make anymore noises."

Her delicate footsteps led to a door opening and closing. The men knew that the routine of her crying, walking, opening and closing the door was a prelude to the main action, whatever the ghost chose it to be. Pencils and paper clips started moving and the men stepped just outside the booth to protect themselves from flying objects. They were wise to have done so when papers started lifting as if an invisible number of fans had been turned on. The velocity of the wind floated the boxes with the reels still in them and caused them to circle the room like someone had dropped a cyclone right in the middle of the booth.

As they watched the force of the power, the men stepped back and covered their mouths and ears. The noise sounded like a plane engine as the rpm's revved to the point where a person could not see the individual propellers any longer. It was a whirlwind of objects in the booth: papers flying, boxes and reels bumping into each other and film spinning off the reels on the projectors.

Then, as if someone turned on the reverse button, the spinning objects stopped in midair and flew the opposite direction. Papers that had been scattered on the floor and counters floated high then dropped into organized piles. The film that had been pulled from the projector reels, retracted and spun back into place. The cardboard boxes dumped the reels into their correct daily order on the racks then one box fit into a bigger box until all the boxes were stacked together against a blank wall. Chairs that had toppled over were standing upright. The usually cluttered table in the middle of the room was clear of any objects.

As suddenly as it had begun, the action in the projection booth stopped. The men stepped back inside the room and could not believe their eyes. Table and counter tops were clean with short stacks of papers organized and ready to file or throw away. The tools were in their proper places, either hanging up or placed in toolboxes.

One clipboard for each day was in sequential order on the wall opposite the splicing counter. An ad for the Bon Marche Beauty Salon was clipped on the clipboard for that day. Across the ad, the name KITTY was hand written in big black letters.

Oz had to laugh at the craziness of the situation. "Geez, I wish I had a ghost who was into me and cleaned up my office." He thought about what he had just said and qualified it. "I gotta take that back little ghosty," he said as he sheepishly grinned and looked up. "You are one powerful female spirit and I got that this was a display of your sorrow over your sister and at the same time, you showed the clue about the beauty shop. You want my friend Rex to become proactive and hunt for answers about your murder."

"But what does the Bon Marche ad with KITTY written on it mean?" Rex asked himself. "Am I supposed to go there and talk to Kitty? I think that's what the message on the clipboard means. Is that what you think it means, Oz?"

As Rex's teacher, Oz said, "Let's make this an easy lesson. Why would she go to all that trouble to give you a clue about the beauty shop? She wants some answers! And you are the man she's counting on to find the answers. Yes, she wants you to go to the beauty shop and have Kitty give you a hair cut. You'll strike up a conversation and you'll put the drawing of Zizi—aka Therese—on her beauty table. Tell Kitty no one can find Zizi and see what she says. Either she'll be mum or she'll talk your ear off."

Oz warned Rex. "What you witnessed today is just a little sample of the power of your ghost. You cooperate with her when she gives you a message and she's gonna treat you right. If you choose to ignore her and keep saying it's a police matter, you're gonna see some powerful examples of a woman scorned. I'm telling you, man, it's not gonna be pretty. Just know that I'm good for a bouquet of posies at your funeral in case you choose to do nothing."

CHAPTER TWENTY-ONE

The Orchid

It had to be done and Rex forced himself to walk to the Bon Marche, go through the doors and up the escalator to women's wear, lingerie, the café and the beauty shop. He shifted feet as he lingered at the reception desk. A lady with two-toned hair stepped behind the counter and said, "May I help you?"

He put the ad on the counter and said, "One of my friends left this note for me to get my hair trimmed by Kitty. Is she here?"

"Sure, hon. Have a seat. She's just about done with a client."

Two-tone woman looked over at station two and saw that Kitty was only doing a comb out on a woman who appeared to be close to ninety-years-old and had hair the color of dirty chalk that reached past her bony shoulders. Kitty's job was to smooth it back into a bun and stick some fancy sequined flowers through the side of the bun. The woman came in each week to have her hair pulled back. Not washed. Just pulled back. Rex imagined Kitty would be doing the woman's hair exactly the same way for her appearance in her casket at her memorial service.

He shuttered and tried to think about what his conversation with Kitty would be if she was uncooperative about discussing Zizi—Therese. He told himself that not everyone would give him the information he wanted but he had to start somewhere and Therese's ghost wanted him to start with Kitty. There was no doubt about it.

'OK, hon. Go on over to Kitty at station two. She's ready for you," the receptionist pointed to a smiling Kitty, who had multiple colored hair in shades of red, bronze, orange and yellow resting on short brown puffed hair with lots of points on her bangs and in front of her ears.

"Hi Rex," Kitty said as she extended her hand. "You want a trim today?"

"Yes. I'm afraid my work schedule has kept me from getting my hair cut on time. I got this note from a friend who said that I should come see you." Rex showed Kitty the Bon Marche ad with her name hand written across the ad.

"Do you have any idea who left this ad and note for you?" Kitty thought it was amusing.

"We're always kidding each other at the theatre so this was a hint that I needed a hair cut," Rex said as Kitty wrapped a smock around his upper body and tied a bow behind his neck.

"At the theatre?" Kitty asked.

"I'm one of the projectionists at the Capitol Theatre. I show movies just about every night," Rex said.

"Wow. How fascinating," Kitty said. "I want to hear all about it after we get your hair washed."

"Oh great," Rex said to himself. "She wants me to talk when I came here to get her to talk. Fine then. I'll talk a little then ask her to tell me about her clients, especially Therese, who she thinks is Zizi. I'll tell her that Zizi used to be a regular customer at the theatre. She disappeared for a while then came back. Now she's disappeared again. I'm concerned and need some background on her so that we can find her. I guess I could say that I'm kinda smitten with Zizi because she's so beautiful. Yeah. That'll work. If I can just keep her talking like she's doing now while she washing my hair, that'll be great."

Rex was settling back in the chair at station two and Kitty was hunting for the right scissors and comb to start on his hair.

"You have really thick hair. What a nice color, sort of auburn. Would you like a few highlights on top to make it appear that you've been out in the sun?" Kitty asked.

Rex thought to himself, "If the highlights will make this session last longer then I better do it."

As she started trimming his hair, she said, "See, right across the top and in front, just a few strands of highlight. What'd you think?

"Sure. Go ahead," Rex said.

After Kitty came back from mixing the bleach for his hair, Rex began his story about Zizi. While Kitty was applying the bleach to individual strands of his hair, he said that Zizi was gone then came back and now is gone again. He said that he got to know her a little and was concerned about her being gone again. He said that he knew she had a boyfriend who was in politics. Maybe they ran off together, he wondered. He asked Kitty if Zizi was a client of hers. He knew his question was taking a big chance that she might clam up so he put the drawing of Zizi on her beauty table.

Kitty picked it up and said, "Yeah, that's Zizi. She is my client and a dear friend. You say that she's disappeared again? She just came back from Montreal and didn't mention any plans to leave Yakima again. Now, I'm really worried about her. You really think you can find her?" Kitty wondered.

"If I have some information about who her boyfriend was or is, I could see if he's missing too. If he is then I'll know that they ran off together. If he's not missing, then we got a big problem because Zizi's missing and she hasn't told anybody that she was going back to Montreal or on vacation," Rex said. He knew that mentioning Montreal meant that he was privy to Zizi—or Therese's—private life. It meant that she actually was a personal friend of his.

"Okay hon, it's time to wash the bleach out before I finish your trim. Let's go get 'er washed," Kitty said. The two of them returned to the wash station and Kitty said, "I'm gonna tell you some stuff about Zizi and it's gotta be between you and me, okay? Maybe it'll help you find her."

In the next few minutes, while she was trimming his hair, Kitty mentioned, "Zizi was a stripper who came from Seattle to work at The Corral, which she did for a couple weeks. Then she met her boyfriend and he said she didn't have to strip anymore as long as she was his girlfriend. He was married but told Zizi that he was not happy with his wife and planned to divorce her. Zizi assumed that the two of them would get married after his divorce. She use to see him at a special rendezvous place every Monday night and anytime he found spare time during the day. He wanted her to be ready to see him at a moment's notice."

The trim was almost complete and he could see that Kitty was making it last as long as she could. Her next client was reading a magazine while she was waiting by the reception desk.

Kitty continued. "She told me her guy was a judge. That's how he could get so much time off but she didn't know if he was connected to the Seattle mob. Well hon, that's about all I know. Come back and tell me what you found out," Kitty said. She looked up at his new highlights and said, "You look ten years younger, like you've been to the beach."

He said, "Thanks. It's nice to receive a compliment from a woman." After she gave him a hug, Rex walked over to the receptionist to pay his bill and leave Kitty a nice tip.

On the walk back to the theatre, Rex wracked his brain to figure out what the next step should be. It was his guess that the judge eliminated Zizi because she knew too much; she was threatening him and she was pregnant with his baby. The question was how was Rex going to find out which judge was her boyfriend and how would he find evidence to back up his guess?

As Rex entered the theatre lobby, Sharon saw his tipped hair and her mouth flew open. "Who did your hair? I love the highlights she put in your hair. Ooo-la-la! You're going to have all the groupies following you everywhere."

Rex joined in the teasing and said, "What can I say? God blessed me with beautiful hair!!"

Oz was setting up the reels for the night when Rex walked into the projection booth. "So how'd it go with the hairdresser?"

Rex told him the gist of what Kitty said and the two of them wondered out loud what the next step would be in finding which judge was Zizi's lover.

Oz said, "By the way, I didn't know you were interested in indoor plants."

"I do have a garden every year. But I've never brought a plant up to the booth because there's not enough natural light and the dark nights are so long," Rex said.

"Well then," said Oz. "Who brought you that beautiful orchid?"

Rex turned around to see what Oz was talking about. A tropical orchid in shades of purples and vanilla sat on the splicing counter. Because the flowers, stems and moss were so perfect, Rex touched a leaf to see if the plant was real. Orchids came from some other world than the Yakima Valley, a world of lush rainforests, rivers and wooded jungles with steamy temperatures. Rex loved orchids more than any other flower but he didn't buy them because they always died. He was happy to see such a perfect specimen and sad that it would not survive Yakima's dry climate and the theatre's dark interior.

A lavender colored card was attached. Rex opened it. It was signed *Z—Z.*

CHAPTER TWENTY-TWO

The Snitch

"How could you separate yourself from a woman whose life we knew was in jeopardy?" Lt. Paganelli was trying to hold his temper in check when he grilled officer Kusske. "Your first mistake was walking those few blocks instead of driving her to the hotel and parking the squad car in front. The kidnappers would not have made an attempt on Madam D'Anjou's life if they knew that she was guarded every second.

"All I can say in my defense is that Louise D'Anjou was within a few yards of the front door of her hotel. I told her to run to the hotel and call you." Officer Kusske was not willing to take 100% responsibility for the abduction of Louise. "I saw her run for the front door before I pursued the man who was shooting at the first runner. There was a murder about to take place and I felt it was my duty to prevent that from happening."

Lt. Paganelli countered officer Kusske's defense. "The man who orchestrated the sting knew that you were expecting an assault on Madam D'Anjou. He was very clever and arranged to separate you from the person whom you were supposed to be guarding. Then he had a second team kidnap her."

"Did you ever wonder how the kidnapper found out about the murdered woman's sister and the evidence she left with the police department?" officer Kusske asked. "Let's examine Louise's schedule. Last night, she went to the 9 p.m. movie at the Capitol Theatre. The staff was able to detain her until you got there. The only other person beside yourself who knew where you were going and whom you were going to question, was the police operator who contacted you."

"During the night, Sharon Meyers from the theatre kept line-of-sight on Louise through the night. I was sitting outside her door until you arrived this morning. You took her to breakfast in a public place so anyone could have seen her then," officer Kusske said.

"You walked her to the police station rather than taking her there in a squad car so anyone could have seen her and thought it was Zizi or Therese. Once you arrived at the station, you had your secretary make her tea. Your secretary also contacted the person in charge of the cold case boxes. So there are two more people who knew something was up with the Therese D'Anjou murder."

Kusske was now asking the questions. "Ask yourself, where did Therese's birth certificate, passport and letters go? In the cold case box? In your desk drawer? In the safe deposit box? We need to find those papers, immediately."

Officer Kusske said, "After the chase, I rushed to the Commercial Hotel and the receptionist said that she had not seen Madam D'Anjou come into the hotel. I showed her my badge and said that I wanted to see Louise's room. She took me there and opened the door with her key. The room was as empty as was Therese's room when we went there the day after her murder. I called you and you called the rest of the CSI team, who searched the room and found nothing."

In opposition to Lt. Paganelli pointing the finger at him for bad judgment, officer Kusske said, "The sting was already active by the time Louise and I walked out of the police department because her room had been emptied. If the actors hadn't distracted me to run after them, they would have found another way to eliminate Louise. I think they would have shot her and maybe me too."

"All due respect, lieutenant, what you need to do is examine who the mole was on this case that is presently in your police department. That person is still here and giving confidential information to the Seattle mob or to the man who had Therese D'Anjou murdered."

"You're using me as a scapegoat and I resent that because I have an impeccable record. Look in your own backyard and find out who the snitch is," officer Kusske stood up and walked out of Lt. Paganelli's office.

Lt. Paganelli hated to admit it but officer Kusske was correct. The murderer had planted an informer in the department who would give him pertinent information about Louise D'Anjou. She was a dead woman the minute she arrived in Yakima. Or if she was alive, no one would ever know the answer.

It wasn't deliberate. And one couldn't say that there was a snitch who was paid to pick up information by the mob or a crooked judge. It was simply gossip—something to talk about among employees of the Yakima Police Department who knew Lt. Paganelli was looking for any information about the murder of Therese D'Anjou. When the sister from Montreal showed up, that was big news for the gossipers who talked about it in the coffee room, clubs and courtroom corridors.

Added to the gossip was information about the evidence that the sister gave to Lt. Paganelli: the letters, birth certificate and photos. Cold cases rarely turned around like this case had done said the gossipers but the evidence was there to define who Therese D'Anjou really was.

There was all kind of speculation about who the killer was. The fact that Therese had been garroted implied that it was a Mafia hit. It was a hit all right. The killer was on someone's payroll and the method of murder indicated that Therese's murder was one of many.

But who was her boyfriend, the gossipers wondered? It had to be someone very powerful in Yakima to be able to hire a hit man. Someone who had complete control of an ex-stripper and who had enticed her to be his mistress. It had to be someone who had a lot of money and who had confidence that the police would never connect her murder to themselves. They had been careful. They had been thorough in removing all evidence from her hotel apartment. That took teamwork, organization and employees who were also confident that there could never be a connection between the murder and them.

The gossipers had it all figured out. But the one thing that they didn't count on is that the person responsible for Therese D'Anjou's murder had listened to the gossipers and believed that her sister had enough evidence to lead the police to their doorstep. The sister had to be eliminated and her disappearance had to happen at the first opportunity.

Police made mistakes and that's exactly what happened when Lt. Paganelli took Louise to breakfast in public. That's what happened when officer Kusske walked her to the hotel. They made fatal mistakes and wound up pointing fingers at each other.

So far the score was the murderers—two: the police—zip.

CHAPTER TWENTY-THREE

The Shadow of Your Smile

Rex expected the orchid to shrivel and die. Instead, it flourished in the dark theatre and seemed to have odd behavior. Not just a plant, it was an entity and Rex almost expected the orchid to speak to him. If he moved from one side of the room to the other side, when he looked up, the flowers were always facing him. "That's impossible," he would say to himself. "Flowers cannot move in that way."

Was the plant watching him or was he becoming paranoid by having another living thing in the tiny room with him? He was expecting to receive a shipment of reel boxes that morning and decided to put the plant on the outside of the doorway to the projection booth so he'd have more room.

After he had carried the boxes up to the booth and filed all the new reels for the week, he was ready to take a break. He stepped out of the booth and looked at the orchid plant. It had shriveled and it's luster of purples, magentas and pinks had faded into shades of browns.

"Oh my word," Rex said out loud. " What have I done?" He picked up the plant and put it on the splice table. The soil didn't feel dry yet he poured cool water from his thermos and made sure the soil was wet. "I've got to go downstairs," he spoke to the plant. "Nature is calling. Please get better."

Expecting the orchid to die like every other orchid he had owned, Rex walked down the stairs. Sharon was cleaning the glass on the candy display case and Rex asked her, "Did you send me an orchid yesterday?"

In her usual annoyed attitude with Rex, she said, "In case you haven't noticed, I work behind a candy counter. That's a minimum wage job. I hope I'll get promoted but until that happens, I am struggling to pay my rent. The short answer is no, I didn't send you an orchid. Don't they cost close to a hundred dollars or more? Again the answer is no, dear Rex. Your girlfriend sent it to you, probably."

"My girlfriend?" Rex said. "What're you talking about?"

"The ghost! She's your girlfriend! No one else sent you the orchid, silly. We love you but none of us are in love with you. And this is a very strange conversation about the ghost being in love with you, so if you'll excuse me, I have to clean out the refrigerator."

"What did it matter that Sharon was talking nonsense?" he mumbled to himself. "I'm gonna toss the orchid when I return to the projection booth and that'll be the end of that! It was dead anyway." With that thought in mind, Rex returned to the booth and stepped inside.

The orchid seemed to have come back to life. The colors were vibrant and buds appeared that Rex didn't recognize as being on the plant when he had taken a break one hour prior.

"What the... ?" Rex stepped to the right and the flowers slowly turned toward him. He stepped to the left and again the flowers followed him. "This is spooky," Rex whispered to himself. "This plant is like a little dog following its master. I don't know if I can live with a plant that seems to be in love with me!"

Just then, the lights flickered. He checked all the plug-ins and they were firmly pushed into the electric sockets. Maybe he had overloaded the electric switch to the projection booth. While he rubbed his chin, he knew that didn't make sense because the projectors weren't running. A ceiling light was on as well as a lamp that was sitting on his splicing table. He left the two lights on, sat in his rolling chair and poured himself some hot coffee from the second thermos.

A flicker caught his eye again. His hand that held the thermos was frozen in the air after he poured his coffee. Slowly, he placed the thermos on the table and put in the plug. He was super alert and waiting for any kind of movement. A fly. A floating paper. A book sliding off the counter. He had not heard the usual crying, walking, door opening and shutting that usually preceded ghostly activity. He thought to himself that if the ghost had changed her strategy, he still wanted to be out of the booth until her usual chaos stopped.

The next flicker did not move between him and the splice lamp. It was a shadow or else he was losing a portion of his sight. He could not see the lamp as surely as if he had a blind spot in his eye even though he could see everything around it. He blinked his eyes, closed them and removed his glasses. He rubbed his eyes, put his glasses back on and deliberately looked at the splice lamp.

The shadow moved to the right then to the left. It backed away completely so he could see the lamp clearly. Then a woman's left hand with wide open fingers slowly moved in front of the lamp. That hand pulled back and the right hand moved in front of the lamp.

Rex jerked back so fast that he knocked over his chair. His intake of air and coffee at the same time caused him to cough and choke and all he could think about was running out of the projection booth. He made a move toward the door and it felt like his body was leaning into a hurricane with a fifty-miles-per-hour force pushing him back. Since there was no definable form he could touch to push out of the way, the force let up the moment he stepped back and sat in his chair.

The overhead light and splice lamp dimmed as a luminescence filled the room and stars twinkled above him. He could hardly breathe while he watched a shadow of a female form materialize just a few feet from where he was sitting. Considering the havoc the ghost had caused in the last few weeks, Rex understood that at any second he could be in the middle of Zizi's whim to destroy the room and everything in it including himself. She was a force to be reckoned with and he was more afraid at this moment than he had ever been in his life.

Her shadow approached him and he watched as two dark hands slipped under his palms and lifted his hands and arms up to the height of his shoulders. The sensation was similar to floating in water where his arms were buoyant as long as he relaxed. He pressed down and resisted. His arms floated downward as they would have if he'd been in water. As soon as he relaxed again, she lifted his hands up again then slowly brought them down to the arms of his rolling chair.

The room continued to be in a state of illumination but he could no longer see her shadow. Just as he was wondering what was next, he felt enough pressure under his armpits to lift him on his feet. Rex didn't try to resist because he knew that she would not allow him to escape the room. He was her prisoner and the best he could do was try not to panic.

Now that he was on his feet, his radio clicked on and he could faintly hear tunes that he was somewhat familiar with because they were theme songs to movies that he had shown.

Rex looked at his hands and arms. They were in the position of a man holding a woman while they were dancing. Parts of his limbs were covered by a shadow and he could feel pressure of a woman's body against his chest, his shoulder and part of his neck and lower jaw. The scent of Chanel 5 wafted in the air and as he turned his head toward the shadow on his chest, the scent became more intense.

When he felt his body shifting from side to side, he didn't fight the pressure from the ghost's body. He no longer felt panicked. Rather, his body seemed to be floating in a gentle current. "Just relax and go with it," he told himself.

The volume on the radio increased slightly as Rex heard Frank Sinatra sing a tune that caught his attention. It was *A Shadow Of Your Smile,* the theme song from a movie called, *The Sandpiper*—a love story with Elizabeth Taylor and Richard Burton. She was a single mother who fell in love with a married principal. Their love was forbidden and tragic, a love that could never be *conpleter.*

The shadow of your smile
When you are gone
Will color all my dreams
And light the dawn
Look into my eyes
My love and see
All the lovely things
You are to me
Our wistful little star
Was far too high
A teardrop kissed your lips
And so did I
Now when I remember spring
All the joy that love can bring
I will be remembering
The shadow of your smile

Although Rex could feel the pressure of her body against his, his attempt to embrace her was similar to embracing a gentle velocity of water or warm air. He did not want his heart to reach out to an entity that he could never bring back to human life. Zizi—Therese's—life was in another world. Forever.

Instead of speaking to him out loud, her words came to him in thoughts.

"Rex, don't be afraid. I am with you whenever you need me to be near you. I know no dawn or night. I have no boundaries. At my bidding, I am all the seasons and all the holidays and all the memories and all the future memories to be made. This is what it means to be eternal. I want you to be in my world but for now, I will be in your world."

"Please be my warrior and find the man who murdered me. I will help you. It is only right that he will live in a different world than me, a world of fire and eternal anguish."

"Please Rex, be my avenger. Be my angel of mercy."

As quickly as she had appeared, Zizi faded and Rex stood in bewilderment while the overhead light and splicing lamp came on. "Was it a dream?" he asked himself. He looked around the room and the orchids were no longer on the splicing table. Everything was back to normal.

Stage lights. Photo courtesy: Leonard La Lumiere.

CHAPTER TWENTY-FOUR

The Concours d'Elegance

When Rex returned to his booth on Saturday, a sheet of paper with schedules was underneath his coffee cup. It was a list of court trials for the week in the Yakima County Courtrooms located across Third Street from the Yakima Police Department and county jail.

Rex went down the stairs to the lobby and saw Mike Hansen. "Say, Mike, I wonder if I could talk to you in private."

"Sure. Step into my office," Mike said knowing that he didn't have an office. He used Al Mallone's office most of the time and all the time when Al didn't come to work. "What's up?" Mike knew that Rex did not ask for "a talk" unless there was a new adventure or project coming up.

"It's about the murderer of Zizi Zeigler—the lady who was murdered here in the theatre? We found out her real name is Therese D'Anjou and she was from Montreal, Canada. We also found out that she was the mistress of a local judge."

"We? Who exactly is 'we'?" Mike was smart in catching details.

"Oz has been in touch with Lt. Paganelli about Therese and also about the disappearance of her sister, Louise. I guess that satisfies the 'we' when I tell you the latest development of the cases."

"Very interesting. I know you have something up your sleeve about Therese's case. SPILL!" Mike said.

"If we can find the judge that she was having an affair with, we might also find out who was working for him and therefore who was assigned to murder Therese, aka Zizi." Rex was ready for the next step.

"Sounds reasonable. How are you planning to find that judge?" Mike asked.

"We need to attend several courtroom trials and hope that we'll be struck by something that will tell us that a particular judge is the one. Maybe we'll follow several judges and see what kind of cars they drive. You'd be able to identify some of the cars you saw when the men picked up Therese at the theatre wouldn't you?" Rex asked.

"I'm sure I could narrow it down. We could start with the kind of cars the judges drive to work by looking in the parking lot and getting the numbers on their license plates. We need to be there when court is out and they go to their cars. We could set up a watch team by following the judges or judge that we thought was suspicious. We'd have to be nearly invisible when we do this. I guess we'll take turns in the actual parking lot so a particular judge doesn't recognize us. What's the next step after that?"

Rex said, "As a matter of fact, we need to get in the primary suspect's office and go through his drawers or files and look for Therese's passport, citizenship papers and her address book. Also, if he has a book where all the people who work for him are listed and any proof that he paid them for Therese's murder and her sister's abduction, that would be enough evidence to nail him."

"Pray tell, how're you going to get into any judge's chambers?" Mike asked.

"No problem actually getting into a judge's office because Oz has a bump key and also a set of lock picks. That's less of a problem than distracting the bailiff or night guard," Rex said. "The best way to get in the judge's office is to have a legitimate reason to present to the judge's clerk, like posing as a repairman."

"Well, all this talk isn't going to get us to first base. We've got to go to some courtrooms and become familiar with the judges, their names, what times they come to and leave work, who their clerks and bailiffs are, what they drive and where they live," said Rex. "Most of the judges go to their chambers at 8 a.m. this Monday so that means we need to be in the courthouse parking lot, check the names on their parking spots and see what cars park in those spaces. If we see classic expensive foreign or vintage domestic cars, then those will be the judges we need to further check on. Maybe we'll only see two or three that fall into that category."

Part of the privilege of being a judge was to have a specific parking spot in the small lot adjoining the courthouse so the judges could come in a side door and take the elevator up to the third floor to their respective courtrooms and chambers.

Mike had done some research on what the maintenance men wore so early Monday morning, he was dressed appropriately to fit in with the cleaning crew. He checked the printing on each parking spot for judges, made notes of their names. The theatre already had a set of walkie-talkies, which he and Rex could use for their investigation.

The plan was that they would write down any judge who drove a vintage car. When he entered the courthouse, Mike would buzz Rex and describe the judge who was approaching the elevator. Although Rex could clearly see the judge coming in, no other person could hear what was said on the walkie-talkie. Immediately, Rex would get on the same elevator with the judge and nonchalantly follow him until the judge entered his chamber where his name was printed on the door.

Oz planned to repeat the same procedure for the next judge entering the building. Once Rex and Oz knew the name of the judge, the team could connect the name and location of his courtroom. They could also connect each judge's name to their car and hunt for the location of his house in the phone book to check for vintage cars that Mike might recognize as the cars that picked up Zizi.

However, that plan never happened because only one judge drove a black 1959 Mark 2 Jaguar into his parking space. The classic car had wire wheels and modified curved fenders, so typical of the grace of Jaguars built in the 1950s. Although most Americans recognized the Mark 2 as a Jaguar, the British police forces used them because of the automobile's small size and ability to reach 125 miles per hour. It's owner, Judge Roger McCarthy, exited the car and was dressed in a fashionable manner that equaled the expensive luxury of his prized vehicle.

Rex heard Mike's voice on the walkie-talkie. "The judge is entering the building right now. He's dressed in a European tweed jacket and black pants and carrying a black briefcase. Follow him."

Rex shadowed Judge McCarthy into the elevator and kept a few paces behind him to see where his chambers were located and who his clerk and bailiff were. After general business with his clerk, the judge entered the Superior Courtroom for a hearing at 9 a.m. The case involved a driver who had the right of way to drive into an intersection after the traffic light turned green. Another person drove through the last seconds of a yellow light that turned red and was T-boned. Both drivers were suing each other and Rex watched every move the judge made and took notes on his method of dealing with the heated situation.

Rex concluded that the judge was conducting business-as-usual and he could not really get a feeling as to whether this particular judge could have ordered Zizi, a young woman, who was carrying his baby, to be murdered. There had to be some other clue that could give him a clear reading of Judge McCarthy's guilt.

Lady luck came their way when the Yakima County Fairgrounds hosted a spring Concours d'Elegance of mid-century classic cars, both foreign and domestic makes. This was no ordinary neighborhood or general auto show. In fact, it was a rare occasion that the Concours was held in what was considered a pedestrian venue.

The three men from the Capitol Theatre compared general auto shows to neighborhood movie theaters. They thought of the Concours in comparison to the Capitol Theatre, which was considered to be the finest artisan's opera and vaudeville theatre in the Pacific Northwest.

Special judges, who were experts in classic automobiles, were selected to decide whether each vehicle surpassed the original purchase condition regarding mechanical restoration, paint, plating, upholstery and interior colors and fabrics selected to match the color and lineage of the car. Rather than being driven on the road, the cars were only driven from their transports to the staging arena where errant bits of dirt, grass or pebbles were removed from the tires and under carriage. The cars were museum quality representations of eras where automobiles were built for comfort and beauty rather than being mass produced with the singular idea of making a profit.

It was a perfect opportunity for Mike to see if he recognized any of the cars as being one of the get-away cars in the alley that picked up Zizi.

The men walked separately as they toured the cars, which included Duesenbergs, an Alfa Romeo Spider, several Mercedes Benz, Jaguars, a Rolls-Royce Silver Cloud, and a Ferrari Aston Martin Rapide Race car in the foreign division. Mike also saw a 1940 Packard Convertible, a 1938 Buick Convertible, a 1960 Ford Thunderbird and several hot rod Chevys and Fords in the domestic division.

After one hour, the men met near the north entrance of the agricultural building in order to compare notes. Mike said, "I saw the judge that we've been searching for. That's Judge McCarthy, who is showing his classic Jaguars."

"Did you see any cars that you recognized?" Rex asked Mike.

"Not only did I see two cars that I recognized from the alley, I also saw a couple of the men standing with him who picked up Zizi. None of the men ever saw me because I was standing in a door alcove outside the theatre as I smoked a cigarette. Once I saw a car drive up, I immediately put out my cigarette so they couldn't see any smoke. I think I'll go strike up a conversation with the judge."

Before Rex and Oz could stop Mike, he was approaching a silver, 1959 Jaguar MK IX Saloon called "The Queen Mum", according to signage that was printed about the history of the car on a poster in front of the car. He walked around the car, turned and faced the second car, a black 1952 Jaguar Mark IV. He shook his head in genuine admiration at the beauty of the elegant automobile and looked up to see the judge smiling at him.

He was tall, slender with slicked back hair. His head was narrow like an ornament on the hood of a car. He had an arrogant persona, one of entitlement and privilege. When the judge conversed with Mike, he never looked at the person he was talking to. Instead, he looked at some place on Mike's face and not his eyes.

Acting as if he thought the judge was also a car buff, Mike said, "These two cars are definitely the most beautifully designed cars of the show. Do you have any idea when the judges will present the awards?"

"So glad you're enjoying the Concours. I've had these two cars restored nearly to perfection and they are both my pride and joy," the judge said.

In a surprised tone of voice, Mike said, "Are you the owner of these two Jaguars?"

"Yes. I'm Roger McCarthy and these are my treasures." The judge must have repeated that he was the owner of the classic Jaguars several times that day.

Mike engaged the judge in a conversation about himself and his other classic cars with the pretense that he also was a car buff and wanted to get into showing cars but didn't have any idea how to get started. He recognized the cars that the judge was describing as the same cars that picked up Zizi, aka Therese.

Mike continued the charade of being a car buff. Out of his hip pocket, he slipped out a photograph of a candy-apple red and white 1957 Buick Century Caballero. "I own the same model as this Buick and am in the process of restoring it. I carry this photograph to remind myself what the possibility can be with the car that I'm restoring."

The judge encouraged Mike and gave him a card that listed Judge Roger McCarthy, his postal address and chamber's phone number. There was no mention of his home address or phone number.

"I see these gentlemen who are staging the car for you. Does an exhibitor always have to have this many helpers?" Mike asked.

"One is a mechanic. But the other three understand the finer points the judges are scoring and they know that I want to make sure that there isn't one grass blade on the car. So these gentlemen double check everything for me," the judge explained.

Getting to the photographs, Mike asked, "It would be great if I could stand beside you and have one of my friends take a photo of you and your cars. Then if it's okay with you, I'd like to get one of you and each of your cars. I'm going to put your photos on my bulletin board to give me inspiration to finish my car."

""I'd be honored," the judge smiled again.

"I'll go tell my friend what I want. Just a sec," Mike said.

After Mike pretended to tell Rex about the judge and the cars, he said, "See that guy in the maroon shirt and black pants? He's the killer. Don't look at him!!! See if you can get some clear shots of him too. But take one photo of me and the judge then a couple of him alone with his cars."

"Got it," Rex said and appeared to set up the camera. He took continuous photos of the man who Mike said was the killer before Mike and the judge were ready.

After Mike shook the judge's hand, and walked with Rex to the domestic classic cars, Oz joined them. He'd been out of sight for fear that the judge might recognize him.

Oz touched Mike's folded arm and under his breath said, "Are you telling us that all this time you knew who the killer was?"

"I'm alive aren't I?" Mike said. "I had no intention of holding this information forever. But now that I see that the killer is associated with the judge, I can truly make an accurate identification. Even then, I knew my ID of him wouldn't be enough. I'm sure he has an alibi and the judge has arranged to protect his men. We just have to hunt for incriminating evidence. Once I tell the police who the killer is, you might as well make plans to come to my funeral. What we have to do is set up a sting so the police think they're the ones who're discovering the killers."

Rex added, "At least we know what direction to go. We got the judge. We got Zizi's killer. That's a pretty good start."

Capitol Theatre, street side. Photo courtesy: David Lynx.

CHAPTER TWENTY-FIVE

The Freezer

After Saturday's Concours d'Elegance, the men drove down Yakima Avenue to The Freezer to have a burger and fries at prices they were use to paying, rather than being obligated to pay for the gourmet food that was offered at the car show.

Oz said, "Mike, you made great progress with the judge at the car show and even got his card." He turned to Rex and said, "Hopefully, the photos that you took will turn out and show a clear photo of the judge. He said that those men who were dressed in polo shirts worked for him and that included the guy you identified as Therese's killer."

"I'll give a couple of those photos to Lt. Paganelli so he can search for the identity of the killer in the mug shots album. There's no way I'm going to the police station to do that. I'd probably be killed before I got back to the theatre. The next thing is that we have to be sure Therese's passport and other stuff is in the judge's possession. Let's hope they're somewhere in his office because if they're hidden in his house, I don't think the three of us would be safe going on his property considering he has bodyguards with guns."

Always the joker, Rex said, "I can just see the headlines. OOOPS! When three men from the Capitol Theatre stepped onto Judge Roger McCarthy's property and were snooping around, guard dogs bit them then resident bodyguards shot them because they were believed to be burglars. Oh Well! Their funeral is a bring-your-own-bottle potluck and will be held in the Capitol Theatre on Monday at 5 p.m. followed by the 6:30 p.m. movie. No charge for the movie."

Oz laughed and said, "I don't know about you guys but I'm not going on the judge's property. I'll help you get in his chambers and if Therese's stuff is not there, man, there is no way I'm going to risk my life and go any further on this deal. I'm warning you to stop getting deeper into this investigation. Let the police handle it!!"

"Yeah. Yeah!" Mike dismissed Oz's warning.

Rex came back at Oz. "Why don't you try dealing with the ghost's rages when we don't do what she wants! You've already seen the havoc she is capable of causing!"

"Hey man, let'er tear up the whole theatre. I'm not going to jail to appease a goddamn ghost," Oz was getting fed up with the whole investigation and felt that the more information they found, the more their lives were in danger.

"It's simple," Rex said as he took another bite of his special burger with onions. "We need to get into the judge's chambers as repair men but we have to figure out what needs to be fixed before we approach the clerk."

Oz warned. "Don't you think the bailiff will stop you?"

"Once the clerk is agreeable to letting us in the judge's chambers to repair something, the bailiff's not going to be a problem. Repairs are made all the time," Mike said.

"Count on his file cabinets being locked. So you better take the lock picks. Do we need to have a practice session with those picks?" Oz looked between Mike and Rex.

Both of them said "yes" at the same time. Rex added, "We can't tell the lieutenant to go after the judge unless we know for sure that Therese's ID papers and her passport are in his chambers. We're not gonna take them. We just need to know that they're in his possession."

"That's understood. So what reason would Lt. Paganelli have to search the judge's office?" Oz asked.

"If the lieutenant found incriminating evidence that connected Therese to the judge, he would look further and that would include the police searching his office and his house." The answer seemed as if Mike wished things would happen that way but in reality Rex and Oz were not convinced that the plan was that simple.

"What incriminating evidence do we have? The crooks took everything out of Therese's apartment."

"Do you still have her earring?" Oz asked Rex. "We could plant it in the judge's car, then anonymously notify the lieutenant that the judge is a person of interest in the murder of Therese D'Anjou, aka Zizi Zeigler."

"Thanks to the ghost's sense of humor, every time I need to show the earring to someone important, she turns the earring into a screw. I can just see us notifying the lieutenant to go hunt in the judge's car for Therese's earring and all he can find is a brass screw. Does the expression, 'we're screwed' come to mind?"

All three men laughed at Rex's joke.

"In all seriousness, you know that we can't do that. The lieutenant knows that I have the earring because I tried to give it to him. If he finds it in the judge's car, he'll know that I planted it," Rex said.

Rex continued. "Now that the earring issue is settled, let's talk about what kind of car the judge would drive to work. He probably would not drive one of those classic cars we saw him showing at the Concours."

"I know that," Mike said. "The only reason it was important to see the judge and his fancy Jaguars is that those two cars were brought to the alley and I saw Therese get inside both cars. You can bet that he will drive some sort of expensive classic car to work."

The wise one of the bunch said, "Okay gentlemen, we're getting ahead of ourselves. Let's just find out if Therese's stuff is in the judge's file cabinet and go from there. I don't have the answer to how we can come up with probable cause for the lieutenant to get a search warrant. I think the best strategies are to show him the photographs of the judge and the killer as well as to tell him that Therese's passport is in the judge's chambers. Let him figure out how to get a search warrant. There's gotta be a point where we turn this deal over to him."

Mike and Rex were silent as they pushed their paper plates to the side of the table and finished their Pepsi's.

"The greatest dangers are that the judge will get wind of our suspicions and will destroy Therese's evidence. To tell you the truth, I don't know why he would still have anything that connects her to him. Then the other danger is that he'll find out that I can identify the drivers of his cars that picked up Therese. That's what I'm truly scared about. I know we're kidding around here but I'm not kidding when I say that my life is in danger. If anything happens to me, guys, I want you to nail the judge for me. Will you?" Mike looked from Oz to Rex for support.

Oz put his hand on Mike's shoulder and Rex put his hand on Mike's other shoulder. "You can count on us to protect you but you and Rex have to stop taking chances with the judge. He will not blink an eye when he gives the order to take you out. Promise me that you will step back and let Lt. Paganelli take over the investigation."

Mike smiled and said, "Once we find the goods in the judge's chambers, we'll notify the lieutenant and let him run with the case. We have no choice but to watch him do his job. But if he doesn't come through, I'm not gonna let the killers get away Scott free."

CHAPTER TWENTY-SIX

The Meeting

First thing on Monday morning, Mike Hansen took a leap of faith as he dialed the number for the Yakima Police Department.

"May I speak to Lt. Paganelli? This is Mike Hansen from the Capitol Theatre."

After Mike's phone call was transferred, the lieutenant came on the line. "Mike? Have you got new information for me?"

"Louise D"Anjou left something here at the theatre that might give us a clue about her whereabouts. I can't make heads or tails about it. Do you read French by any chance?"

"Mostly I know basic Italian but I could probably get the idea of what she's written. Can't you bring it to the station?" the lieutenant asked.

"I'd rather that you decide if this information has any value."

"I'll be here all morning. Just drop by and let me take a look at it," the lieutenant didn't understand Mike's reluctance to come to the police station.

"Well, I might have been mistaken after all," Mike said. "Maybe what I have won't help after all. It was just a hunch. Sorry I called." He hung up the phone.

It was clear that Mike was not going to bring any information to the station so the lieutenant had no choice but to drive the few blocks to the Capitol Theatre. He parked right in front of the historical theatre, got out of the squad car and approached the front doors. He pushed two of the heavy doors and they were locked. On the third try, he pushed a different door and it opened to the grand lobby. Mike was waiting for him.

"What's this all about?" the lieutenant asked.

"Follow me, please," Mike said. Leading the way, Mike walked down the main aisle toward the stage. Up the side stairs, the men were momentarily on the stage. Mike walked across the stage and into the wings where he descended the stairs that led to the dressing rooms. He entered the largest dressing room, historically used for the star of the show, where a table and chairs were sitting in the middle of the room. There was a tablet on the table with a rather long, handwritten letter. Mike picked it up and handed it to the lieutenant. It said:

Lt. Paganelli,

We are going to write to each other right now rather than speak. I will destroy what we've written to each other after we exchange information. Please read this letter and write your response on the tablet.

I can identify Therese D'Anjou's killer. I saw him drive up in a black Jaguar to pick up Therese on March 1. I was smoking in the alley at the time and he didn't see me because I was hidden in a door alcove. When he came out of the theatre, she was not with him. Her body was discovered within an hour after he left.

I saw him again at the Concours d'Elegance just recently at the fairgrounds. He was attending Judge Roger McCarthy's two Jaguars along with three other men who appeared to be working for the judge. Rex acted like he was taking my photo alongside one of the cars but what he was really doing, was taking photos of the judge and the killer. I have several photos that you're going to look at right now. The killer is the man with dark hair who is wearing a maroon polo shirt and black pants. You may take the best photo and I will keep the others. I will not come down to the station and go through the mug shot books. Once the killer or the judge find out that I can identify the killer, I will be dead. You have a snitch at the police station so I'm afraid to come down there.

You will have to go through the mug shot books yourself to identify the killer. DON'T LET ANYONE KNOW WHAT YOU ARE DOING OR I WILL BE ELIMINATED JUST AS THERESE AND LOUISE WERE KILLED.

From now on we will refer to this man as the "honoree" for the pretend surprise birthday party you are planning at the theatre. Will you agree to this arrangement before I show you the photos?"

Lt. Paganelli wrote, *"Yes, he is the honoree."*

Mike showed the lieutenant clear shots of the faces of the judge and the men who worked for him. Mike wrote, *"Do you see Judge McCarthy in the photos?"*

The lieutenant wrote, *"Yes."*

"He ordered Therese's murder because she was pregnant and probably because she threatened to reveal that he was a crook. The honoree choked her with a wire!" Mike wrote.

"It looks bad for the judge," the lieutenant wrote.

"Unless he destroyed them, the judge has Therese's passport, her citizenship papers and her address book. That's what her sister said."

"Probable cause," the lieutenant wrote.

"To search his car, his office, his house?" Mike wrote.

The lieutenant check marked all three choices.

In a low voice, Mike said, "What are your plans for the honoree?"

"You've given me all the pertinent information. I'll have to think about what the final plans are for the party. I'll be in touch. For now, I'll say, 'Mum's the word!' the lieutenant put his index finger up to his mouth and pretended to lock his lips and throw away the key.

CHAPTER TWENTY-SEVEN

The Judge's Chambers

Mike knew things moved slowly at the police department and frankly, he didn't have much faith that Lt. Paganelli would make this new information a priority although the finger of murder was clearly pointing at Judge Roger McCarthy. Being a can-do person, Mike approached Rex about a plan he had in mind.

"What's the plan?" Rex asked Mike when the two of them got together for coffee in the lobby.

"I heard a couple of florescent tubes were out in the judge's office and needed to be replaced. Some of his electric connections needed to be checked. Amazingly enough, I have a couple workman's jumpsuits and some info as to when he won't be in his office," Mike said.

"Right on!" Rex said.

"Are you ready to go now? He won't be in his office all week. The theatre has a panel truck for our ladder and other equipment. I got a general work form from The Bindery and I'll fill it in so it looks official. We'll present this form to the clerk, get in his office and check his desk and file cabinets for Therese's passport and her other papers." Mike had it all planned out and Rex was ready for the investigation.

The men parked in the south lot where all the marked parking spaces were located. There was no security guard in the lot or in the courthouse. Both men looked like a maintenance crew as Rex carried a ladder and Mike carried the florescent tubes and a toolbox. Instead of taking the elevator, they climbed the stairs to the third floor where the judge's courtroom and chambers were located. The court clerk was busy at her desk and the bailiff was talking to a couple of his buddies about fishing on the

Yakima River the next weekend.

Mike did the talking. "Morning, Ma'am. We're here to fix a few electrical problems in Judge McCarthy's chambers. Let's see," Mike examined his work order. "Florescent tubes need to be replaced and he's got a dead outlet."

The clerk took a look at the work order that Mike handed her. "Looks good. Okay gentlemen, his chamber is down this hall. Second door on the right. You can't miss it. His name is on the glass. Here's his key. He won't be in today so you can take your time."

"Thanks, Ma'am," Mike said and the men walked down the hall and opened the judge's chamber. The men closed the door and put a chair under the doorknob to make sure that they were not interrupted. They could easily say that they had to move furniture around to set up the ladder. Mike had brought the lock picks and immediately got in the judge's desk drawers. After pawing through his papers, he wrote down his bank account number and his social security number.

Rex was on the ladder and unscrewed the panel that covered the florescent tubes, which were all working except one that did need to be replaced. He was busy with that job while Mike got into each of the file cabinet drawers. The bottom drawer had the usual manila files except there was space behind the files where a stack of papers covered a large shoe box. Mike placed the stack of papers on the floor, lifted the shoebox out of the file cabinet, placed it on the table and opened the lid.

Therese's passport, her citizenship papers, her address book were there. Hidden under her passport was a miniature black book that contained names, addresses and phone numbers. Frank Colacurcio's number was in there and it was the only name that Mike recognized. Businesses and their owners were listed, including taverns, massage parlors, dirty bookstores and restaurants. Mike returned all the items to the box in exactly the same order that he found them. He placed the box back in the file cabinet and covered it with the short stack of papers.

"Rex," Mike said. "Mission accomplished. Let's get outta here!"

The men left the office, returned the key to the clerk and walked out of the courthouse and into the reserved parking lot to their van. The phone number he had written on the work order was the phone number for the Snoqualmie Pass report.

On Monday, a week from this day, he knew the clerk would tell the judge that the workmen had replaced his florescent tube and fixed his electric outlet. The judge might not think twice about it since there was a florescent tube that needed to be replaced. On the other hand, the judge might become suspicious that a couple men were snooping in his office. That was a dangerous situation for Mike and Rex because they had a feeling that the judge's man who eliminated Therese would find out they were the men who got in his office. The other fear was that the judge would destroy Therese's passport and papers. They had both risked their lives and they needed to contact Lt. Paganelli immediately.

After the men returned to the theatre, Mike called the police station and asked to speak to the lieutenant. "Say Lt. Paganelli, I wanted to talk to you about the final details of the birthday party. I wonder if you could stop by and give me your guest list. I have some info for you on the prices so you can make some choices. Could you drop by in fifteen minutes?"

"I'll be right there. I've got my list." The lieutenant dropped everything and knew that Mike and Rex had some critical information for him.

When the lieutenant arrived, he pushed in the same front door of the theatre that he had opened into the lobby. Once again, he found himself in the theatre's lobby and Mike and Rex were waiting for him. This time he followed them into Al Mallone's office, which was Mike's office at times.

Mike instructed the lieutenant to check the following written information.

> "Lt. Paganelli,
>
> We found Therese's passport, her citizenship papers and address book in the bottom drawer of the judge's file cabinet. We also found a small address book with names, addresses of business owners and men's names you might recognize, one of which was Frank Colacurcio. We also found some women's names that sound like strippers: Candy, Bitty, Tara and Gizelle. Therese's name was in the book too. This information ties the judge to Therese and implicates him in her murder."

The lieutenant wrote on the tablet. "*How did you get into the judge's chambers?*" then looked at both Mike and Rex.

Mike wrote. "*We dressed like repair men and handed a fake work order* to Judge McCarthy's clerk. She gave us the key to his chambers."

"*What about the bailiff?*" the lieutenant wrote.

Rex jumped in and wrote, "*He was having a conversation with another man about fishing.*"

"*How did you get into the judge's desk and file cabinet?*" the lieutenant scribbled.

This was a scary question because it fulfilled the definition of breaking and entering. But they had already said that they saw Therese's passport so they couldn't deny that they had broken into the desk and file cabinet. Mike had no choice but to tell the truth and hope that the lieutenant would consider the discovery of Therese's passport and other papers a tradeoff for catching the killer and his boss.

"*While Rex was replacing one of the florescent tubes, I used a set of lock picks to open the desk drawers and file cabinet,*" Mike wrote and waited for the fireworks.

"*So Rex, you actually did replace a florescent tube?*"

"*Yes. One of the judge's tubes was out,*" Rex wrote.

In a low voice, the lieutenant said, "Good job, detectives Rex and Mike. I guess the ball is in my court now to arrange for the honoree to receive his surprise birthday cake!"

The tension had passed as the three men broke out in smiles.

Mike said, "Oh yeah, we're gonna have us one big surprise party!"

—

The next evening, Lt. Paganelli waited until everyone in the department had left their desks for the night. He browsed through the mug shots in the first photo album with no luck. The criminals' faces and their histories were familiar to him. The snapshot from the car show was clear enough that a match would not be a problem. Just to make things a little easier, he cut a small circle out of a sheet of typing paper and placed it over the snapshot so that only the honoree's face was showing.

He photocopied the altered photo then enlarged it three times its original size. The resulting picture of the man was not as clear as the original but with a few connecting dots, he was able to redefine the man's features.

He found the man's photo and his bio in the second mug shot album.

Originally from the Seattle-Tacoma area, the man's name was Lorenzo Calucci. Along with the Colacurcio family, his grandfather had been one of the produce farmers in an agricultural valley called garlic gulch, which became the location of Boeing Field Airport. He learned the art of intimidation in school along with his buddies who participated in juvenile crimes. Things got serious once he no longer was classified as a juvenile but the men he worked for always protected him from prosecution.

The idea of protection money was prevalent in the historic district where Pike's Place Market was located because massage parlors, peep shows, dirty book stores, strip joints and prostitution johns were in danger of prosecution from the law. Protection money insured that the beat officers would look the other way and judges would be lenient if protection money was paid.

If a business failed to pay protection money, their businesses were damaged or the owner was injured. Same thing held true for money that needed to be repaid to loan sharks. The borrowers were often felons and certainly not able to legitimately borrow from a bank. Loan sharks were the only quick source of available money and high interest. Failure to pay both the principle and interest could result in personal injuries of the most painful kind. Lorenzo Calucci was an expert at collecting money from businesses or personal loans. He was a man who asked no questions except to know who to injure or whose business to damage if the owner did not pay for protection.

His occupation was listed as a bodyguard. Charges of assault were met with a slap on the hand from judges and probation was the only penalty that was listed on his criminal record.

According to the Concours' photographs, Lt. Paganelli could see that Calucci was working for Judge McCarthy. Unfortunately, there was no evidence to prove that he was responsible for killing Therese and Louise except Mike Hansen's testimony. Unless Mike was willing to identify Lorenzo Calucci in a line-up, the lieutenant couldn't bring the killer in.

In order to find current information on Lorenzo Calucci, Lt. Paganelli contacted the Department of Motor Vehicles. Lorenzo Calucci lived in the Lower Valley just off Lateral A, a small highway that originated from a fork off Highway 97. The Lower Valley of Yakima County was known for a vast production of soft and hard fruit, hops and vineyards.

At the same time, the lieutenant checked Judge McCarthy's address with DMV and found that both men's addresses were nearly identical. The judge lived at 5801 Fort Road and Calucci lived at 5802 Fort Road. The only explanation was that both men lived on the same property in separate residences.

"*Very curious,*" thought the lieutenant. "*The judge is not in the fruit business although his property is surrounded by apple orchards. Mike has shown me that the judge's hobby is classic cars so he must have a car barn. I don't think Lorenzo Calucci is a car mechanic so what is his connection to the judge? The only thing I can figure out is that he's a bodyguard and he must do jobs that the judge doesn't want to do himself.*"

"*I do know that he picked Therese D'Anjou up on Monday nights. And her sister disappeared after a sting with officer Kusske. So the judge has a team of mobsters that he can call on to do his bidding. Maybe Lorenzo Calucci is in charge of getting the needed men for illegal jobs. Seems risky for a judge to be involved in mobster activities. Right now, I don't know the why of the judge's actions. I just know that he is connected to Therese's murder and Louise's disappearance. In theory, it sounds like I have enough probable cause for a search warrant but I don't think it's enough. I must have solid evidence for a conviction and I'm going to find a way to get it!*"

CHAPTER TWENTY-EIGHT

My Foolish Heart

When Rex returned to the projection booth, he was beat. As soon as he stepped into the booth, he inhaled the fragrance from an orchid that was sitting on the splicing counter.

"What the…? I thought you disappeared!" he shook his head and looked around the tiny room expecting to see other signs that the ghost had been in his space. He found himself talking to the plant as if it was a person because that's what it seemed to be, sort of a plant and sort of a person, since the flowers turned in Rex's direction as he moved around the booth.

"Did you know that Mike and I got into the judge's chambers today? Yeah, we did. I was surprised at how easy it was. We found your passport and other papers, " Rex said as he sat in his rolling chair and spoke to the orchid as if it was Therese.

"Once the judge returns to his office, there's a good chance he'll suspect that someone has been snooping around. All he has to do is check with his clerk to find out who's been in his chambers this week. He'll look at the work order and have his clerk call the phone number Mike wrote down. It's pretty funny because when his secretary calls that number, she'll get a report for weather conditions on Snoqualmie Pass. Then he'll know that two fake maintenance men were in his chambers looking for your papers."

Rex checked himself and realized that he was speaking to a flower.

"I don't know what I'm doing speaking to an orchid as if you are a person," he looked straight at the plant. "I must really be a mental case," Rex mumbled to himself.

Rather than making a move to pick out the reels that would be used in the movie that night, Rex seemed at a loss as to what to do about his work and Therese's case. Holding a pencil and stroking a tablet on the table, he was doodling, which was unlike Rex. He was a man who stayed on top of tasks that needed to be done. He was a man who was busy with the job or busy planning how he was going to do the job.

The picture that he was drawing was a woman's face. Although it appeared to be a cartoon at first, he kept sketching the details and could see that it was beginning to look like Therese. Although he couldn't say that he had a photographic memory, he remembered just about everything that he saw and heard. When it came to mechanics, numbers and sequences, his thought processes were far above average intelligence. He did not believe in nonsense and that was the category that he put the ghost in. Not that her ghostly activities had no meaning. That wasn't it. He could only understand what he could see and touch.

When the sketch was finished, he held the tablet up and checked it for accuracy. It was the best he could remember about Therese since he saw her briefly the night she was murdered. He put his hand on his mouth and wondered why God would allow her to have such a tragic childhood. Finally, when she was pregnant and wanted to turn her life around, Rex couldn't understand why God allowed her to be murdered in a way that terrified her during the last moments of her life. Rex couldn't help but feel that if he had known about Therese's desperate situation, he would have saved her.

He was confused at the surge of emotions he was experiencing this night. Lt. Paganelli had good intentions and knew who was responsible for Therese's death. Then why wasn't he stepping into the judge's office and confiscating Therese's passport, her papers and the small black address book? Rex wondered if he had to lead the police by their noses to the evidence?

He reached over and turned on his radio only to hear ballads and love songs. "Great," he thought. "Exactly what I need to lift my mood out of the dumps!" The lyrics and soft music caused his throat to ache with loneliness. He realized the romantic part of his life was missing. "Why am I thinking about this now?" he asked himself. "I can't remember ever needing a woman to love before tonight."

While he was thinking of turning off the radio, he could feel sufficient pressure on his palms to lift his hands as if he was floating in a bathtub.

He easily could have jerked his hands back but he allowed the invisible pressure to lift his arms and body.

"Are you here, Therese?" Rex spoke softly to the ghost for the first time. "If you are here, can you speak to me?"

He felt air as warm as a person's breath by his left ear. "I am here," the ghost whispered. "Dance with me," she said and Rex could feel the pressure of her body as she shifted from side to side.

"I want to see you," he said softly. "I will protect you and avenge your murderers. Just let me see you," he implored her.

As the light in the room dimmed, a luminescence around the edge of the room appeared, like sunbeams going up instead of going down. Against the backlighting, he could see that Therese's silhouette was slender but athletic and he felt that she could have run like a deer if she had lived near a meadow.

Nat King Cole's melodic voice was singing *My Foolish Heart* and the lyrics and dreaminess of the ethereal lighting lifted Rex's spirit into a different world than he had ever experienced. As he and Therese's ghost swayed to the music, he could see her face and arms clearly for a moment at a time then she would fade back into a silhouette. At times, he could see all of her clearly and he was afraid that when the music stopped, she would disappear into a wisp of air. For the moment, Rex and Therese were synchronized in their movement to the music.

The night is like a lovely tune,
beware my foolish heart.
How white the ever constant moon,
take care, my foolish heart.
There's a line between love and fascination,
that's hard to see on an evening such as this.
For they both give the very same sensation,
when you are lost in the passion of a kiss.
Your lips are much to close to mine,
beware my foolish heart.
But should our eager lips combine,
then let the fire start.

For this time, it isn't fascination,
or a dream that will fade and fall apart,
It's love this time, it's love, my foolish heart.

As soon as the music ended and the radio disc jockey began a sales pitch for a local musical event, Therese's apparition and the luminescence of the room faded so that only Rex's desk lamp remained as the sole light source. He didn't cry out for her because his logical mind understood that she was trapped in a different world than his world. His mind understood the difference. But his heart was truly gripped with longing for an entity who could never return as a real person.

CHAPTER TWENTY-NINE

Fort Road

In the foothills of the Cascade Mountains, there was a meeting, trade and cultural center for prehistoric tribes of Indigenous peoples of the Americas from areas all around the state of Washington. Located in an old oak grove watered by natural springs, the site was used as a trade center and campground for the various bands of Native Americans that made up the Yakama Indian Nation.

In 1850, Civil War General Robert Garnett erected Fort Simcoe to house troops to keep watch over local Indian tribes. In 1869, the military turned the fort over to the Yakama Indian Agency and the site was converted to an Indian school. The Yakama Indian Agency managed its affairs until the early 1900s when the 200 acres were developed into Fort Simcoe State Park in 1956.

The interpretive center, the original commander's house and two officer's buildings with period furnishings were open to the public from April through September. The roads that led from the city of Yakima to Fort Simcoe were Highway 97, Lateral A and Fort Road, all the way through the village of White Swan. A person could own several hundred acres of fruit orchards, mint or alfalfa fields, hop fields or vineyards yet have a compound hidden from public view with no questions asked. Only a helicopter could truly get a bird's eye view of a person's house, barns or activities. Without a hint of suspicion, it would be easy to live a life of isolation and that's precisely what Judge Roger McCarthy chose to do.

Both in their fifties, he and his wife had an arrangement. She wanted to live in Yakima on Scenic Drive, an exclusive area of custom-built expensive homes located on a ridge overlooking the city. Her days were filled with bridge parties, tennis at the Yakima Tennis Club, and social events of high society. She had all the amenities of a prestigious house, car and expensive clothes and jewelry.

On the other hand, the judge was a hunter and fisherman and had a compound on Fort Road that was built for the pleasure of outdoorsmen and classic car enthusiasts. He had several car barns where his cars were kept in a climate and dust controlled atmosphere. There was also a mechanic's shop, where cars were repaired and detailed. All show cars were driven occasionally because the judge did not believe that his cars were only museum objects. Since he employed car buffs to clean the cars, he enjoyed driving them whenever he wanted. Fruit trees surrounded the compound on Fort Road but the main house, barns and yard were enclosed in an electronic fence and remote controlled gates.

Lorenzo Calucci, who was employed by the judge as a manager of the compound, lived two hundred yards from the main house. Calucci's passion was motorcycles and sports cars. He had his own triple car garage and kept his Harley Davidson "hog", and an old Harley plus two sports cars available for use at all times. The money he earned from Judge McCarthy was given to him under the table, so to speak. The judge was listed as his landlord, nothing more. But that was not the whole picture. Calucci was the judge's strong-arm man. He met people-of-interest at the airport and acted as the judge's bodyguard when necessary. For several months, he had picked Therese up at the theatre and brought her to the Fort Road compound and was part of the sting in capturing Louise D'Anjou. He knew where her body was and so did the judge. He was simply following the judge's orders and was paid handsomely.

In order to establish an occupation that was recognized by the Internal Revenue Service, Lorenzo Calucci worked at The Alaskan Corral in a management position. He was in charge of entertainment and often brought in entertainers from Seattle. The most unusual duo that he brought from one of Frank Colacurcio's strip joints was advertised as "Two of the Most Beautiful Girls In The World!" Verissa and Celeste were formerly men who wrote a book called: SEX CHANGE, which told the story of men who changed their sex to become two of the most beautiful and complete women in the world. The ad encouraged customers to see the girls dance at The Corral nightly from 5 p.m. to 2 a.m. Calucci liked to keep the entertainment interesting at the club and he had an abundance of connections in the Seattle-Tacoma area to import any girls he wanted.

In Seattle, Therese D'Anjou had used the name, Zizi Zeigler, when she was an exotic dancer who was famous for her partially nude dancing in a three-part routine. In the first part of the dance, she appeared in a skimpy sequined bikini top and slit skirt. She teased the audience and simply took off her full-length gloves. In the second part of her dance, she took off her skirt to reveal a string bikini. And in the third part of her strip tease, everything came off behind two giant fans She allowed the audience to have an occasional glimpse of her totally nude body, which she quickly covered with huge ostrich feathered fans in a similar manner to the famous strip tease dancer, Sally Rand, who began the tradition using fans. Every time she danced, Therese, who was known as Zizi, received a standing ovation.

Lorenzo Calucci wanted Therese to be a headliner at The Corral. She consented to perform for only a couple weeks. During that time, Judge McCarthy saw her famous strip tease dance and charmed her into becoming his mistress. He rewarded her financially and bought her fine clothes, jewelry and a luxurious place to live. He wanted her to be available to him. Therese didn't need the judge's money because she was earning top dollar as a performer. However, she was ready for a change and saw the arrangement as a way to marry her lover as soon as he divorced his wife; at least that was his promise to her.

That was one of the secrets that Lorenzo Calucci kept private regarding the judge's personal life. He was a careful man about his work, discreet and secretive. The darkest secrets of the people he worked for were recorded in his memory and could be used as blackmail if the occasion called for it.

The movie, *Easy Rider*, with Peter Fonda, Dennis Hopper and Jack Nicholson, was a bit hit in the 1960s. The girls at The Corral choreographed a strip act to Steppenwolf's signature tune in the movie called: *Born To Be Wild* and after they rode Lorenzo Calucci's new motorcycle on stage, the fireworks started with booming music and wind machines blowing the girl's clothes off. The audience went crazy for the act. The lyrics described exactly how Calucci was feeling as he revved his motor to higher and higher speeds.

Get your motor running
Head out on the highway
Looking for adventure
In whatever comes my way
Yeah, you know I'm
Gonna make it happen
Take the world in a love embrace
Fire all of your guns at once and
Explode into space
I like smoke and lightning
Heavy metal thunder
Racing in the wind
And the feeling that I'm under
Like a true nature child
I was born to be wild
Born to be wild
I've have climbed so high
Never want to die
Born to be wild
Born to be wild

Unless the judge had a special assignment for him, he worked at The Corral until after hours and was on the road before 3 a.m. During clear weather, Lorenzo Calucci rode his 1965 electric blue Harley-Davidson back to the compound. The "hog" weighed 700 pounds but felt solid under him once he built up speed. He still had an older model Harley but the brand new Electra-Glide had an electric starter rather than requiring a rider to kick-start the big V-twin engine, which could be temperamental.

One of the reasons he enjoyed living on the Yakama Indian Reservation out on Fort Road was the long stretch of road, which enabled him to race his motorcycle at close to 100 miles per hour. He dressed in black leather gloves, chaps and a motorcycle jacket. Helmets were not required in the 1960s and Calucci elected not to wear one. Instead, he covered his mouth with a bandana and wore aviator glasses to avoid the sting of being hit by flying bugs.

Fort Road was lined with *descansos*, a Spanish word for a resting place. They were roadside memorials that commemorated a site where a person died suddenly and unexpectedly, away from home. Unlike a gravesite headstone, which marked where a body was laid, the memorial marked the last place on earth where a person was alive. Usually the memorial, a simple cross with the person's name and decorated with plastic flowers, was created and maintained by family members or friends of the person who died. To Calucci and most drivers on Fort Road, the *descansos* were merely decorations rather than a deadly warning of human catastrophe. Not even Lorenzo Calucci believed he would die on the road.

Fort Road had a roller coaster lift and dip roadway with severely slanted shoulders and in some cases, no shoulders where a car could safely pull over without landing in an irrigation ditch. Many of the *descansos* were created as a result of drunk drivers crashing a car with a whole family being killed.

Lorenzo Calucci disregarded other people's tragedies and was often the cause of their injuries and in some cases, their deaths. He was like a wolf in pursuit of his prey. There was no sense of regret or feeling about causing others to suffer when he was assigned to kill someone. It was simply a job that needed to be done that he would get paid to do. He was clever about not being discovered and used a garrote whenever possible because it was a homemade instrument of death that the general population, including the police, were not familiar with and could be cut up and destroyed.

About a month after the abduction of Louise D'Anjou, Lorenzo Calucci had finished his shift at The Corral. It was a spring night and the sky was clear with weather conditions that were perfect for his ride back to the compound. He was careful about the speed limits through Union Gap and even after he turned right on Lateral A. When he turned right onto Fort Road, he knew he had a five-mile ride before he reached the compound. There were no Yakama Reservation Patrol cars on Fort Road that night and he guessed they were busy with gang related shootings or stabbings in Toppenish.

It was usual for him to travel at speeds of eighty miles per hour between 3 and 4 a.m. Usually, there was no traffic on the road unless there had been an Indian pow-wow in White Swan. But this night, he could not see any headlights or taillights so he felt free to race as close to 100 miles per hour as his Harley could go. He knew the advertisements said that the Electra-Glide could reach 110 miles per hour and he figured what better time than now to see if the motorcycle could reach that speed, even for a second or two.

After the first mile flew by, no longer could he distinguish anything but the white lines on the side of the road and the yellow lines in the middle of the road. As the dips and lifts in the road began, Lorenzo Calucci's motorcycle flew above each rise in the highway as he raced down Fort Road at ninety-miles-per-hour. He descended into the next dip and suddenly realized there was a person standing in the road slightly to his right. No, it wasn't only one woman. It was two women! My God, it was Therese and Louise D'Anjou flying at the motorcycle with their faces grotesquely decomposed in death. He had killed the two women in the last couple months and wondered how they could appear on the road.

As he swerved to avoid an impact with the apparitions, his motorcycle changed lanes and he was headed toward oncoming traffic. Because of the dip he'd been in, he failed to see a truck that had pulled out of a dirt road between two orchards, had turned right and was proceeding toward Lateral A.

When Calucci saw that he and the truck were going to collide, he leaned heavily to the left side of his motorcycle with the hope that he could avoid a collision by sliding out of the way. The impact between the truck and the motorcycle crushed both vehicles beyond recognition. The drunken couple in the truck was instantly buried in twisted metal. Lorenzo Calucci's leg was pinned under the weight of the Harley as he slid into an irrigation ditch. He lived long enough to realize that his beloved 700 pound Harley was resting on his chest and submerging his entire body under three feet of water.

CHAPTER THIRTY

New Descansos

It was May 15 and the day began before the sun came up when John Bevins was delivering Thursday's Yakima Herald-Republic to his list of subscribers who lived along Fort Road. He had to travel on the wrong side of the road at times in order to stick the paper in the tubes under a subscriber's rural mailbox.

At the top of one of the rises in the road, Bevins looked down upon a grisly scene of a pickup that was so severely smashed in front that it was folded like an accordion. He was already running the moment his car screeched to a halt. There seemed to be no movement when he approached the truck and as he moved around it, he yelled, "Are you alive?"

He thought he heard a squeak or a slight scream and as he looked closer, he made eye contact with a passenger in the truck who was still alive. He ran back to his car and got on his walkie-talkie. His wife was on the other end and could make a phone call if needed.

In the years that Bevins delivered papers, he had come upon car wrecks on a regular basis. Most were fatal and in some cases, a car or truck would be abandoned and he could see the people he assumed were the drivers walking across a field to a farmer's house. He always shook his head because he knew those drunk, and possibly injured, drivers would be met by guard dogs at the edge of the farmer's property.

"Martha, Martha come in," John called after activating his walkie-talkie.

"I'm here. What's up?" Martha answered.

"Call the Yakima Sheriff, the fire department and the tribal sheriff. We got a bad accident one mile west of Sam's place. We need at least one ambulance and something to cut open a smashed truck. A passenger is still alive. Bring a tow truck. It's a big mess. Thing is, I don't see the other car that hit this truck. I'll look around and maybe I can find it."

Martha said, "Roger and out."

Bevins opened his trunk and pulled out a crow bar then rushed back to the truck and tried to wedge open the metal where he could see the passenger's face. The man was either dead or unconscious and Bevins was thankful that at least he was not suffering.

He heard sirens in the distance and knew that help was on the way. Even with a crowbar, he could not wedge open the twisted metal of the truck so he simply stood back and looked around. "Where was the other vehicle?" he wondered. Looking down at the skid marks on the highway, he followed the rubber to a trench in the dirt by the side of the road that led to an eight-foot deep irrigation ditch.

As Bevin's looked down in the ditch, he brought his hand to his mouth and gasped at the sight of a man with black hair who was dressed in black leather lying under the water with a twisted electric blue Harley Davidson resting on top of him.

"Jesus God, have mercy!" he whispered. He turned back to look down the highway toward the blinking red and blue lights that were just over a couple rises. All he could do was wait until the sheriff's car, the fire truck and ambulance arrived, and then he gave his information to the sheriff. A forensic photographer was busy marking all evidence with numbered tags and taking photographs.

The order of business was to try to wedge the wreckage open and get the lone survivor out of the twisted truck. Once the efforts of the fire department loosened the man from the truck, the only thing he could manage to say was, "Find motorcycle." Bevins directed the Yakima Sheriff to the ditch as the tow truck showed up.

When the sun was about to rise over the tops of the apple orchards, cars had gathered on both sides of the road and a deputy had to direct traffic. After the passenger of the truck was inside the ambulance, the vehicle headed toward Lateral A then back on Highway 97 toward St. Elizabeth's Hospital in Yakima.

After the tow truck pulled the smashed truck to the side of the road, it backed up to the ditch. The mechanic connected a huge hook to the chassis of the motorcycle, dragged it off the top of Lorenzo Calucci and pulled it to the side of the road. A second ambulance had arrived and the EMTs were lifting and dragging Calucci's body up the side of the ditch and on to a stretcher.

The sheriff asked the coroner to sign a death certificate before the body could be released to the morgue. During the process, the sheriff examined the contents of the dead man's wallet and said, "The motorcycle guy is Lorenzo Calucci who works at The Corral. He lives on Judge Roger Mc-Carthy's property in a house just a couple hundred yards from the main residence here on Fort Road. When you take his prints, you're gonna find they match the prints that're registered with the FBI. He's got some assault charges that didn't amount to much. But I suspect those charges are the tip of the iceberg. Know what I mean? Be sure and contact Lt. Paganelli. I think he's gonna run with the information on this guy."

Both the coroner's car and the ambulance displayed their blinking lights as the two vehicles exited the scene and headed for the Yakima County Morgue. The forensic photographer continued to take photographs as the tow truck loaded the damaged truck and motorcycle.

Lt. Paganelli was notified enroute by the ambulance driver and he was waiting at the coroner's office when the ambulance and the coroner arrived. After the EMTs slid the gurney out of the ambulance, the lieutenant lifted the sheet and looked at Lorenzo Calucci's face. He spoke to the coroner and said, "Give me a call when you have him cleaned up. I'm going to get some information on him and contact a couple people then I'll be back to hear the particulars on this man's death."

Before he returned to his office, Lt. Paganelli walked into the courthouse and up to the third floor to see his mentor, Judge Edward Simmons, in his chambers. The judge was in his mid-seventies and not looking forward to retirement. He was always interested in the lieutenant's cases and the two of them were like a teacher and student. "I need a bunch of search warrants, Judge Ed," the lieutenant said.

"I got a stack of 'em already signed right here. Take what you need and come back for more if the situation calls for it," the judge said. "Anyone I know?"

The lieutenant's tongue was tied momentarily. "If things go as planned, you will be shocked with these couple cases like you've never been shocked before. That's all I can tell you. I've got the ammunition with these search warrants and you're gonna see some fireworks in the next twenty-four hours. Trust me!"

"Dear boy," the judge was patient with his former student. "I have seen every human condition known to man and God. I have seen the most incorrigible human behavior before my bench. Granted, what I have seen doesn't compare to what the forensic photographer has seen. But I doubt that whatever direction you're going, will affect me more than a general Hhrrummmph!"

"Thanks for the search warrants. I'll put them to good use and we'll see if I can get more out of you than a Hhrummmmph" the lieutenant pointed the warrants at the judge and smiled.

CHAPTER THIRTY-ONE

The Morgue

"Hello Mike, this is Lt. Paganelli, I'm afraid the birthday party's been called off. I'm at the Yakima County Morgue in the same room with the honoree. I need you to come down to First Street and make sure this is the honoree you had in mind when we were planning the party."

Mike said, "We've discussed this before, lieutenant. I'm not coming to the morgue. Now if you'll excuse me, I have a delivery truck out in back waiting for me." Mike gently but firmly hung up the phone, closed his eyes and rubbed his face at the turn of events.

He actually did have a delivery truck waiting for him so after he hung up, Mike walked to the receiving area behind the stage. As he was helping the deliveryman carry in supplies, a black and white Yakima Police squad car pulled up beside the delivery truck and two officers got out. Mike wanted to run but got a grip on his feeling of panic and stood still.

After the officers walked up the stairs, one of the men got behind Mike and one stood in front of him. "Mike Hansen?"

"Yes," he said.

"Lt. Paganelli wants us to transport you over to the morgue to make an identification of a deceased man," the officer said.

"Are you arresting me?" Mike asked.

"Not at all. We're simply giving you a ride to the morgue and we'll bring you right back. Let's get in the car," the front officer said and turned toward the stairs. If Mike had any idea about turning and heading away from the men, he would be looking into the face of the officer just a couple steps behind him. Rather than using threatening language or force, the officers were intimidating only because of their proactive presence and Mike had no choice but to get in the squad car.

In the meantime, Lt. Paganelli got the low down from the coroner as they both looked down at Lorenzo Calucci's naked body with a sheet covering him from his knees to his neck. The coroner had performed an extensive autopsy, had taken his fingerprints and a sample of his blood.

The coroner began by saying, "Lorenzo Calucci was a healthy thirty-two-year old male. His cause of death was a severe impact to his whole body. His skull and spine have been crushed. His leg was pinned under the weight of the motorcycle as he was skidding on the asphalt. As a result, from his hip down to his foot was shattered. Once he slid into the irrigation ditch and his 700 pound motorcycle landed on him, he must have taken a couple breaths because his lungs were filled with water."

"His prints and blood work?" the lieutenant wondered.

"I sent out his prints and should be getting a response any minute. I haven't had time to do his blood work. So I'll do that and send you a report. I didn't smell alcohol on his person so he was not intoxicated. It puzzles me that he was driving in the oncoming lane. Maybe something scared him and he was trying to avoid hitting it," the coroner said.

The lieutenant said, "Once we see the forensic photographs, we'll be able to tell how fast he was going. If he did see something in the road, and tried to avoid it, because of his high, speed even a slight change of the bike's front wheel overcompensated his attempt to avoid the object."

Both men turned toward the parking lot door when they heard some voices. Once the squad car arrived, the officers exited their car and opened the door for Mike. "Just go to that door and wait," one of the officers instructed him.

Lt. Paganelli stepped out of the morgue and joined Mike and the officers. In a low voice, Mike said, "I told you the reason I didn't want to come to this place or the police station and now that you've forced me to be here, I'm just as good as dead."

"Mike," the lieutenant said. "Try to calm down. I know what you feared and I can assure you that 98% of that threat is laying on an autopsy table in the morgue."

"Are you telling me that the guy who killed Therese is dead?" Mike's eyes widened.

"That's what I'm telling you. Once you ID him, we'll have probable cause to search both his place of work and his residence," the lieutenant said.

"This guy was working for the judge. Are you going to search the judge's chambers and his residence?"

"Yes. The information you found will be confiscated and we'll probably bring charges. But we have to move today. The judge will return from his vacation on Monday. We can search even after he returns but it we'll have no interference today." After a momentary silence, the lieutenant said, "Ready to go in?"

"I'm ready," Mike said.

They both entered the autopsy room and saw the coroner dressed in a white coat. He was standing beside a man's body that was laid out on the stainless steel examination table. To the coroner, Lt. Paganelli said, "This is Mike Hansen and I'd like him to identify the man on the table. Will you be a witness to his comments?"

The coroner said, "Yes, I'll be a witness."

"Mike, will you identify this man?" the lieutenant said as he looked at the body.

"I saw this man pick up a woman who we thought was called Zizi Zeigler from the Capitol Theatre on several occasions when I was standing in an alcove of a theatre doorway in the alley smoking a cigarette. The last time I saw him in the alley, he parked a vintage Jaguar between the theatre and the back of the Wilson Building and Commercial Hotel. He went into the theatre as usual and I thought he was going to escort Zizi back to the car like always. But when he came out of the theatre, he was by himself and drove away."

Lt. Paganelli asked, "Is that the same night Zizi was found murdered in the theatre?"

"Yes, her body was discovered one hour later," Mike said.

"Is there any other time that you saw this man?"

"I saw him dusting a vintage Jaguar that Judge Roger McCarthy was exhibiting at the Concours d'Elegance. I asked the judge if this man and the three others who were dressed in polo shirts and black pants worked for him. He said yes. I took several photographs of the judge and this man at the car show."

"Do you know what this man's name is?'" the lieutenant asked.

"No. I don't know his name or anything about him except I saw him in the alley and at the fairgrounds. I've never spoken to him," Mike said.

"Thank you, Mike. The officers will take you back to the theatre," the lieutenant said.

After Mike was escorted to the squad car, the coroner asked the lieutenant, "What's next?"

"Hold his body as long as you can. We'll see if we can find his next of kin to claim his body. I've got his wallet now with his driver's license and we'll go from there."

Lt. Paganelli remembered Mike's warning that there might be a snitch in the police department so he was secretive about telling anyone what his investigative moves would be. He had several search warrants and by the end of the day, he was confident that he would have enough evidence to prove that Lorenzo Calucci murdered Zizi Zeigler, also known as Therese D'Anjou.

He suspected that Louise D'Anjou's body was buried somewhere on the judge's compound and would put a hundred dollar bill on the table and bet that she also was garroted, like Therese. If he could find the garrote used in these two murders, it would prove that Lorenzo Calucci murdered the two women. Judge McCarthy had motive to order the murders and the lieutenant would have great pleasure in throwing the judge's uppity butt into jail for the rest of his life.

CHAPTER THIRTY-TWO

The Box

Lt. Paganelli knew that everything he did from this point forward would be questioned in court. So it was important that his searches were sequential. He began with Lorenzo Calucci's office at The Corral. He took a forensic photographer with him so that any evidence could be photographed where it was found. He did not want to be accused of planting incriminating evidence.

Officers Kusske and Murphy followed him in a van. The lieutenant wanted items found during the searches to be double checked and photographed before he picked them up and boxed them as exhibits.

"Yeah, sure," said the manager in charge at The Corral when Lt. Paganelli showed him a search warrant and told him to unlock the door to Lorenzo Calucci's office. The lieutenant had gathered the keys that were in Calucci's pants and jacket pockets and tried a couple keys to unlock his desk and file cabinets.

Besides a hand gun, several bottles of bourbon whiskey, a few marijuana joints, pornography and nude photos of every imaginable variety, two of the most valuable items were an address book that included Judge McCarthy's name and Zizi Zeigler's name, phone number and room number at the Chinook Hotel. His bank account statements that listed deposits and withdrawals would prove to be valuable because the lieutenant would match the judge's cash flow and bank statements to see if they corresponded with Calucci's financial activity.

Anticipating some extended time to examine all records and items in Calucci's office, officers Kusske and Murphy began packing the contents of the desk, the file cabinets, photographs and personal items. There were several photos of Lorenzo Calucci and Frank Colacurcio together in Seattle nightclubs and The Corral. The boxes were loaded into the van and taken to the storage warehouse of the Yakima Police Department. Once the boxes were stored, the team went across the street and up to the third floor where Judge McCarthy's chambers were located.

When the lieutenant stood in front of the judge's clerk's desk and hadn't yet said a word, she said, "Lt. Paganelli, the judge isn't in today. He'll be back on Monday. Would you like to leave a message for him."

"Mary, I'm here on official business. I need you to open the judge's chambers for me," the lieutenant said.

She smiled because she thought this scene was a joke. When the lieutenant held the search warrant up, her smile faded and she opened her desk drawer to get the key to the judge's office. "Can't you wait until Monday?" she complained.

The lieutenant reached for the key. She reluctantly handed it to him and he said, "Your work is finished for the day. Get your purse and leave the building." The four men stood by her desk until she got her purse and headed toward the elevator. Just a slight indication from the lieutenant's eyes clued officer Murphy to escort the clerk out the front door onto Second Street.

After entering the judge's chambers, the lieutenant used one of the smaller keys on the chain to open the file cabinets. He kept the attention of the forensic photographer and prayed that the incriminating box would be there as reported by Mike Hansen and Rex Marvel. In the bottom drawer of the cabinet on the left, there was a space behind the files where there was a stack of miscellaneous papers. With each step, the photographer took a picture. The lieutenant removed the papers to reveal a shoebox, which he took out and placed on the desk. He lifted the lid and saw Therese D'Anjou's passport, her citizenship papers, her pink address book and a packet of photographs.

There was also a black address book with the judge's name neatly printed on the opening page. The first names that the lieutenant looked up were Therese D'Anjou and Zizi Zeigler. The phone numbers and room numbers at the Chinook Hotel were the same. There were quite a few women's names that sounded like either hooker or stripper's names. Lorenzo Calucci's number at The Corral was also listed as well as his home number and address on the judge's property.

One unexpected item was an envelope from a local photo studio filled with photographs of the judge and Zizi and a few photos of her dancing on stage with her huge fans. The judge was embracing the girl known as Zizi in most of the photos and appeared to be in love with her.

In the desk, the judge had a daily calendar so the lieutenant checked every Monday night and where a notation of ZZ was made. There were other nights when the same notations of ZZ were made. Unknown to her, the judge was also seeing some of the strippers who were listed in Lorenzo Calucci's black book.

Finding Therese D'Anjou's passport, her papers and the photographs were the first pieces of evidence that truly connected Judge McCarthy with the murdered woman. However, there was nothing in his office that belonged to Louise D'Anjou. The lieutenant hoped that he would find additional evidence against the judge at his compound because he knew that it would be unlikely that a murder weapon would be found in either Judge McCarthy or Lorenzo Calucci's offices.

Per the lieutenant's instructions, the contents of the judge's desk were packed in boxes, as was the shoebox with Therese's passport, papers and snapshots. Since there was such a large volume of papers to examine, the lieutenant put a police padlock on the judge's chamber door and would have a forensic investigator go through the paperwork within twenty-four hours.

Time was of the essence and he and the team needed to drive out to Judge McCarthy's compound. Although the crimes were committed in the city of Yakima, the judge's compound was in Yakima County and also on the Yakama Indian Reservation. The Yakima County Sheriff's Department and the Yakama tribal officials needed to be involved. After a phone call, the heads of the three departments had a quick meeting.

"I know this investigation of the judge's compound is in your departments," the lieutenant said to the sheriff and tribal sheriff. "I need to go with you because I know what we're looking for."

"No problem," the officials said. "Do you know if the judge has an electric fence around the compound? Or guard dogs?"

"Pacific Power can shut his electricity off from the road. Let's alert them that a service truck needs to meet us out there. As far as guard dogs? I wouldn't doubt that we're gonna run into some monsters. How about the

K-9 Unit? They could handle the dogs. I also would like a special police dog that can sniff out a cadaver. I have a suspicion that the body of Louise D'Anjou is buried on the judge's property," the lieutenant said.

He added. "The judge might be on his property with a bunch of his thugs. So we need the men need to wear bulletproof vests just in case there's a gun battle. I suggest that we have one team for the judge's house and one team for Lorenzo Calucci's house and one team to act as security to watch for intruders. We're looking for anything of Therese's in the judge's house and hopefully a garrote with some nice fingerprints on the handles and a trace of Therese's blood on the wire, in Calucci's house."

The sheriff said, "We're going out there nice and quiet. No sirens. Part of the team will lie back until we clear the way. I'll be able to call them when they're needed. I want the back of the property covered so that when I do enter the front perimeter, if the judge is there, I want to give him a chance to cooperate."

Police cars, vans, dog kennels and trucks—the whole works was moving out to Fort Road. This was judgment day and Lt. Paganelli was prepared to go to war if that's what it took to avenge the murders of Therese and Louise D'Anjou.

CHAPTER THIRTY-THREE

The Compound

Like wolves gathering before a hunt, members of the Yakima sheriff and police departments met briefly in the parking lot behind the police department on Second Street. Each man was given a map of the compound and what the initial plan was. They were cautioned that Judge McCarthy might be in his house and that he might have a number of bodyguards who would be armed.

The K-9 Unit was put in charge of handling guard dogs as well as providing a cadaver dog to see if the body of Louise D'Anjou could be located on the judge's property. The sheriff had received word that the power company trucks were on their way to the road outside the compound and would turn the power off if needed.

The sheriff spoke. "Make no mistake. We are going to Judge McCarthy's compound to arrest him for ordering the murder of Therese D'Anjou. If we find the body of her sister, Louise, on his property, there'll be two counts of first-degree murder. Just remember, he has everything to lose and will be desperate to escape. We have to make sure that he is healthy when he's taken into custody so he can be tried in court for his crimes. Don't be a hero in this operation. Protect yourself. At the same time, we need to make sure that when we leave the compound, the judge will be in the back of a squad car. So men, we have an important job to do today so let's get started!!"

After a brief cheer, adrenaline was in the air as the men got in their cars and vans and followed the sheriff's car toward Highway 97 and into the Lower Valley. As the procession of law enforcement cars passed by the fields of Yakima Valley, life on the farms seemed so orderly with hopes for a profitable crop as men labored at twining hops, picking asparagus, planting corn and other field crops. Orchards were acres of trees covered with pink and white blossoms and seemed as if they came out of a child's dream of candy land. The Lower Valley paradise appeared to be without a worry in the world.

Reality checked in when the Yakama Tribal Police met the procession at the corner of Lateral A and Fort Road.

The plan was that an unmarked car would drive past the compound to see if there were any visiting cars parked there or if there were any people moving around. After a couple drive-bys, it was determined that there was some activity and most probably the judge was in his house or in one of the car barns. The fancy rod-iron gate was shut and there was a tall black iron fence around the perimeter.

The power company was given the green light to cut off the power, which they did. Within five minutes, a man dressed in an Hawaiian shirt and matching slacks opened the main gate and walked out to the road toward the lineman who was perched at the the top of the pole.

"Hey man," the judge's bodyguard looked up and yelled at the lineman. "What the hell is going on? We've lost our power in every building and need to have that power come back on, immediately." Within seconds, an unmarked car drove up to the bodyguard and two policemen grabbed the man, took his handgun, cuffed him, read him his rights and charged him as an accessory to murder. He was forced into the back seat and taken to a paddy wagon for safe keeping until the sting was completed.

In the meantime, a unit of three men dressed in camouflage outfits had secured the back perimeter of the compound. They looked like hunters and blended in with the dry grass and weeds that hadn't been burned yet. An officer from the dog unit was also dressed in camouflage and ready to dart any guard dogs. They could hear a couple of dogs barking and running toward them. By the time the two Rottweilers approached the back fence, the K-9 unit officer had raised his tranquilizing gun and fired at each of the dogs. They both went down peacefully and he said, "I'll stay with these two just to make sure they stay down until the sting is over. I doubt that there are any other guard dogs because they'd all be together."

No bodyguards followed the dogs so the three camouflaged officers went over the fence and worked their way to the back of the car barns.

There was no one in the barns or the mechanic's shop. One of the officers sprinted toward the second house, looked through the windows and could not see anyone inside. Using a glasscutter, he sliced a section out of the glass on the back porch door, reached through and opened the door. Crouched down, he waited to see if he could hear any movement and heard nothing but crows flying overhead as they squawked and looked down on the scene then landed in a couple tall cedar trees to watch the action.

Rather than the backdoor leading directly into the house, the camouflaged officer found himself in a breezeway that led either to the garage and workshop or into the house. He turned the knob to go into the garage and workshop and the door opened. He was able to move around in the dark room and found himself in a shop with motorcycle and car parts. He switched on his flashlight and looked at tools above the workbench that were clamped in place on the wall. He had never seen a garrote before and it took a minute for him to recognize the three garrotes that were hanging on a hook right in front of him.

Two of the wires had wooden waterski handles on each end. The third garrote had sections of rubber hose on the ends with the wire threaded through the inside of the hose parts and knotted tightly. As curious as he was to pick up the garrotes, the officer knew that the forensic photographer had to take photographs of the instruments of death where they were hanging.

The other two camouflaged officers had reached the back of the house and could hear Judge McCarthy having a conversation with two bodyguards.

"Where's Reno?" the judge asked the men.

"He went out to talk to the power lineman and hasn't come back," said the tall man whose face looked like he been the loser in a lifetime of boxing matches.

"So he's disappeared? Are you saying that he didn't walk back in the compound after talking to the power guy?" The judge wanted details.

"I don't know what to tell you except he's not here," the boxing loser said.

"I don't hear the dogs," the judge said. "Look out the back door and see where they are."

The second man walked outside to check the back yard and whistled for the dogs. When he walked around the corner where the two camouflaged officers were pressing themselves against the house, they grabbed him. One of the officers wrapped his arm around the man's neck in a chokehold and applied pressure until he passed out. They gagged him and cuffed his hands behind his back. The whole scene was being watched through binoculars by the sheriff as he hid in the apple orchard surrounding the compound.

After a five-minute pause, the judge began to pace. "I heard Enrique whistle but I don't see him anywhere when I look out the window. What the shit is happening?"

Ready to recognize that two men and two dogs had disappeared, the judge's last bodyguard said, "Something's going down!" He pulled his gun out at attention and started peeking through the windows that faced Fort Road. "I don't see any cars but I can just feel that we are surrounded by cops."

"You could be right. Mary, my clerk, called me and said the police had asked for the key to my office. If they got in there and found that box, it connects me to Therese. But it doesn't prove that I murdered her. Let's not panic. I'm a judge and there's got to be a reasonable way out of this situation," the judge was babbling to himself.

Just then, the sheriff's car drove up and passed through the open gate. Several squad cars followed him and formed a semi-circle. The officers used their cars as shields as they pointed shotguns, rifles and handguns at the front and side of the judge's house.

Judge Roger McCarthy realized that there was no way out for him. The best thing to do was to surrender and let the battle take place in court rather than risk being shot. The preponderance of evidence rested squarely on the prosecution's shoulders. Even one vote in favor of his innocence, would kill the case against him. He was confident that there wasn't enough proof to tie him to Therese D'Anjou's murder. It was simple. He didn't murder her.

Before he stepped out of the front door with his hands up, the judge said to his bodyguard, "You have nothing to fear. They have no case against you or me. We'll both be released before the day is over. Stick with me and you'll be okay."

Judge Roger McCarthy walked out of the front door of his house smiling and with his hands in the air. "Gentlemen. Gentlemen, let's sit down together and talk about whatever the problem is. I have no idea why all these officers are here. I think you've got some incorrect information about me and I know we can work things out."

Before he finished his little public relations speech, the two camouflaged men from the side of the house, rushed forward and pulled both the judge and the bodyguard's arms behind them and cuffed their hands behind their backs. The bodyguard's handgun was lifted and kicked away from him.

The sheriff stepped up to the judge and said, "I'm arresting you for the murder of Therese D'Anjou." And to the bodyguard, the sheriff said, I'm arresting you as an accomplice to murder. You both have the right to an attorney... ." The sheriff repeated the Miranda code to each man. Two officers escorted the judge to a squad car and two other officers escorted the bodyguard to a second squad car.

The investigative team entered the judge's house and turned on the lights. Lt. Paganelli walked into the master bedroom and searched the closet. He pulled out several nightgowns, robes and casual women's clothes. His assistant bagged them and left them temporarily on the bed. Then the lieutenant looked at the contents of jewelry and items on the judge's dresser.

Right in the middle of a silver velvet cloth covering the dresser, a sparkle caught the lieutenant's eye. It was Therese's gold earring with a one-carat diamond. This time, the earring didn't change to a screw. This time, the earring dazzled and reflected the spotlight shining down on the dresser.

CHAPTER THIRTY-FOUR

Louise

W hen Lt. Paganelli picked up the earring with his handkerchief, he examined it and thought about the time that Rex brought the so-called earring to the police station. When Rex opened his handkerchief, all he was holding was a brass screw. The lieutenant was an expert at reading people's body language and he observed that Rex was truly surprised at seeing the screw rather than the earring. And now the earring was here.

There was no way that Rex could have brought the earring to this compound and placed it on the judge's dresser. The matching earring was in the evidence box at the police station so the lieutenant knew in his heart that this earring he was holding was, in fact, the same earring that Rex found in the Capitol Theatre.

How did it get from the theatre to the judge's dresser?

The lieutenant was a Catholic who believed the stories about miracles in the Bible. He never discussed his religion or God or the possibility that there might be a world where entities had powers that man would never have as long as they were alive on earth. It was a theory that he would not admit nor would he ever have a conversation about it. He didn't have the answer to how the earring got to the judge's dresser. He just knew that Therese's earring was the final evidence that she had been in the judge's bedroom. It connected her to the judge and there was no denying that fact.

"Lieutenant, you've gotta see what we found!" Officer Kusske startled Lt. Paganelli out of his reverie. "Follow me to Lorenzo Calucci's house."

The crime scene investigators were like a swarm of bees on every house and barn on the compound. The guard dogs had been put in kennels and were on their way to an isolation section at the police dog compound in

Yakima. Their fate did not look good.

Once the two men reached Lorenzo Calucci's house and garage, officer Kusske led the lieutenant into the tool shop. A photographer was already taking photographs of the three garrotes hanging on a hook along with a variety of tools.

"If I'm not mistaken, sir, one of those garrotes is the murder weapon that killed Therese D'Anjou.

"I hope that no one has touched these wires." The lieutenant knew he was looking at crucial evidence in Therese's murder.

"No one has touched the wires although we sure have been looking at them," officer Kusske said.

"I want you to be in charge of wrapping these wires very carefully and keeping them in your possession until we get back to the police station. Will you do that?" The lieutenant looked at officer Kusske.

"Shall we combine these wires and Therese's earring in the same evidence box?" officer Kusske asked.

"Yes, those are the two most important items. I think that a number of things will be packed in the van and we'll just lock everything else so a CSI team can take their time to thoroughly look for additional evidence," the lieutenant said. "Tell the officer of the K-9 unit that I'm ready for him and his dog. I'll wait right outside this house for him."

Within five minutes, an officer and a large German Shepard dog walked up to the lieutenant. "Lt. Paganelli? I'm officer Dan Gress and this is my dog, Jack."

The dog seemed happy and looked at this handler as he sat quietly waiting for instructions on the task at hand. He was a very big dog and totally black, without the buff legs so common on most German Shepard dogs.

"Has your dog ever found a buried body before?" The lieutenant thought the goal of finding Louise was a long shot since he had no garments for the dog to sniff in order to clue the dog about what he was looking for.

"Jack seems to be sensitive to the smell of any dead animal. We've buried some road kill in the most unlikely places and gone back a couple weeks later to see if he could pick up the scent. So far, he's had a 100% success rate. In fact, I noticed after we arrived here and I took him out of his kennel and let him look around, he was sniffing the air. So he must have smelled something," officer Dan said.

"What about finding people?"

"He's never been asked to find a buried person but he's found a couple dead street persons. So he knows what a dead human smells like."

"What did he do when he found the dead people?" the lieutenant was curious.

Dan said, "He backed up from the smell and started barking. We told him good-boy. So I'm eager to see if he can find your missing lady. Would you like him to try?"

"What's your plan?" the lieutenant wondered.

"First, I'd like to take him through each house and barn. She might be buried under the floor. Then I'm going to take him off the leash and follow him around the property. I know the front gate is closed and he can't get out to the road. So I'll watch him search for whatever attracts his nose."

"Okay, let's start with Judge McCarthy's house then the second house and attached garage. Finally, we'll go into the car barns. Officer Murphy, here, will clear each structure before you enter. He's on his way over to the judge's house so let's walk over there and see if Jack picks up anything," the lieutenant said.

The dog was patient and acted as if going through each house and car barn was a simple job. He did pause at one of the cars and sniffed the back door area of a vintage Jaguar. Officer Dan opened the door to the car and the dog lifted up on his forelegs and gave a thorough sniff but didn't bark. Once the structures had been completed, officer Dan walked over to Lt. Paganelli.

"There's just one more outbuilding and it's way over near the back fence. Looks like an old pump house. I recognize the big outhouse shape because we had one just like it on my dad's hop farm. Would you like me to check it?"

"Might as well check everything. Seems like it would be a good place to bury someone since it's the furthest structure from the houses and barns. Mind if I walk with you and Jack?" The lieutenant was getting a feeling about the old shed.

"Let's go!" The minute officer Dan said that, the dog started getting pumped and looked at his master like any good bird dog would do before he was sent out to hunt for pheasant. No difference to the dog but a big difference to the police officers because it involved a human being who was murdered.

"Jack, go!" officer Dan tossed his arm forward as if he was throwing a tennis ball. The dog responded like a rocket and covered the ground between where they were walking and the pump shed in a few seconds. The dog circled the shed with his nose near the ground then he raised up on his forelegs and sniffed between the loose sunbaked boards. The two officers watched when Jack backed up and barked as he circled the shed. He'd charge the shed then repeat his action of backing up and barking. His tail was high and curled over his back as it shimmied rather than wagged.

Lt. Paganelli activated his walkie-talkie and said, "Bring in the ambulance to a shed at the furthest end of the property. Make sure you have a body bag. It looks like the K-9 dog has found Louise D'Anjou. We're on our way to make an identification of her body. Tell the photographers and the sheriff to get over here ASAP. Roger and out."

By the time the two officers reached the shed, they could smell something fowl like a dead bird stench, only different.

"Good boy, Jack. Good boy!" Officer Dan was loving up his dog and trying to calm him down at the same time by making him sit.

The shed was padlocked and rather than kick it in, the lieutenant wanted the photographer to chronicle every step of the discovery of Louise's body so he had to wait until a gang of crime scene investigators arrived. The photographer got photos of the dog and the locked door. The ambulance driver had a crowbar stored with the spare tire and wedged the hinges off the sun baked and rotting shed. Once the door was off, the stench of a human body made everyone step back and cough in a gagging reaction.

The dog barked and struggled to get loose from officer Dan. "I'm going to take him back to Yakima. He's done a good job for you and I don't want to aggravate him with this smell and all these people."

While the rest of the police and sheriff's force was busy with the body, Lt. Paganelli turned toward officer Dan and his dog, Jack. "Will he let me touch him?" he asked.

"Sure. Give him a pat on his head and he'll appreciate the attention." Officer Dan scratched his dog's head and the lieutenant joined in.

"That's a good dog. You found her all by yourself. Good Jack!" The dog looked up at officer Dan to see if the man touching him was okay. The lieutenant stepped back and the dog and his master headed toward the front gate.

Lt. Paganelli turned toward a gruesome sight of a woman's body in a shallow grave. She was covered with dirt and the ambulance drivers had rolled her on her side in order to get a blanket under her so they could lift her up and bring her outside.

In the meantime, the coroner and sheriff had arrived and were watching the procedure. The sheriff had to sign a paper that Louise was dead at the scene before her body was zipped into a body bag. Although there was no next of kin to identify her, the lieutenant recognized her dress and sweater and the way she wore her hair pulled back in a short ponytail. She had a deep line around her neck and the lieutenant figured that Lorenzo Calucci had murdered her with a garrote.

It appeared that the same man killed both sisters and now he was also dead. Lt. Paganelli did believe in karma—as in 'just desserts'. He didn't know how it would happen but the lieutenant had an eerie feeling that the judge would not live long enough to testify before a jury of twelve of his peers.

CHAPTER THIRTY-FIVE

The Judge

Placing a Superior Court judge in lock-up was a problem especially since the charge was first-degree murder.

There were four floors at the city hall jail also known as the Yakima Police Department. The men stayed on the third floor; the women stayed on the fourth floor. Overflow inmates could be jailed on the other two floors.

The judge could not be housed with other inmates or they would see him as a scapegoat who represented the system and beat him to a pulp. Their attitude was that judges and juries had no problem telling them that they had to spend the majority of their lives locked in a cell. Now they felt it was the judge's turn to see how they felt and they would make sure that he suffered like they were suffering.

Fortunately, one of the floors was vacant and the judge had the privilege of being placed in a larger cell where he would be safe from other inmates. He was not allowed to eat with the general population so his food was brought to his cell. When the guard was given permission, the judge could walk up and down the hall of the fifth floor since the doors were locked and there was no way he could escape through the barred windows.

Although he promised his bodyguard that he would protect him, it was an empty promise. Once the man was taken into custody and placed with a group of other inmates, there wasn't a thing the judge could do. His efforts were focused on finding an attorney who rarely lost a case, someone who he had favored in his courtroom. There was only one man who fit that description and his name was Lee Cartier, pronounced in the French manner—car—tee—ay.

The Cartier family members were famous French luxury jewelers and watch manufacturers. In fact, a member of their family created the first wristwatch. The company had a long and distinguished history of serving royalty, as well as stars and celebrities. King Edward VII was crowned in 1902 and in 1904 he honored the Company with the Royal warrant of supplier to the Royal Court of England, particularly for making tiaras.

Although Lee's lineage was aristocratic, his talent was not in jewelry making. Rather, he discovered that he had the gift of conviction and not many people were immune to his abilities to convince them of just about anything he imagined. He chose his clients carefully with a quiet knowledge that he could win the case even though the odds were stacked against his client. He made headlines in Northwestern newspapers and features in national magazines. The judge couldn't have chosen anyone to represent him who was more qualified than Lee Cartier.

The judge loved the finer things in life, particularly his vintage Jaguars. He also loved beautiful jewelry and upon closer examination, Therese's gold and diamond earrings were a simple Cartier design and came directly from Paris where the Cartier family and business resided. The judge gifted his wife with similar pieces of jewelry, which were kept in a safe in a hidden room adjacent to their bedroom.

The evidence against the judge seemed overwhelming and Lee Cartier began his defense conferences writing down every conceivable charge that the prosecution might have.

Therese's earring and many of her garments were found in the judge's closet at the compound. He was having an affair with Therese D'Anjou and paid her rent at the Chinook Hotel. Naively, she allowed him to keep her passport and other papers "safe", as she described it. When she found that she had no freedom, she threatened to leave him and return to Montreal and she wanted him to return her passport. He said that he would give her passport back to her but he had one excuse after another just as his excuses were endless when it came to divorcing his wife.

Once he found out that she was pregnant, Lee Cartier suggested that the prosecution would say the judge wanted to eliminate her from complicating his life. She threatened to tell his wife so that the wife would leave him. Then she and the judge could be married. When he refused to divorce his wife, Therese became impossible to handle. Finally, she simply wanted to return to Montreal and once she received her birth certificate, she would have a new passport made.

The prosecution would bring up the abduction of Therese's sister, Louise D'Anjou. She did bring Therese's birth certificate, a letter saying that Therese was dating a judge and photographs of the two sisters. Her body was found on the judge's property and the prosecution would say he had motive to eliminate her.

Lorenzo Calucci was the entertainment manager for Frank Colacurcio, owner of The Corral Bar. Calucci also worked for the judge and lived on his property. Three garrotes were found in his workshop and were being tested for blood matches for the two sisters. If the blood types matched the sisters, the prosecution could easily prove that Calucci murdered the women. At the same time, he had no motive to kill them because he had no relationship with either woman.

When all the odds seemed against him, Judge McCarthy wondered what could possibly be in his favor?

It was true that overwhelming circumstantial evidence had convicted many people. However, in the judge's case, Lee Cartier made a list that rebuked every charge against the judge.

He was guilty of having an affair with Therese but that was not against the law. He had no contact with her the night she was murdered.

He never had contact with her sister, Louise. And even though her body was found on his property, he did not kill her and he claimed that he had no knowledge that she was buried in the old pump house.

Lorenzo Calucci did work for him and did rent a house on the judge's property. He was hired to take care of the judge's cars even though he was not the mechanic. Mostly, he aided the judge when he attended classic car shows. He did errands for the judge and picking up Therese at the theatre and bringing her to the compound was one of his jobs. The work he did for Frank Colacurcio was his private business.

Lee Cartier planned to say that the judge was surprised that the garrotes that killed Therese and Louise were found in Lorenzo Calucci's tool shed. They weren't found in the judge's possession or in his house so how could he be charged with Louise's murder?

Lee Cartier said, "Those are the charges against you and in rebuttal, I've outlined our defense. At no time did the police or sheriff find a murder weapon in your house or your possession. It's conjecture that you paid

Lorenzo to kill Therese and Louise."

The judge responded. "The women's blood will match the blood on those garrotes. Calucci had no relationship with the women so what was his motive for killing them?"

"That's not our problem. There's no witness who heard you order Calucci to kill the women and there's no request in writing. It's their word against your word and you are a judge with an absolutely clean record. You already know what I'm going to say when I tell you that we only have to create reasonable doubt with one juror who doesn't have enough empirical evidence for a conviction. There was no smoking gun in your possession and that's in your favor."

"Sounds good. Now what can we do about getting me outta here on bail? I'll strictly stay at my house on Scenic Drive," the judge asked.

"If the judge orders a million dollar bail, I think we can manage it. He'll know that you are not a flight risk and you want your name cleared as soon as possible. You're in luck. All the judges know you and have recused themselves from your trial. One judge, however, has convinced all concerned that he will be impartial."

"Who is the judge?"

"Judge Edward Simmons."

"He's a former law instructor and Lt. Paganelli was one of his students," the judge said.

"That's why he will be extra careful about being impartial. He doesn't want anyone to say that he favors Lt. Paganelli. He's not the one bringing charges. He's simply a witness and he cannot say that you were in possession of a murder weapon."

At the judge's arraignment, Lee Cartier was correct. Judge McCarthy was not a flight risk. No murder weapons were found in his possession. He could easily make the bail and he promised that he would stay under house arrest at his Scenic Drive home. His wife was not there any longer. But the court returned a promise by saying that they would visit him with no notice just to make sure he stayed at home. The airports had been notified of his restriction and if he was caught driving to another state, he would lose his bail and would be put into the general population immediately. An additional charge of escape and eluding the police would be added to the charge of first-degree murder.

Although Judge McCarthy was professionally humiliated with the double murder charges, he was also an opportunist and saw a positive outcome resulting from his notoriety. He could write a book about all the experiences and various cases he handled throughout his life. His famous books, along the same lines as John Grisham's books, could lead to speaking engagements. He could even begin the book while he was in house lock-up.

He had made himself a roast beef, tomato and onion sandwich. While he was eating his sandwich, he wrote a list of stories that he thought audiences might enjoy hearing during his tour of speaking engagements. The sandwich was particularly big and juicy and he was having trouble eating with one hand and writing with the other hand.

Just as he bit into the end of his sandwich, a burst of swirling color appeared before him out of nowhere. My sweet Lord, he recognized the moving figure that was circling his head. It was Therese's ghost and she was undulating around him then rushing up into his face and causing him to jerk backwards from his insane imagination. Happening in a split second, Therese's ghost bumped him in front and attempted to knock him backwards. He was startled and gasped. The mouthful of beef sandwich lodged in the back of his throat and blocked his windpipe.

Like any person who is choking on food, he attempted to breathe in through his nose and cough the food out. To his surprise, he could not pull any air in through his nose and the more he tried, the more the food was pushed into his trachea.

Therese's ghost continued to circle around him until her apparition put pressure on his throat. The judge could not get air as he stood on his feet to try to run from her terrorizing him. As he knocked over chairs, he began to see black dots swimming before his eyes. Black dots and Therese's smiling swirling face were the last things on earth that Judge McCarthy ever saw.

CHAPTER THIRTY-SIX

Return to Montreal

"Rex, this is Lt. Paganelli. I wonder if I could come to the theatre and have a meeting with you, Mike and Ozzie. I have some information about Therese and Louise I think you might be interested in. Did you say 1 p.m. for the meeting? Yes, that time would work for me. See you then."

Per usual, Lt. Paganelli pushed one of the heavy front doors of the theatre and found himself in the lobby with all three men waiting for him. Mike said, "Let's go in the conference room. I made some coffee and we can have a little talk."

The four men filed into the conference room and sat in rolling chairs around the large round oak table. Without asking, Mike poured four cups of coffee and already had milk and sugar on the table with spoons and napkins. He'd bought a box of doughnuts and passed them around. No one hesitated to take one and if they wanted another one, there was plenty to go around a couple more times.

Lt Paganelli ate half of his doughnut and drank half of his coffee. As he was dusting the sugar off his fingers, he said, "I wanted to give you an update on the murders of Therese and Louise D'Anjou. First, we had to make sure we had their blood types and I'm glad we did that because both their blood types were on two different garrote wires that we found in Lorenzo Calucci's tool shed. He murdered both women."

Rex asked, "What was his motive?"

"He had no motive. He knew Therese from her strip tease dancing in the Tacoma-Seattle area in Frank Colacurcio's clubs. She stripped at The Corral for a brief amount of time. And he picked her up from this theatre and took her out to the judge's compound. That's about it."

"What about Louise?" Mike asked.

"No. He didn't know her at all. He just did what he was ordered to do by Judge McCarthy," the lieutenant said while watching the surprise on the three men's faces.

"Well, why don't you nail the judge's butt?" Oz said.

"I'm afraid the god of karma has done that for us," the lieutenant said.

"What happened to him?" Rex asked.

"He choked to death eating a roast beef sandwich. He'd been dead a few hours when an officer checked his house. That happened yesterday and he's at the morgue right now. We're waiting for his wife to ID him and move him to a mortuary." The lieutenant was eyeing another doughnut. The death of a crooked judge didn't stop his appetite.

Oz, the wizard of the Capitol Theatre, said, "So we've got two dead women. Innocent sisters who just wanted to be reunited back in Montreal. And we've got the murderer and the man who ordered the murders. All four are dead. Wouldn't these statistics make a great movie?!!!" He looked at each man to reciprocate his enthusiasm and they did.

Always the pragmatist, Mike asked, "What's next?"

"The women have been cremated. Therese because we thought she was Zizi Zeigler and no one claimed her body. And we cremated Louise because she had already been buried and we had to lift her body to determine the cause of death. I'm going to send the two tureens of ashes to Montreal to their father, Roland D'Anjou. He will have the family and friends gather and have a proper funeral then the sisters will be buried side-by-side."

There was a moment of silence except for the chewing of doughnuts and loud sipping of hot coffee. Oz said, "Anything else, lieutenant?"

The lieutenant rubbed his mouth and leaned forward in his chair. Looking down, he said, "Would you like to have a memorial ceremony for the two sisters?"

"Is this sanctioned by the Yakima Police Department?" Oz asked.

"No. I just thought that these two sisters have been through the worst circumstances right here in Yakima and I wanted some way to say that we're sorry before I send them home. What do you guys think? Rex?"

"Let's do it before the 9 p.m. movie on Monday. We can have cake and coffee in the lobby and hold the audience before they go into the theatre.

We'll imagine that the two sisters are listening to us and we'll bid them farewell. What could we do in their honor?" Rex looked around.

"Put two ghost lights on stage during the night?" Oz said.

"What's a ghost light?" the lieutenant asked.

"Just in case someone needs to enter the theatre during the night, it won't be totally dark. So two lights, one for each of the sisters, would be a nice tribute. What do you all think?" Oz asked.

"Sounds good," Rex and Mike said at the same time.

"I'll play *The Godfather* that night in a sneak preview. There's a beautiful wedding song called, *Speak Softly, Love* that Al Martino sings," Rex said.

"Woo woo!" said Mike in mocking Rex's incidents with the adoring ghost of Therese.

"I'm going to have to kill you if you do that again," Rex smiled and grabbed at Mike's throat. "The ghost's little love scenes will be leaving with her ashes. We're finally going to exorcise Therese so she can have some peace."

Monday night arrived and Rex had a cake made that had two cartoon sisters holding hands and flying with their angel wings back to a little city of butter cream buildings with a sign that said, 'Welcome to Montreal.' Each person who routinely went to the late movie on Monday nights was given a candle. They took turns putting their candle on the cake and three people were assigned to light the candles. Everybody gathered around the cake and blew out the candles. Then the group applauded and Mike cut the cake. Lt. Paganelli got the first piece.

As soon as everyone filled their cups with 7-Up, they raised them up and said in unison, "Therese and Louise, may you rest in peace!" Everyone applauded then ate their cake and partied with each other. They were the Monday late night movie family. In some cases, these moviegoers were the only family that some of the people had. And for this special night, that was okay.

CHAPTER THIRTY-SEVEN

The City of Yakima

After the memorial service for Therese and Louise in the lobby of the Capitol Theatre, Rex assumed that the ghost had truly been exorcised. In the following days, he didn't hear her crying, walking or opening and closing a door. No more orchid plants greeted him as he entered the projection booth. And when he looked in his Folger's Coffee tin to see if Therese's gold and diamond earring was still there, a brass screw was the only thing in the can.

Rex didn't want to try to find out where the earring was. Really, he had mixed feelings about not being able to be the most important person in the ghost's existence. "That's crap," he admonished himself. "Get a grip on what you are feeling. You miss the ghost. At the same time, you feel relief that she will never bother you again. Which is it? You want her or you don't want her? Her attention feeds your ego. Think about the situation. The only way you could be with her is to BE DEAD! You need to find a real live woman to love and forget about the ghost!"

At the same time Rex was having a conversation with himself, the phone rang. It was Mike and he said, "Rex, take line two. It's Lt. Paganelli."

"Lieutenant? What can I do for you?" Rex couldn't imagine why the lieutenant was calling him.

"It's about Therese's gold and diamond earring," the lieutenant said. "The sheriff and the police departments went to Judge McCarthy's compound a few days ago because we had probable cause to search his house. I found an earring on the judge's dresser that matches the earring Therese was wearing when she was found dead. I remember when you tried to bring me an earring that you found in the theatre that you thought was

Therese's earring. Do you still have that earring?"

"Let me ask you a question before I answer," Rex said. "Exactly what day did you go out to the judge's place?"

"Just a few days ago, on Friday," the lieutenant answered.

"That day, I was very busy yet I had a nagging urge to check the coffee can where I kept Therese's earring. I opened the lid and all that was there was a brass screw. The earring was gone. The answer is no, I don't have it," Rex said.

"Considering how impossible it would be for you to step onto the judge's property, much less enter his house, did you put Therese's earring on his dresser?" The lieutenant already knew the answer.

Rex said, "First, I don't know where he lives. And no, I did not put Therese's earring on his dresser. By the way, why didn't you ask me about this at our meeting the other day?"

"Let's just consider how the earring situation would look to your buddies at the theatre. You found an earring in the theatre and brought it to me, except it turned out to be a screw. You've been keeping the earring in a coffee can, except it's not there anymore because I found it in the judge's bedroom. You didn't put it there. The earring moved from your booth to the judge's house. Is there any way that you could have explained that at the meeting?" The lieutenant continued. "That's a hypothetical question because I don't want to admit that the ghost moved it. When a person has experiences with imaginary people, psychiatrists call that person schizophrenic. And you and I wouldn't want our colleagues to think that we believe the ghost was real, now would we?"

"Lieutenant, I don't know the answers to your questions. I think you need a rest since four people in your investigation have died, a couple from mysterious causes. I don't know what you have to do today but I have a delivery truck waiting for me. So I'm going to wish you a good day." Rex gently hung up the phone.

That was the last time Rex and Lt. Paganelli had a conversation about Therese or her ghost. For the next few years, Rex received special gifts when he would arrive at work. At first, he asked Sharon or Mike if they left a candy bar or chocolates from Boehm's Candy store on his counter right by his coffee cup. They would look at him as if to say, "We didn't leave you a thing. Guess who did?" Their implication was that the ghost would leave him candy, cookies, poetry, a flower or even a bag of freshly ground coffee. He didn't see the ghost but he felt her presence on a daily basis.

He thought, "What could it hurt if she leaves these tokens of her affection for me? I like it. I just don't want her to show herself to me and try to tempt me to join her in her world."

The weeks and months turned into years. In 1973, the phone rang in the projection booth and Oz was on the line. "Rex, come on down. All of us need to have a meeting."

Once Rex came down from the stairs and into the lobby, Oz stuck his head out of the conference room and said, "We're in here, Rex. Come on in."

After everyone settled into their chairs, Oz began his speech. "I've got some good news and some bad news about the theatre and it's future. All of you have made requests about supplies you need that you haven't gotten. You have seen that our movie population has dwindled to half of the people who were coming here only a couple years ago. We are not pulling in enough money to pay our utilities and now, we will not be able to pay you guys." Oz looked at the sad expressions on his theatre family's faces.

He continued. "The Mercy family cannot afford to finance the repairs that are needed for this theatre. As much as they regret it, they are forced to sell the theatre and hope someone or some organization will buy it. Otherwise, everything will be sold in the theatre then the building will be demolished and turned into a parking lot."

Mike said, "What about the community groups that've been renting the theatre for their productions? That should be bringing in some money."

"They're the only reason we haven't locked the front doors. The good news is that this situation is temporary because the Allied Arts Council and the strong support of local citizens have convinced the city of Yakima to purchase the building for a complete restoration. Their plan is to use the theatre as a community arts center. I'm guessing that would include theatre productions and maybe movies too. The Arts Council is so cool. Know why?"

Everybody chimed in. "Why?"

"They found a way to register the Capitol Theatre on the National Register of Historic Sites. Guys, because of the theatre's historical significance, the sale has a good chance of going through so that the City of Yakima will own the theatre. Volunteers are gonna find a bunch of ways to raise money for the repairs that are desperately needed."

"As soon as workers come into the theatre to begin the renovation, we can't have any visitors for productions or movies. Sorry Rex," Oz said.

Rex responded. "I'm out of a job? How about Mike and Sharon?"

"I'm the only one staying," Oz said. "Mostly to supervise the restoration. Al, of course, will be in and out of his office to keep track of the work and what was repaired. Don't worry, guys, uncle Oz is looking out for the three of you. Here are some job possibilities for each of you." He handed each of the trio a typed piece of paper with a list of job availabilities.

Jed's Sporting Goods Store on Yakima Avenue was the most attractive retail operation to the threesome. Mike was a good administrator and good with customers because he genuinely knew the sporting gear business. Sharon was hired immediately to work in sport's shoes and hiking gear. Rex still was an expert on bicycle mechanics and was put in charge of mountain and racing bikes as well as rider's gear and bike accessories.

It was time to say goodbye to the theatre for the time being and Rex felt as if he was losing his family and the job he loved the best—showing movies. It wasn't a grand endeavor but it required passion and a lot of technical knowledge.

Rex was not sure that there would be an opportunity for him to work at the theatre again. He lingered and touched the projectors for the last time. Just as he was about to lift his hand, a gust of wind blew into the booth and slammed the door shut. Papers were lifted and tossed until the room was with filled with typing paper confetti. Jars and tins were swept off the shelves and suspended in the whirlwind. Rex headed for the shut door to escape the twirling paper, coffee cups, scissors and broken pieces of film.

As if he was facing a sixty-mile-an-hour wind, he could barely stand upright much less take a step toward the door. All he could think to do was crawl under the table in the middle of the room for shelter.

His radio clicked on and Nat King Cole was singing *The Shadow Of Your Smile*. Rex felt pressure under his arms as if he was a baby being lifted by his mother and made to stand on his two feet. He felt the ghost's body against his and his arms were placed in a slow dancing position. The ghost's head rested on his shoulder as she caused the two of them to sway from side to side.

Rex knew he was helpless to resist the ghost's romantic hold on him for fear that she might tear him apart so he didn't allow himself to think about escaping. She smelled good, felt good and he was melting in her embrace. In a glowing moment, Therese revealed her whole person to him and she was wearing a silvered sleeveless gown that shimmered as if it was covered in thousands of stars. Her skin was flawless against her auburn long hair. The picture of health, her autumn colored eyes, long lashes, white teeth shown in contrast to burgundy colored lips. She looked lovingly into Rex's eyes as if he was the light of her life.

As he wrapped his arms around her and attempted to hold her as close as possible, the music stopped and the papers, cups, tins and filmstrips glided to their normal place in the room. She had vaporized and the door creaked open.

Rex walked out of his projection booth and out of the theatre.

Front of the Capitol Theatre. Photo courtesy: David Lynx.

CHAPTER THIRTY-EIGHT

Jed's Sporting Goods

Working at Jed's was a culture shock for Rex.

He was a man who enjoyed darkness and solitude in his make-believe world of movies. He lived vicariously through the characters in their adventures of history, crime and romance. While his theatre family struggled with their personal relationships, Rex never experienced infatuation, bonding with a woman, attempting to work out problems and trying to recover after the relationship failed. The staff at the theatre had no problem telling Rex about their failed relationships and seeking his advice regardless that he'd never had a romantic relationship with a woman, except the ghost.

Maybe that's what was so charming about him. He had no preconceived notions about people based on their gender, race or religious preferences. He'd seen every conceivable personality type on the movie screen and how the other characters in the story handled people and situations. Even though the actors had memorized their lines from a script, they knew exactly what to say and what to do. In Rex's mind, that's precisely how the world worked.

Working in a retail store required Rex to keep an upbeat public persona as he interacted with customers. Rather than just repair bikes, he was expected to initiate sales in a friendly manner. He kept a perpetual smile on his face even when explaining the most difficult concepts to a customer. His manager watched him have a one-on-one conversation with each customer as if that person was the only person in the world. It took a very short amount of time for customers to ask for Rex to advise them as they learned to ride longer distances on their bikes.

He spent his days off attending local movie theatres and even assisted the projectionists on a volunteer basis. The theatres knew that Rex could show their evening movies if a projectionist called in sick or wanted to take a vacation. In the absence of their projectionist, the theatres paid him. He decided that he would stick with Jed's for one year hoping that there would be a possibility that he would be reinstated at the Capitol Theatre or one of the other theatres in Yakima. If that didn't happen, he would make a move to Seattle and find a job in one of their grand theatres as a projectionist.

During an ordinary day at Jed's, a young woman approached Rex about buying a mountain bike. He thought she looked like a high school cheerleader but she said she was a women's tennis coach at Eisenhower High School and taught Psy. Ed. It turned out that she and Rex had graduated from high school around the same time, she from Ike and Rex from First Christian.

"I remember your brother, Lance, was an outstanding football player and our team had trouble during the games because he was such a fabulous runner," Laurie said.

"No doubt about it," Rex agreed. "Lance was one of a kind. If you wish, I can pass your phone number on to him."

"Oh no, I didn't mean to imply that I am interested in getting in touch with him. He's the only one in your family that I know. I'm just making conversation," she said.

Laurie could see that Rex was pleasant but lacked skill at social interactions with ladies. As a single female who was pretty and physically fit, she was use to men hitting on her and making sexual innuendos. She was not a game player when it came to relationships. At the same time, she was a competitive person who was mature in her encouragement of others attempts to improve their skills at sports, even if that meant trying to win while competing against her.

In their conversations, Laurie and Rex talked about their interest in riding bikes and she found out that Rex also had a mountain bike. "I think I could really improve my riding skills if I had someone to ride with. Would you like to go biking with me on Sunday on a trail by the Yakima River?"

Rex had never experienced a real date and certainly had never been asked by a woman to spend time together. Accepting a riding adventure with Laurie seemed like it would be fun so Rex said yes.

They met and spent some time talking about their bikes before Rex led the way along a fairly even graveled trail. After about a half hour, Rex stopped and checked with Laurie to see how she was using her gears. There seemed to be a lot of people walking the trail this Sunday so part of the challenge was to ride around them safely. They passed by a small lake and decided to stop and walk out on a pier to see if they could spot perch or trout. Laurie had brought some sandwiches and Rex found that he was nervous eating in front of a woman. Beside his mother, Sharon was the only other female that he'd ever eaten a meal with. But he didn't consider her to be anything more than an adopted sister.

Laurie was different. It would take many Sundays of bike riding before Rex got enough nerve to ask her to go to a movie with him. Since he had helped in the projection booth at most of the movie theatres in Yakima, he thought she might like to see what a projection booth looked like. He was right. It was as if she went into magic land when she was looking around the booth at the Liberty Theatre and he saw that she was impressed at his natural knowledge of the equipment. It was the first time she could see that he was truly relaxed because he was in his element of a dark movie theatre.

It had been a little over two years since he had left the Capitol Theatre and he yearned to walk inside and see if they were making enough progress that there might be a possibility that he could return as the projectionist. He asked Laurie if she would be interested in seeing the interior of the theatre. She answered with great enthusiasm and he gave Ozzie a call to see if it would be okay for the two of them to visit the theatre on the evening of Tuesday, August 19. Rex had that day off and Laurie was not in school yet.

A carpenter's truck had parked in front and one of the heavy doors of the theatre was open. Rex and Laurie walked into the crimson-colored lobby, which still smelled like popcorn. Even though the concession stand display cases were empty, it seemed like Sharon was simply on a break and would return with boxes of candy, ice cream bars and bags of popcorn kernels that needed to be popped.

The light in Oz's office was not on so Rex assumed he must be inside the theatre. "Let's go into the theatre. We can enter through this door." Rex held the door open for Laurie and as she took a couple steps down the main aisle, she gasped at the wonder and beauty of the theatre. The luxury of the carpeting and lush fabric covering the seats, the vastness of the height of the ceiling and the hand painted murals gave her a sense that she was in Italy viewing artwork by Michelangelo. The gold gilded fancy carved columns that flanked the stage seemed more like the finest artisan's work that one might find in an opera house in New York City. She looked at the opera boxes and thought of President Lincoln attending his last performance at the Ford Theatre before John Wilkes Booth shot him.

As Laurie walked further down the aisle, she looked from left to right and back again to take in the scope of the stage, the proscenium opening and heavy velvet curtains. She was mesmerized by the artwork and grandeur of the stage and domed ceiling. Rex was delighted at her appreciation of the theatre that he loved and hoped that Oz was ready for him to return to work. This was the only place in Rex's life where he felt completely happy.

"Rex!!" Oz walked on stage from the left wing and skipped down the side stairs. "So good to see you, buddy." He gave Rex a hug and knew it would embarrass him to be part of a public display of affection. "Who's this little lady?" Oz already knew the answer.

"This is Laurie," he kept the introductions simple. To Laurie, he said, "This is Oz, the manager of the theatre. Sort of like my uncle. Sort of like my brother. He acts like he's my mother and my father. I guess you could say he's my family rolled into one person." Rex was not shy about voicing his affection for Oz, the wizard of the Capitol Theatre. Laurie has never been in the Capitol Theatre and from the look on her face, she is fascinated by our treasure."

Rex couldn't help himself when he asked about getting his job back. "Say, how is the remodeling coming and when can I come back and show movies again?"

"Nothing like getting to the point," Oz chuckled. "Well, there is some good news. The Allied Arts Council and the City of Yakima began working together to transfer the building to public ownership. A guy named Walter Lewis from Twin Y Corporation assisted the city of Yakima in negotiating the purchase of the theatre. We have a few more things to complete but generally things are going well and you'll probably be able to show movies again and photograph art exhibits."

Rex was looking back toward the main floor and two balconies. He looked to the highest point in the theatre to see if the projection booth was still standing.

Oz recognized that Rex needed some time to visit his booth and dust a few things off before Laurie went up there.

"Laurie, why don't I show you around while Rex goes up to his booth and cleans things up a bit before you visit up there?" Oz suggested. "Rex, would that be okay with you?"

"Come on up in about twenty minutes?" Rex invited Oz and Laurie. "I'll see if the coffee is still good and if it is, I'll make some in the coffee maker. Oz, you have any cookies?"

"You know I always do. I'll bring 'em up. See you then," Oz said and went into his narrative tour guide rhetoric.

Rex climbed the stairs and entered his booth. He turned on the light and walked over to the Folger's coffee can and lifted the lid. Only the brass screw was there. Then he walked over to the radio and turned it on to see if it still worked. As the music came on, he found a clean cloth and began to dust the counters.

Within seconds of Frank Sinatra's voice crooning the lyrics to *My Foolish Heart*, a puff of wind blustered through the door and slammed it shut. Stacks of papers lifted and swirled. The posters on the walls strained and tore through the tacks. They flopped and lifted as if waving bye-bye. Once again, Rex attempted to dive under the table but was prevented from bending over as if he was facing a rocket of water.

He knew what the ghost wanted and decided it would be better to dance with her and get rid of her before Laurie and Oz came up to the booth. How could he possibly explain the relationship he had with Therese's ghost? It was a love phenomenon that he craved and yet, knew would destroy him. He could feel her slender body melting into him as they swayed to the music. The scent of Channel 5 wafted from the ghost's body while she laid her head on his shoulder. Last time when they danced, as soon as the tune had finished, Therese's ghost evaporated into air.

But this time was different.

Rex felt as if his body was in a vice that was moving up toward his neck and throat. The pressure squeezed his trachea and he attempted to pull the ghost off him but there was nothing solid to grasp. It was an enigma. He was being strangled and could not pull the force away from his neck.

"*My world,*" the ghost put those words in his head rather than speaking them as living people did. "*You are coming to my world and we will be together forever, my love.*"

"Stop this immediately," Rex struggled to talk. "I have a live girlfriend and I want to get married and have a family. I can't do that with you because we're in two different worlds. I love you but it's hopeless."

"*You will be in my world and we will be lovers forever,*" she whispered in his mind. "*Relax and let me end the miseries of your world. I know you are frightened, my darling, but it will all be over in a couple minutes.*"

Rex started to panic as he grabbed his neck to pull her body away from his throat. He tried to run but stumbled into the table in the middle of the room. He pulled at the latch on the door to escape being choked to death but the knob shattered out of the door. Like a drowning man, he began to lose consciousness and struggled to inhale a tiny amount of air.

Oz and Laurie arrived at his door and Oz saw Rex holding his neck while he twisted and rolled from the counter to the table and knocked over the reel case. He clung to the projector to avoid passing out on the floor.

They could hear the roar of a tornado as the room was filled with paper and ceramic cups and filmstrips lifting in the swirling air. As the velocity of the wind in the booth increased, film reels snapped out of the shelves and bumped into Rex's head and shoulders. Oz lifted his leg and bashed in the door with his foot. He grabbed Rex and yelled, "Run! Go to the stairs!" The threesome headed for the stairs and Oz put one of Rex's arms over his shoulder and helped him move as quickly as possible. "She's trying to kill you, man, so you and she can be together forever. Run Rex! Don't let her take you to her world."

Oz could feel Rex slipping into unconsciousness because the ghost increased the pressure around his neck. By the time they reached the stairway door, Oz had to drag Rex's limp body. Finally, with Laurie's help, Oz draped Rex over his back while holding onto his arms in front. The velocity of the ghost's tornado rushed ahead of Oz and slammed shut the door so that the trio was trapped on the highest balcony.

"Pull the fire escape door open," Oz yelled at Laurie. Barely able to crack the door, she used her body to keep it open as the ghost tried to blind her with whirling sand and debris from the alley. Oz and Rex barely made it through the door before Laurie could no longer wedge her body against the wind pressure. Her skirt got caught as the door slammed shut and without thinking twice, she unzipped the fabric and rushed down the stairs with only her underslip on.

By the time, Oz reached the fire escape to the mezzanine level, the door to the theatre was open and all seemed calm. No wind. No ghost. It was an invitation to enter the theatre but Oz was smarter than the ghost's little deception and he continued down the metal fire escape stairs until the trio reached the alley.

"Oz laid Rex down and observed that his tongue and desperate mouth were no longer gasping for air. As Oz held Rex's upper body in his arms, Rex regained consciousness and looked up at his theatre uncle and new girl friend with a question on his face. He smiled, rubbed his neck and said, "What happened? I feel like I've been in a wrestling match and came out the loser!"

Always the wizard of the Capitol Theatre, Oz said, "No, my man. You're not the loser. You're alive and that makes you the winner."

CHAPTER THIRTY-NINE

The Fire and Reconstruction

Oz had to make a decision that night.

Rex was clearly the object of the ghost's attention and anyone who got in her way of possessing him was in danger of losing his or her life.

It took about fifteen minutes for Rex to realize what had happened. The purplish-crimson abrasions around his neck were testimony to the intensity of the ghost's intention to pull him into her world. The irony of the situation was that even if she had killed Rex, the ghost was not in control of the after-life of eternity. In her case, she had been murdered and because of the violence to her person, she had not passed completely to the next world. She intended to kill Rex the same way she was killed, by strangulation. To her way of thinking, Rex also would not have a complete passing and therefore would be with her.

Who could really know how things worked on the other side?

Oz said, "Listen Rex, you know I love you but if you step in the theatre, particularly the projection booth, I'm afraid that next time you won't make it out alive. You see what I'm saying, man? It's no good for you to go back into the theatre."

"I don't get it," Rex said. "We had a beautiful memorial party for Therese and Louise in the lobby and raised our glasses in their honor. Even Lt. Paganelli was there. In fact, he suggested the party. I thought the party would end the appearances by the ghost. What more could we possibly do to give her peace?"

"You're right. That party was a send-off for the sisters as far as we were concerned. It made sense to us but we're not up-to-date on ghostly thinking or behavior. What can I say? We've done it all like you said," Oz rubbed his chin.

Laurie jumped into the scene. "What has just happened? Are you two seriously talking about a female ghost going after Rex?"

Oz responded by saying, "It's a long story, Laurie. A girl was murdered here in the theatre and she turned into a ghost who's been after Rex. No one can say why. Maybe it's 'cause he's such a charming guy!" Oz laughed at his own joke and Rex joined in too.

"Or, or maybe it's 'cause I'm so darn good looking!" Rex added to the joke and flinched when he laughed because of his sore neck.

Laurie wasn't laughing. "You two are nuts. I barely know you, Rex, and here I find out that you've got a thing going with a ghost? It looks like she's going to be a part of your life but she's not going to be a part of my life. I'm sorry that you're hurt, Rex, but I'm not sticking around. I'm going to call my brother from the café around the corner to pick me up. Don't call me. You're both too weird for me!"

After the men watched Laurie walk away and disappear around the corner, they were silent. Neither one could think of anything to say.

Rex was suddenly concerned for Oz's safety about going back into the theatre. "I don't want you to go back into the theatre either if you think the ghost is gonna hurt you."

"She's not after me, man. It's you she wants. Tonight, I'm going to lock the theatre and let her cool off. What I'm really concerned about is that if she can't have you, she might just figure out a way to destroy the theatre. Have you ever heard the saying, *'Hell hath no fury like a woman scorned.'* "

Oz must have been clairvoyant because on the same hot evening of August 19, 1975, he smelled something that was suspicious but he locked the theatre temporarily. Just as a precaution, he called the fire department and upon their investigation, nothing was found. Everyone went home with the thought in mind that the old building truly needed to be thoroughly checked. No one could know that the destiny of the historic theatre was in the control of a force beyond this world.

During the quiet of the night, the unattended spark from a short in a wire on the ice machine ignited the wall socket. If a person had been in the same area at the time, the smoldering wallboards could have easily been extinguished. Since the time frame was during the night, the small fire spread into the most combustible parts of the lobby and traveled up the walls and into the seating areas.

The open space between the mezzanine and the orchestra level seating, which was designed by Marcus Priteca for acoustical reasons, was enclosed during a past remodel. One of the reasons the fire destroyed the theatre was that this enclosed chamber was unknown to the firefighters, who thought the area was contained. On the contrary, the fire was hidden. When the flames broke out of the sealed enclosure, the wooden balcony supports, mezzanine floor and the roof became engulfed in an inferno.

From there, the fire roared through the theatre's interior and destroyed everything but the basement dressing rooms, the stage area and fly gallery, the steel balcony supporters and the bottom portion of the façade.

When interviewed at a later date, Oz could not tell reporters from the Yakima Herald-Republic that he believed the ghost deliberately set the fire. She had proven that she was capable of manipulating objects and Oz was certain that she was angry with Rex for rejecting her efforts to bring him into her world. Once Oz saved Rex, she set out to destroy the one thing in his life that he truly loved, the beloved Capitol Theatre.

Within a matter of an hour, Frederick Mercy, Sr.'s dream of a grand theatre, which featured vaudeville and other performing arts, went up in flames. It was the largest theatre in the Pacific Northwest and the pride of Yakima. The result of the ghost's anger was devastating to the destruction of the Capitol Theatre but she did not count on the community pulling together to create a new theatre.

During the fire, the firefighters went back into the stage wings to save a Steinway grand piano, which had been signed by Henry Steinway, the president of Steinway and Sons.

The top portion of the façade had fallen into the burning interior and shattered into pieces. Architect, Bill Paddock, sifted through the burned wreckage to salvage anything he could find. When he discovered parts of the façade, people at the scene heard him say, "We'll need these broken pieces from the front of the building to restore the theatre!" Because the theatre had been placed on the National Register of Historic Sites, there were hundreds of pictures taken just before the fire that could be used as guides for the restoration.

After the fire, the Capitol Theatre Corporation formed a charitable trust and entered into a matching fund agreement with both the city and county to develop a 2.4 million dollar funding package to rebuild the theatre. With a 1.6 million dollar grant from the Economic Development Administration, and insurance resources, restoration began.

A company that was famous for producing architectural terra cotta facades, Gladding, McBean and Co. was hired for the restoration of the façade. The company was applauded for some of the most significant historical landmarks in the world such as the architecturally stunning Stanford University. Gladding, McBean specialized in firebrick, roof tile, fancy clay tile, chimney pipes and ornamental garden pottery. The State Parks Department Office of Historic Preservation donated sixty thousand dollars to help with the total bid of $174,000. to restore the façade.

In the stage area, the fly gallery stored the entire height of scenery above the visible stage and used pin-rails before or during performances. Since sandbags counterbalanced the weight of heavy pieces, the system required the creation of a storage *stage house* or *loft* that was usually as high or higher than the proscenium arch. Both the fly gallery and stage house were untouched by the fire.

The cartouche is a decoration at the top of the proscenium arch resembling the prow of a ship. At the base of the cartouche was the vaudeville impresario, Alexander Pantage's small face, which was said to be counting the number of people in the theatre, otherwise described as *counting the house*. Using pre-fire photographs, his face was recreated and once again, Mr. Pantage watched the audience as they entered the theatre in order to see how much money he would make during that performance.

In the mural about the muse of art, Mr. Tony Heinsbergen, the mural artist, painted himself in the brown jacket. In a different mural, he painted his dark haired wife dressed in a green dress.

The Grand Drape, which weighed 2,000 pounds, had a hand painted cornucopia design and was different than the original country scene on the old "main rag", another name for the large red curtain. An asbestos fire curtain was stored in a pocket on the topside of the stage in case of a fire.

The stage floor structural timbers and three outside walls of the stage house were only slightly damaged by the fire. New support columns in these walls enabled a new rigging grid and a mechanical room on the roof. The grid contained almost five miles of manila and wire rope for the new counterweight system. The south stage still contains the original giraffe doors where animal acts were transferred from cages to the stage. Over two hundred lighting instruments were used on stage or in the front of house lighting positions.

Oz was particularly impressed with the lighting and sound system, which were controlled at the back of the main floor theatre. The projection booth, located in the center of the upper balcony, housed two follow-spots instead of projectors. So Rex was definitely out of a projectionist's job but had every possibility of becoming a lighting specialist.

The curved walls of the theatre allowed sound to be channeled up instead of bouncing. Acoustics in the Capitol Theatre were considered to be some of the best in the Pacific Northwest.

The orchestra pit was in front of the stage. The whole unit raised and lowered to the basement, allowing the orchestra to set up their chairs, music stands and instruments before the unit raised enough to be hidden from the audience as they played music for the performances. The elevator transported road equipment down to the dressing room level. During the reconstruction, the elevator was purchased from the 5th Avenue Theatre in Seattle where it had been in use for many years. When raised, the lift also formed a thrust adding approximately 450 square feet to the stage.

The opera boxes on either side of the stage were considered the best seats in the house during the vaudeville performances because the action took place at the front of the stage. Today, most shows happen toward the back of the stage. And people no longer sit in the opera boxes. Instead, side stage lights have been placed in the front of the boxes and are operated by the lighting director.

Historical duplicates of the theatre's ornamentation were created in fiberglass using molds cast from pieces that were discovered in the ruins of the debris after the fire. In the case where there was nothing left to use, new pieces were handcrafted in California using photos of the Capitol interior as guides. These included the cartouche and the top parts of the two columns flanking the stage.

Molds were also cast from features at the Roxy Theatre in Tacoma, another Marcus Priteca theatre. Two men came from the Inservac Firm in Toronto, Ontario to set up a production assembly line with a local crew of twenty people in a Hollingbery and Sons hop warehouse to reproduce thousands of plaster pieces. The gold gilding all around the theatre is a gold leaf painting technique that was painted by volunteers from Yakima during renovation.

After the fire, the carpeted lobby was replaced with a new marble lobby, visually enlarging the space. The concession stand near the entrance of the old theatre was eliminated. The original floor of the main audience level was wood and one of the many features that caught on fire. During the renovation, concrete was poured at a slightly slanted angle as the base of the orchestra level seating area. Curved rows, with added space between the rows were used on the main floor to aid good sight lines. By eliminating the center aisle of the old theatre, audience traffic flowed more smoothly toward the sides of the main floor.

The fabric on the auditorium seating that became engulfed in flames was replaced by 1500 chairs from the Daughters of the American Revolution Hall in Washington D.C., which was built around the turn of the century. Although the hardware, padding and springs are new, the backs, seat pans and end standards were original and recaptured the older, elegant décor of the original theatre. Jean Jongeward, the interior design consultant, selected the seating upholstery to match the theatre's carpeting, which she designed.

Capitol Theatre Fire Collage located in theatre lower level.
Photo courtesy: Leonard La Lumiere.

The mechanical room was the major portion of the lower level of the theatre along with some dressing rooms that were not connected. Mr. and Mrs. Ted Robertson donated a grant of $300,000. which paid for the excavation of the space between the mechanic's room and the dressing rooms and added space for the Robertson Room, which was used for receptions and after-theatre functions. Administration offices were moved from the front lobby to the lower level.

Every day, Al Mallone and Ozzie Goldstein checked the progress of the construction, not that they had the final vote on any particular part of the process. The restoration brought together the best of the grand old style with newly constructed necessities that allowed the theatre to satisfy code requirements and operate efficiently with every conceivable safeguard to prevent future fires.

If a fireman made a list of all the things that could go wrong in the old theatre, replacing the wiring on the ice machine probably wouldn't be included on the list. Yet, that one spark cost the community over four million dollars to replace Yakima's historic treasure.

The Robertson Room: Donated by Mr. and Mrs. Ted Robertson.
Photo courtesy: Leonard La Lumiere.

Thanks for the Memories

Beside the beautiful stage and seating area reconstruction, there was one feature that took center stage. In 1920, Tony Heinsbergen had painted the original four murals: the muses of comedy, tragedy, music and art.

After the fire, Bill Paddock called Mr. Heinsbergen and asked him a very important question. At age eighty-three, would he be willing to repaint the murals that he had painted on the dome in 1920? Heinsbergen agreed to do the murals with one stipulation. He would paint the four muses on four canvases at his Los Angeles studio then have a construction crew adhere them to the panel that surrounds the rectangular relight in the center of the dome. In turn, he would retouch the seams so the finished murals would appear to have been painted directly on the dome. In addition to painting the mural, Heinsbergen was responsible for all the auditorium painting and the associated color selections.

While he was awaiting the completion of the ornamental plaster pieces that would be installed in the dome, Heinsbergen designed and painted two murals in gold leaf on the wall space behind what would become the mezzanine concession stand because he said that wall "needed a little life."

One of the complaints heard most often with the construction crew was that occasionally their tools were misplaced or mixed up with other worker's tools. "I am meticulous about my tools and have marked each one with my initials," one of the head carpenters complained. "Now I find my drill in your tool box. Did you just flat steal it?" The men would appear to be coming to blows.

"Look man, I don't know how your drill got in with my stuff. I want you to look in your tool box and see if my hand sander is there." Reluctantly, the first carpenter did look and found the second carpenter's hand sander.

It didn't seem like a big deal until Mr. Heinsbergen mentioned to Oz that he was missing his box of touch-up paints and a collection of fine art brushes.

"I have to continue the mural colors so the audience can't see the seams that I'm working on. We've got to find that box of paint tubes," Heinsbergen complained to Oz. On second thought, he said, "I've heard a rumor that there's a ghost named Shorty in this theatre who was a former janitor. Didn't he hang himself because of a love situation?"

Oz had to answer in the affirmative.

"So Shorty is the famous ghost of the Capitol Theatre who moves things around?" Heinsbergen smiled as he looked at Oz. "He is annoying but the idea of a male ghost is rather amusing!"

As soon as Heinsbergen's accolades to Shorty were spoken, a hefty gust of wind filled the seating area of the auditorium. The men on scaffolds, who were adhering the canvases to the panel, sat back on their haunches and raised their arms and hands to protect their faces from the flying sawdust and chips of wood left by the carpenters.

"Go to the wall by the stairs!" Oz firmly pushed Heinsbergen against the wall and shielded him from the carpenter's shrapnel, flying papers, ropes and small tools. The rigging system and spotlight cables started swinging as the wind eased then rocketed toward the workers and Oz and Tony Heinsbergen.

Oz yelled, "Shorty has disappeared. Therese is the new ghost. She was murdered right here in the theatre in 1965. She was a beautiful French strip tease dancer from Montreal and it looks like she has taken up permanent residence here at the Capitol Theatre!"

The howling wind immediately died down to a fluff of a breeze then disappeared.

Oz looked around to make sure it was safe to leave the wall. The head workman yelled down at Oz, "What the hell just happened?"

"There's a storm outside. Someone must have left the sliding door to the loading dock open." Oz knew that explanation didn't hold water so he yelled at a couple stage crew, "Hey guys, close the loading dock door. Let's keep the wind out!"

Tony Heinsbergen was wise to the unexplainable phenomenon of the world and in a low voice, he said, "There's no storm outside is there? That was Therese and she wants everyone to know that Shorty's gone and she reigns as the queen ghost of the Capitol Theatre. If her ego is that sensitive, I'd hate to be her boyfriend."

The wizard of the Capitol Theatre commented to a man who knew the truth about the ghost. "Brother, if you ever think of scorning a female ghost, the only advice I can give you is to run for cover."

———

The citizens of Yakima loved their performing arts treasure. They pulled together to save the Capitol Theatre from becoming a parking lot. And when she burned, rather than demolishing the historic building, funds were raised, donations were contributed and artisans from the original theatre returned to restore and improve the interior to its grand beauty.

The Capitol Theatre murals had been Tony Heinsbergen's first creations. The four muses that he painted on canvas and adhered to the theatre dome were his last masterpiece. He passed away shortly after the complete restoration of the theatre.

On November 4, 1978, just 733 days from the beginning of the reconstruction, the Capitol Theatre opened its doors. Governor Dixie Lee Ray and local dignitaries dedicated the theatre to the "continued vitality of the performing arts in Yakima."

Bob Hope, famous Hollywood actor, entertained the crowd with his usual quips. While he was singing *Thanks For The Memories*, Al Mallone, Oz Goldstein, Mike Hansen, Sharon Meyer and Rex Marvel sat together in the first row with Lt. Paganelli as their guest. Rex was particularly happy since Oz said that he wanted him to be the lighting director. Stepping into the theatre once again brought a smile to Rex's face. "I'm at home in this theatre," he said to Oz. "Forever!"

"I'm copacetic with you working here again, man," Oz said. "As far as I'm concerned, we're all one happy family." He looked up and softly said, "Yes, Therese, that includes you too!"

A surprising puff of wind blew sheets of music and programs around the stage and auditorium. Women's hair was blown in their faces and they scrambled to push their hair back in place. With the final breath of air, the ghost of the Capitol Theatre showed the audience and speakers that she would always have the last word. Gently, she settled the sheet music and programs back into their proper places.

Yes, Oz was right! Everything was copacetic at the Capitol Theatre.

Tony Heinsbergen and artists finishing new murals.
Photo courtesy Leonard La Lumiere.

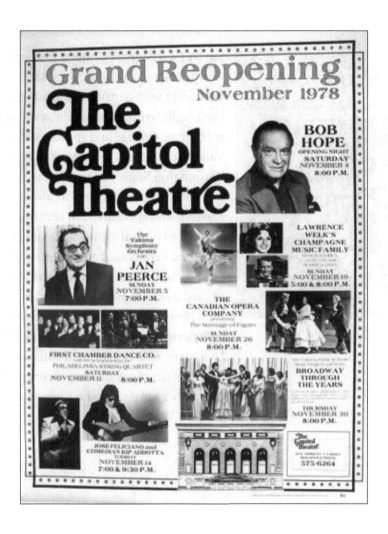

Susan La Riviere is a regional novelist who graduated from Arizona State University with a major in journalism. She taught writing and public speaking at Heritage College and speech at Yakima Valley Community College in Eastern Washington State. She was a correspondent and photographer for the *Yakima Herald-Republic* and specialized in features about the cultural significance of people's activities, ceremonies and events of the diverse cultures of Yakima County. She also worked as an investigative reporter for a local personal injury attorney. Besides being a playwright, she and her husband, Larry La Riviere, who is a musical entertainer, have written songs that are recorded on the CDs in her novels. The La Rivieres reside in Yakima, WA.

CPSIA information can be obtained at www.ICGtesting.com
Printed in the USA
LVOW01s2109170215

427342LV00010B/34/P